~ The ~
INDIGO SUN

Rupa Bhullar serves as the Director of Finance at a leading global corporation that provides digital and financial software solutions. She holds a CFA (Chartered Financial Analyst) Charter and a Post Graduate Diploma in Business Administration.

Rupa was born in India and spent her early childhood years in Jaipur before moving to Chandigarh, the place she still calls home. She relocated to New York in the year 2000, and currently lives with her family in New Jersey.

The
INDIGO SUN

RUPA BHULLAR

RUPA

Published by
Rupa Publications India Pvt. Ltd 2018
7/16, Ansari Road, Daryaganj
New Delhi 110002

Sales centres:
Allahabad Bengaluru Chennai
Hyderabad Jaipur Kathmandu
Kolkata Mumbai

ISBN: 978-81-291-4960-2

First impression 2018

10 9 8 7 6 5 4 3 2 1

The moral right of the author has been asserted.

Printed at Thomson Press India Ltd. Faridabad

Papa, I miss you!
For my sons Karman and Sahej, and
the reason for my joy, my 'Ananda'

Contents

Beauty and Bliss

Beauty is whatever gives joy.

—Edna St. Vincent Millay

*M*AYA gazed at the star-studded night sky, awestruck by its grandeur and vastness. The inviting and dazzling mystery seemed to stretch infinitely in every direction, markedly brighter than it had ever been, or at least than she had ever noticed it to be. Perhaps it was the cool summer night over the vast desert expanse or simply the fact that never before had she made the time to be still enough to appreciate the beauty that pervaded her universe. She felt softly grounded in the stillness within her, gently cradled by the harmony around. The purity of the moment was intensified by the coolness of the white marble she lay upon, as the whispering wind playfully caressed her long golden hair.

Maya felt as tranquil and beautiful as the full moon that admired itself in all its glory. Its reflection danced in joy upon the gentle ripples caused by the fragrant breeze sweeping across the pool. The majestic tree above her seemed to bend over as if to look closer, reach out and pay its reverence to the dancing reflection of the enchanted moon. Everything was perfectly at ease with itself and in harmony with the surroundings. There was no struggle, strife, unease or unrest. Just a peaceful coexistence—a celebration of everything unique in itself, completing and complementing the other.

Maya let out a deep sigh and closed her eyes with a desire to capture this moment and carry it to eternity. As she closed her eyes, she wondered if this was what peace felt like, and was it really peace or just the absence of noise and movement? Whatever it was, it felt good. Just as she grew aware of the joy she felt within her heart, it started to fade, little by little. The harder she tried to hold on, the faster it slipped, like grains of sand slipping through a tightened fist. Her thoughts echoed in her mind, 'The desire to be abundant, the desire to just be binds us as much as it sets us free. Is peace a state of environment, a state of life or a state of mind? Does it arise from fulfilment of a desire, or does it emerge from giving up the very desire itself?' Maya was startled out of her thoughts by the sound of a splash. She sat up and looked over the unsettled water, no longer painting the tranquil picture of the night sky. The moon was still shining brightly and the tree stood gracefully in place, but the stir within the water caused it to deny its abounding beauty. What seemed like an ecstatic reality just moments ago, became a surreal dream, non-existent to the perspective of the baffled pond.

Maya's sweeping gaze caught a little boy on the other side of the pool playing with his prized possession, a handful of rocks. When he noticed the grim look on Maya's face, his innocent joy transformed into regretful guilt. He slowly retreated into the shadows of the night, as if debating whether to flee the scene or admit his crime. Time seemed to have frozen still for the little boy who stood like a deer caught in headlights. The sweet sound of veena from somewhere in the distance seemed to bring warmth and comfort to the otherwise cold moment upon which the young boy's fate hung. He gradually gathered his wits about him, folded his hands and bowed his head in a sincere apology.

Maya smiled and with a wave of her hand, indicated him to come over. The boy slowly started to come forward in unsure, yet deliberate steps, his shoulders still drooping with the remorse of his mistake. He suddenly broke into a profound apology. 'Please do not report me to the hotel management. I understand you are a privileged guest here and nothing within the premises of this hotel should cause you any disturbance. It is late at night and the spot is fairly secluded at this hour of the evening. I often come here to wait for my father. He works here as a darbaan, and when he finishes his shift late in the evening, we walk home together,' the young boy blurted out.

Maya softly said, 'I won't tell anyone, but what is your name?'

The boy had a sincere innocence about him. Maya noticed his tiny worn-out, slipper-less feet peeking from under a white pajama and his head adorned with a bright red turban.

'My name is "Ananda". My mother says it means eternal bliss,' he explained.

He continued, 'Memsahib, I should not be here at this time. If someone finds out, my father could lose his job. We are poor people and work with integrity and honesty. It would be very unfortunate if someone came to know of this incident, please allow me to take my leave.'

With a sudden sparkle in his eyes, Ananda exclaimed, 'For this kindness of yours, I will teach you my secret game of the rocks and the water. It contains the wisdom of the universe and when I have a hard time understanding the answers, it reveals those to me.'

Maya was very intrigued but before she could ask him anything else, the boy turned his back and slipped into the darkness of the night.

At a distance, under a dimly lit fluorescent street light, surrounded by a swarm of mosquitoes and moths, she observed little Ananda sketching in the sand. She smiled to herself, perhaps the sticks and sands have a story for him as well.

Maya was pleasantly refreshed by the brief interaction. It felt like a breath of fresh air, the sweetness of which had successfully cleansed her mind of worries, for the moment at least. She deeply wished to go right back to the sanctuary she had briefly experienced a few moments ago, but realizing it was late at night, she decided instead to make her way back to the room.

Maya slowly arose from her stupor, intoxicated by the release of stress. Her body felt relaxed and her steps were heavy as she gradually made her way over to the winding steps lit with candles and fragrant with jasmine oil. This place had a heavenly feel to it. The steps spilled into the wide open gardens illuminated with carved sandstone lamps. The building stood across—majestic and regal.

In the distance, Maya observed bright lights and colourful attires. She also heard upbeat music and noticed a buzz of happy people clicking pictures and flashing smiles. She gathered this was the much raved about after-dinner cultural performance. A lady she met in the elevator yesterday had insisted that Maya could not leave this place without experiencing the true glory of Rajasthani culture; the colourful costumes and lively dances entertained and rejuvenated the tourist after a long day of sightseeing and shopping.

At that point, it had been the last thing on Maya's mind. But today was different. Somewhere in the back of her mind, a conflict was brewing. Her body wanted nothing more than a comfortable bed and a good night's rest. But in her heart, she dreaded the idea of walking into the room by herself to be flooded with all the painful memories of her hollow life.

She was afraid of herself. Her mind appeared to be her greatest enemy and she shuddered at the thought of being left alone in its company. She neither wanted to think about her past nor talk about it; if only she could drown the noise of her mind in an even greater clamour.

Maya quickened her pace and went straight for the crowd. She pulled up a chair and sank right into it, looking as dejected as she felt. The noise outside seemed to pale in comparison to the tumultuous cacophony that was beginning to erupt within. Maya hastily ordered some wine to aide her combat and help numb her senses. All she wanted at that moment was to wipe out her memory and feel alive again. She closed her eyes, neither paying attention to, nor concerned about the performance. All that mattered was that she wasn't alone with her thoughts.

Just then, she heard the painful steps of her fear approaching closer, followed by a sardonic whisper in her ear, 'It all could have been, only if you had just let it be. It wasn't perfect but at least it *was*.' And in the blink of an eye, she was held hostage by her thoughts and transported back to her glorious yet painful past. Her mind, playing both the devil and the advocate, was racing yet again. From the dark valleys of one dreadfully dismal vision into the tantalizing sunlit peaks of the next, the roller coaster of memories swung her around until finally easing its grip and dropping her into the oversized chair of her 27th-floor office overlooking the gloomy New York City skyline on a cold sunny day. Maya could still hear the distinct knock on the door as the nurse announced, 'Doctor, your next patient is here.' Maya recalled instinctively wiping away that lone cold tear that had discreetly escaped her left eye as she bravely stepped through the doors with an overconfident smile, and her clichéd greeting 'Come on in, so what brings you here on this beautiful day?'

Maya could once again sense the sinking feeling that seemed to have lately become her heart's constant companion. A mist of hopeless despair enveloped her life. She had the qualification and the career of choice, the man of every woman's dream, lived in the most exciting city in the world and was ravishingly beautiful. She had everything, but happiness.

The vision started to fade, making way for the pain of her hollow emotions to resurface again, bringing with it reminders of her beautiful home, her busy practice, the fabulous parties, the exotic vacations, the fun and laughter, the bitter fights, the lonely nights, flashing police cars and ambulances, blood on the floor followed by the dream, yet again. Maya had seen this dream all too often in the last few months for her to write it off.

This dream repeated itself at nights and haunted her during the day, the elusive happiness inviting her to return home. Yet again, she saw that little girl in a white dress, running barefoot through narrow cobblestone alleys, surrounded by towering brick walls and glimmering hot sand. She laughed and the sound of this laughter echoed in every direction. A laughter that seemed to contain eternal happiness. Finally, arriving at an old blue door, the little girl drew a house on the sand and whispered, 'Come home'.

Maya woke up to a gentle tap on her shoulder. Startled, she opened her eyes, her heart was beating faster and her palms were sweaty again. She quickly scanned her surroundings. It was quiet and dark. The performers were gone, as was the crowd. And the cleaning crew was about done picking up the last bits of leftovers and empty glasses. The darbaan spoke in a soft voice that was barely audible, 'Madam, the show is over and it is past midnight,' he said. 'I noticed you fell asleep in your chair. Would you like me to walk you to your room?'

Before he could finish speaking, Maya stood up and hurriedly walked away, realizing she couldn't recall much after she had her first few sips of wine.

In a matter of few short hours, the morning came alive. The pale rising sun filtered through the white khadi blinds. The chirping of the birds grew louder, and the occasional beat of a drum was now more consistent. The loud and lively call of peacocks jolted her awake. She smiled. She noticed the crisp white sheets, the fresh fragrant flowers, and a pair of slippers neatly laid out by her bedside. It just felt good.

Maya climbed over to the edge of her bed and pulled back the blinds to see the most splendid peacock displaying its magnificent plumage on top of the roof. For some elusive reason this morning was different. The day was bright and Maya felt a tiny flicker of joy in her heart. She jumped right off the bed and pulled her hair up in a ponytail. She quickly changed into her shorts and grabbed her camera as she made her way downstairs to the garden.

Maya was greeted by the same darbaan who had offered to walk her to her room the previous night. 'Good morning Madam, hope you are feeling well-rested,' he said with a gracious smile and a reverent bow.

Maya felt a little embarrassed, yet touched by his concern. She bowed in return and said, 'Yes, I am. Thank you very much.'

Following her keen glance over his shoulder, the darbaan smiled and said, 'Peacocks are quite abundant here; you will find them roaming all over the property. That one right there is still very young but will soon grow into his glory. I'm not sure if you are aware of it but the peacock is India's national bird and greatly revered by the people here.'

'Really? I didn't know, but of course, given its beauty, it is quite easy to understand why it was chosen as the national bird,' returned Maya.

'Yes, it is beautiful indeed but interestingly, going beyond its appearance, a peacock is considered a symbol of joy, kindness, spirituality and grace. I guess it can be said that it seems to depict the core value system or the essence of this country,' he clarified.

'How is a peacock a symbol of spirituality?' asked Maya.

'Good question, Madam. The reason it commands this lofty status is in part because the peacock is associated with goddess Laxmi, one of the most worshipped Hindu goddesses that represents wisdom, knowledge and prosperity. Of course, as you will also notice, the iridescent eye of a peacock feather adorns Lord Krishna's Mukuta (headgear), depicting divine wisdom or third eye—a very high honour indeed.'

'Most religious beliefs, especially the Tibetan-Buddhist system consider it as a symbol of transformation of evil into good and suffering into enlightenment. They correlate its message of transformation to the goal of human existence. In fact, our ancestors believed a peacock could eat something as deadly as a snake and remain unharmed by the venom, by transforming it into this stunning iridescence.'

'Interesting!' admitted Maya.

'Well, I believe it is not too far from the western world view. I hear that even in the western world it represents resurrection and immortality—much like, what do they call it…ummm… that which rises from its own ashes?'

'The phoenix?' suggested Maya.

'Yes, that's right, much like the phoenix.'

'I never thought it could hold such a deep significance beneath its beauty. That is a very interesting viewpoint,' said Maya as she leaned sideways to capture an unobstructed view of a stunning peacock in all its splendour.

'Judging by the grand display of its glory, I assume it must be really proud to possess these alluring feathers,' remarked Maya as she picked up a feather off the ground.

The darbaan replied, 'You know Madam, as proud as it is to have these feathers, it knows well it doesn't own these. It enjoys them tremendously while it has them and when the time arrives, it sheds its plumage gracefully, usually once every year. It knows fully that the feathers it is about to shed aren't self-replacing, yet with an unwavering belief in nature, it lets go of its defining possession. From there on, through a process called "molting", nature enables the peacock to regenerate its feathers. That's how life rewards those who believe in it.'

'Fascinating! So now I also know what the "symbol of grace" is attributed to,' declared Maya.

'Well, that is enough about peacocks,' the darbaan concluded. 'I'm sure knowing all this will enable you to appreciate the true beauty of this bird. This way please,' indicated the darbaan as he led Maya around the building over to the other side. 'For some reason, this spot remains their favourite. You can always find them here. Be especially on the lookout in early mornings and on cloudy days, it will perform a spectacular dance in sheer ecstasy.'

As they reached their destination, the darbaan extended his arm and said, 'Here we are, Madam. You should be able to get your best shots here. I will send some fresh lemonade your way, and do let me know if I can be of any other service to you.'

With this, he bowed and left. Maya felt truly ecstatic capturing the bird from every different angle as it walked along the pathway, jumped to the roof and spun around in delight. The performance was mesmerizing. After clicking pictures to her heart's content and refreshed by a glass of ice-cold lemonade, she bid goodbye to the peacocks and proceeded for breakfast.

Maya smiled softly, recalling the words, *It has them but doesn't own them...yet it enjoys them tremendously.* 'How do you learn to enjoy that which you know will not last and how do you give up that which belongs to you, which defines you? Only if we could learn to do that with our possessions, our dreams, our relationships and our own self. No wonder it's so graceful... graceful in accepting and graceful in letting go,' she wondered.

As she walked along, Maya surveyed the lush green gardens at every turn, conjuring up images of men and women over hundreds of years, making promises, asserting their power, professing their everlasting love, claiming the sunset, the moon, the unchanging and the change itself. No trace, no recall. Who were they and where are they now?

Consumed in her thoughts, she almost tripped over a jutting stone, but caught herself in time.

A tiny voice whispered, 'Watch out, Memsahib, looking isn't enough sometimes.'

Maya smiled. 'Ananda, my friend, how are you?'

He suddenly broke into an electrifying grin and his big black eyes shone like the brightest diamonds. There was something about him that did not belong here, something powerful and pure.

'Couldn't be better!' he said with a twinkle in his eyes.

'And you Memsahib?' he questioned in response.

'Much better this morning, almost aligned with the local time. Coming from New York, jet lag can sometimes last an entire week. Thankfully, it wasn't too rough this time.'

Maya asked Ananda, 'Would you like to join me for breakfast?' Ananda replied politely, 'Thank you for the offer Memsahib, but I dare not. At least not here, although you are welcome to join us for a meal anytime. In India, there is a saying, "Atithi Devo Bhava" which means "Our guest is our god". We would be privileged to have you over, anytime at all.'

Maya smiled again, 'I will certainly take you up on that one, but since I am a guest in your country, which is also your home, will you honour me by introducing me to your country?'

Ananda replied cheerfully, 'Sure, there is a lot to see here— Hawa Mahal, Jantar Mantar, Amer Fort...'

Maya interrupted, 'Ananda, I'm not interested in the landmarks...the footprints...the remains. I want to feel the pulse, touch the soul, and experience the true spirit of this land.

'Meet me at 12 o'clock by the pool, Ananda, and be ready as my guide on this journey of exploration.'

Ananda was visibly confused and obviously delighted as he scampered away. Maya treated herself to a glass of fresh watermelon juice and a traditional Indian thali for breakfast. It was immensely rich, delicious and satisfying—kachori, aloo puri, halwa—served on a silver platter decorated with bright green banana leaves and accented with pink flowers.

Maya felt like a princess indulging in the grandeur, opulence, and ease of this place. She headed back to her room to change into her favourite garb—skinny blue jeans and a white Lanvin ruffled shirt. She had been warned upon arrival that beyond the premises of this hotel lies another world, which is orthodox. So, it was best to dress conservatively.

She didn't recall much of the two childhood years she had spent in Jaipur, but for most parts, she knew about the Indian culture based upon what she had read and heard from her family.

Maya was right on time. Little Ananda stood by the pool waiting, shifting his weight from one foot to another as if to keep his special shoes from wearing out. He leaned against the white wall, his gaze steady over the calm pool as if in a silent sweet conversation. The little man was handsome in his pristine white kurta and regal turban, a little too burdensome for his tiny head.

Ananda greeted Maya with his familiar heart-warming smile before questioning abruptly, 'Memsahib, before we embark on this journey, may I ask you something?'

Maya smiled as usual and prompted Ananda to continue.

'Why are you sad?' asked Ananda point-blank, cocking his head slightly.

Maya was taken aback. 'What makes you think I'm sad? I'm happy, smiling and having a wonderful time.'

Ananda elaborated, 'Memsahib, when you said that you wanted to experience the pulse of this place, I was a little confused about what you meant, and while you were gone, I kept thinking about it. Honestly, I was worried where I would take you for that experience. Just then, I observed some ripples in the water and after they vanished, the water became still. Then I noticed an undercurrent—a flow beneath the surface, it was right there, yet so easy to miss. Suddenly, I knew what you meant by "pulse of this place"—the pulse you were looking for is this same undercurrent that remains hidden beneath the surface, visible only to the keen observer.'

'That is sound reasoning indeed. You are very bright Ananda,' expressed Maya.

'Thank you Memsahib but I can't take 100 per cent of the credit for it, it was actually your strange request that got me thinking. You could have simply asked me to be your guide like so many tourists ask Baba. They want to see everything—the palaces, the historic landmarks, the crafts and jewellery, but you didn't ask for any of those. You were searching for what lies beyond them—the pulse.

'Coming back to your question, as I was reflecting upon all this, you walked in with a big smile and I observed that while you were smiling, your eyes were not.

'Amma says that eyes are the windows to the soul, the soul speaks its truth through them...but Memsahib, your eyes are empty...like you can't find your soul anymore...like it doesn't speak to you any longer...like you've lost your pulse.'

Maya was a little offended and felt exposed and vulnerable.

At the same time, she knew what he had just stated so plainly was something most people would neither observe nor have the courage to say—he had hit the nail right on the head.

Maya became thoughtful and her large brown eyes gleamed with welling tears, 'You are right Ananda, I am searching for my soul. Where, is also my question, why, even I'm not sure that I understand. It's complicated.'

Noting the change in Maya's expression, Ananda quickly apologized, 'I did not mean to hurt your feelings, it is just that I felt curious. I wanted to understand what could possibly make you sad.

'What I mean is we have many reasons to be sad. Life brings plenty of hardships and lots of challenges, but we fight to live, to overcome and we celebrate every little victory. But you are not like us. You have everything. I don't understand the reason for this contradiction, so I asked.

'Memsahib, if something is broken, you can fix it and if something is missing, you can create it.'

Maya paused as if to interpret the statement Ananda had just made. Of course, there was an element of truth there but it seemed irreconcilable.

'Ananda, the pain doesn't always emanate from the missing and the broken, sometimes it is the strong and intact reality that crushes a tender dream. Hope exists where a dream exists, despair emerges when the reality distances you so much from your dream, that you can't see it anymore...not even in a distance.'

'Besides, to fix something, we must first know what is broken, and to create something, we must understand what is missing. We go about it the wrong way. Every nail that we hammer in to close the gaps often works to wedge the part further and usually what we spend our busy lives painstakingly creating is the very wall that separates us from our joy.

'You may not get it Ananda, but one day when the wall comes down and the nails fall out, you will see a tiny flower emerging from the ground below. It will smile at the sun and say… "I need no more to be happy!"'

With this, Maya looked down towards her feet and mumbled, mostly to herself, 'Where feelings make us realize, logic can only rationalize… Sometimes we need to close our eyes and be held, more than we need to be awakened and shown the path. We need acceptance more than advice, we need to be wrong in order to understand the right, and we need to lose it in order to know its true worth. Perhaps we fall to rise and to be great and we break in order to recreate.'

She turned her head away looking through the wall that stood there in front of her, speechless, thoughtful, still. Suddenly, she burst out in another one of her feeble attempts at smiling, her eyes deceiving her actions again.

'Okay, forget all that Ananda!' she exclaimed. 'For now, all I can tell you is that I want what you have.'

Ananda laughed heartily. 'Really, Memsahib, you want what I have?'

Ananda laughed almost uncontrollably until tears ran down his cheeks and his stomach hurt.

'I have barely anything,' he said. 'What could you possibly want from me, and what could a poor little boy like me offer to someone who stands so far above me?'

Maya bent down slightly to look directly into Ananda's eyes and said, 'Ananda, my dear boy, you have something that money can't buy, something that status can't provide. You have bliss—the reason your mother named you "Ananda".'

With this, she tapped him gently on his head and said, 'You talk too much...let's go now.'

Kaleidoscope

'The way to do is to be.'

—Lao Tzu

$\mathcal{M}$AYA DECIDED NOT TO REQUEST for the car, she wanted to be one of the locals—the ordinary, the simple, the blissful, the fighter. As soon as they walked out, Ananda bolted into the middle of the busy street and leapt in front of a taxi, literally forcing it to come to a screeching stop.

Maya yelled at Ananda, 'Are you crazy? Heavy traffic pouring in from both sides and you jump right in the middle of it and place yourself directly in front of a taxi barreling down at 60 miles an hour, waving your arms down to stop it! Couldn't you hail it from the edge of the road?'

Ananda looked at her and proclaimed, 'Memsahib, Hukum says you can't live your life standing at the edge. It will pass you by. No matter how dangerous it seems at first you will never learn its ways by observing. You have to jump in, you will learn to adapt to the pace—and yes, there is always a risk but taking the risk, he says, is what makes it a life. We know people die of choking on food but we go on eating right?' Maya was neither impressed by his response nor his actions and certainly not by whoever gave him that piece of advice. She let out an exasperated breath and shook her head in disbelief.

Ananda tossed his backpack into the taxi and sat easy in the front seat next to the driver, while Maya uncomfortably hinged off the edge of the black grimy carpet spread on the back seat of the taxi. She cowered at a closer look, which suggested it might actually have been red and blue at one point in time. As much as Maya wanted to be ordinary, she realized it was loftier in thought than in practice. 'Oh well, tomorrow shall be a perfectly good day to be ordinary,' she declared as she instinctively pulled out her scarf and spread it on the carpet before sitting down and allowing herself to breathe again. She continued to maintain an upright stance, carefully balancing those bumps and brakes to ensure that at all times her arms and back steered clear of any direct contact with the seat.

Ananda was perfectly at home, having conversations about the weather and cricket and the upcoming celebrations with the taxi driver like they had been buddies for life. By now, Maya had tuned them out and was soaking in the city charm while latently maintaining her balancing act. She appeared amused to see this aspect of Ananda.

'By the corner of Bapu bazaar across from the gate is fine,' said Ananda.

The taxi driver parked the car and came around to see Ananda off. They shook hands and talked and chuckled even though the taxi driver was nearly three times Ananda's age. They then hugged and shook hands all over again and laughed heartily one more time.

As soon as Maya took out her wallet, the taxi driver became animated and excitedly waved his hand and shook his head, 'Oh no, Madam,' he protested, 'please put that away! How can I accept money from you? Ananda's aunt is married to my father's cousin's wife's nephew. We just discovered we are related. I cannot accept money!'

Maya was further baffled.

'I understand relationships, but what does livelihood have to do with that? Work is work and relationships are relationships, please accept this money. It's not a good idea for a horse to become friends with the grass, he will get into trouble sooner or later,' she insisted with a polite smile.

The taxi driver flashed an even broader grin, his teeth perfectly orange from the paan he was chewing. Maya quickly stepped back before his enthusiasm splattered stains on her white top, all this while keeping up her perpetual smile.

Trying to manage all the spit collected in his mouth, he tried to explain to Maya through his puckered lips and distorted speech, 'Madam, in India we believe that money is much like the dirt of the hand—today it's here and tomorrow it's gone.'

Maya's eyes gravitated towards the driver's hands, indeed layered quite heavily with dirt. 'Besides,' he continued, 'richness is not measured by the size of your bank account but by the size of your heart. A heart that knows how to give is as rich as a king and despite the greatest riches, a heart that keeps seeking more is poor as a beggar. You see Madam, abundance is not a matter of riches, it is a matter of trust. My heart is the master; I don't question its choices. And then my mind can keep telling me whatever it wants, I refuse to listen. I like Ananda, I will not charge money,' he insisted, as he ran his palm across his neatly flattened hair smeared with a strongly scented oil.

'*Okay bhai, phir milenge,*' he said as he waved to Ananda, and disappeared into the traffic.

'Quite a strange man,' muttered Maya to herself, thinking about how the word 'trust' had been appearing in her life so often lately.

'What was this about Ananda, why didn't he charge us?' questioned Maya.

'I suspect he might be one of those,' said Ananda.

'Those?' asked Maya.

'Yes, those that Baba refers to as "Malangs"—the ones unwise to the worldly ways but true to their heart. Baba tells me that once a person stops worrying for himself and simply follows the generous urges of his heart, life starts to compensate such people through its own means and in its own way. They are taken care of.

'But Memsahib, save your generous urges for humanity, it doesn't particularly work in shopping situations.'

Maya laughed, 'I wasn't born yesterday, Ananda,' and gave him a little pat.

Within minutes, she forgot all about the taxi talk and the driver. She was delighted with the bustle of tiny shops, stalls and vendors, each clamouring for her attention. Before she knew it, she found herself surrounded by a mob of vendors selling everything from scarves to figurines to key chains and incenses. She was like a magnet that attracted all the attention, a little unwanted perhaps.

Maya was overwhelmed with the crowd and the noise, and all at once, felt she would pass out in the heat and congestion. Sweating profusely, she took off her Bvlgari sunglasses, and looked for Ananda, only to find him standing to her side, seemingly entertained. He stepped forward and spoke what must have been some magic words in the local accent, for it instantaneously worked to disperse the crowd. Throngs of vendors and spectators streamed back to their businesses, as they would have from a packed theatre at the end of a movie.

Ananda laughed and offering her a bottle of cold water, said, 'Memsahib, welcome to India!'

'Is that how they greet all shoppers?' asked Maya.

'No, not all shoppers, but you certainly look like you belong to another planet, and a very rich one at that. Actually speaking, I just shattered their hopes of being able to sell a 20-rupee figure for ₹2,000 with their claims of charity to support working women and feeding the hungry. Or perhaps, an attempt to sell you an ordinary stone passed off as belonging to the royal family through the generations, finally to land in your very lucky hands. You are an easy target you know! We need to get you some low-key gear.'

Maya laughed with him and said, 'Why didn't you tell me that before we left the hotel?'

'Experience is the greatest teacher in life,' Ananda preached with a hint of humour. 'Hukum says knowing *why* is often more important than knowing *what*.'

'Of course!' chuckled Maya.

'Who is this "Hukum" that you keep quoting? Is he some kind of a sage or Guru?'

'Don't worry, I will introduce you to him today.'

'For now, the pulse of the Pink city awaits you,' he said as he bowed down and pointed towards the vibrant shops bursting with a colourful display of bandhanis and mirror-work umbrellas. The man behind the counter stepped promptly forward, 'Welcome Madam, let me explain to you the significance of our very special bandhani, this is no ordinary scarf. Limca or coffee?' Maya and Ananda glanced at each other and broke into laughter as they navigated their way through the sea of people, twisting and turning and elbowing and stepping.

Maya got quite a thrill out of this true-to-life shopping experience. She tried on colourful harem pants in orange and blue, red and green. Ananda nodded up and down to indicate a 'yes' and left and right to mean 'no'. And a strange, ever so famous, side to side Indian wobble that Maya wasn't quite sure meant yes or no. She tried on bangles and juttis (sandals) in emerald, gold and silver. She bought little mirror-work dolls and bright cushions. It felt like the world had suddenly transformed into a giant kaleidoscope.

Maya felt the colour seeping through her eyes into her heart. Everything seemed brighter and happier. Ananda showed her how to haggle—'If they ask for 1,000, you offer them 50.'

Maya laughed, 'I've never heard of 5 per cent being a negotiable start!'

'Well, you haven't heard of a 2,000 per cent markup either,' he responded.

They giggled and walked along like children running out of school and jabbering excitedly about the day they had. It was getting hot and Ananda asked Maya, 'Memsahib, how local would you like to feel?'

'As local as it gets,' came the swift reply and they chuckled again. He said, 'Okay, follow me!' They ran to a small shop at the end of the street named 'Pahalwaan Lassi Bhandar', literally translated as 'Wrestler Lassi Shop.'

Ananda ordered two large sweet lassis (yoghurt drink). The shop owner, wearing a white vest barely covering the top of his pot belly, hair slick with scented oil, and the giant moustache twisted upwards at the edges, broke some ice off a huge slab that lay out in the open, and covered it with a jute bag while constantly scratching his big belly. Maya cringed, but looked away as though she didn't see it and it didn't matter. He swatted the buzzing flies with a rolled newspaper just before handing her an enormous silver glass of sweet yoghurt drink with a thick layer of cream on top.

Maya looked at the sheer size of the glass and the thickness of yellow cream in disbelief and with another smile peeking through her eyes, held up the glass and toasted 'cheers'. The drink was nearly a meal in itself. Finished with the enormous lassi, Maya began to feel a little exhausted, 'Let's go sit somewhere for a bit,' she suggested.

Ananda responded, 'Albert Hall museum is just around the corner and it's one of my favourite places to visit.'

'And what is there to do at Albert Hall?' questioned Maya.

'I don't go there to *do*, I go there to *be*,' replied Ananda. 'Baba often brings me here, and for hours, we simply sit and watch hundreds of pigeons flying, we feel the breeze, enjoy the silence. Baba taught me that sometimes just being is the greatest doing,' replied Ananda as his eyes twinkled again.

Maya mused that he was too wise for his age, had an overactive imagination, a knack for storytelling or was actually blessed to have in his life this mystical Hukum who had the right words for every occasion and a Baba who appeared to be nothing less than a great Zen master. Whatever the case might have been, Maya could relate to him better than she could with most other people she knew. It was almost as if they were on a perfectly aligned mental plane. The words he spoke were responses to the silent questions in Maya's heart.

'You are so right Ananda,' Maya asserted. 'A great philosopher named Lao Tzu once remarked "The way to do is to be." Unfortunately, we have become so accustomed to doing things—to-do lists, endless tasks, errands, work, activities—that we've forgotten to experience *being.*'

'I don't even know what it feels like anymore to just *be,*' said Maya sadly. 'It sounds like an alien concept.'

Ananda responded, 'Well, there is nothing wrong with doing as long as it's in alignment with your being.' He continued, 'One day, Baba told me, "Ananda, always remember to be yourself, for when you're being yourself, your doing becomes a prayer, a meditation. You accomplish but don't feel the effort. You expand and move outwardly yet remain centred, grounded and totally at ease within. He believes that the very act of being contains the seeds of your becoming. It is a release, a fulfilment, much like the way a bud blossoms into a flower or a caterpillar transforms into a colourful butterfly. In that moment, the distinction between being and doing is transcended."' Maya listened intently, trying to understand the philosophy that this little boy seemed to have adopted and owned, like he was speaking about a way of inner life rather than the outer.

Maya seemed almost in sync as Ananda continued, 'I have learnt much from Baba and even more from Hukum. And every opportunity that I get, I make it a point to go back and share it with him. We frequently exchange emails. His words inspire me. I like reading them over and over so I print all his emails and save them in this file which I carry around in my backpack.

I'm compiling this collection of emails to serve as my personal wisdom encyclopedia,' laughed Ananda as Maya looked upon the backpack which displayed a worn-out hotel logo.

'In this way, I take him with me wherever I go. So now for the introduction. Hukum,' announced Ananda, pointing towards his backpack, 'meet Maya Memsahib, Memsahib meet Hukum.'

Maya smiled at the backpack. 'Good to meet you Hukum!' and they broke into another spell of laughter.

'So that evening,' Ananda continued, 'after spending the day here with Baba, I emailed Hukum about my experience, wait a minute,' he added with an impatient excitement as he dug into his backpack, fumbling through the pages.

'Found it! Here, read this, you will enjoy it,' exclaimed Ananda as he handed over the worn-out, slightly crumpled piece of paper.

It read, 'Hukum, today baba took me to Albert Hall and introduced me to the experience of being. He also said that being is the greatest doing. I enjoyed the experience tremendously and I think I understand his words somewhat, but how about you? I'm curious to know what you think about it.'

The response continued below, 'Ananda, powerful words, my friend. Remember to remember them, understanding will come with experience. For now, what I can tell you is that *being* need not be complicated. It can be a simple moment when you pause to appreciate that beautiful sunset on your way back home...it takes neither time, nor effort, just a gentle awareness, an attention to the moment...you have to be present there... neither trapped in the past nor a slave to the future. You are being when you break into that heartfelt laughter...when you smile at a stranger, or reach out to someone in need. When you experience a moment fully, you are being. We don't need more to enjoy the stars, to smell the roses, to hug a loved one, to feel the soft breeze and the warm sun. It's not the most momentous occasions but rather these little moments when you feel the most alive. As they say, life is a journey not a destination. Sadly, when you go along the journey with your eyes closed, you arrive at the destination empty-handed.

Wish that your journey through life will be one of doing which flows from your being.

Good luck my friend.'

Maya listened intently to the sound of her own words that fell upon her ears like raindrops falling upon a parched desert as she finished reading the email.

Ananda noticed how the spark in Maya's eyes just moments earlier was beginning to fade, replaced by the jaded dullness of an unfulfilled journey.

Ananda broke Maya's chain of thoughts and said, 'Well, it's never too late! Come on!'

Ananda pulled Maya by her hand as they ran through the huge flock of feral pigeons that scattered and raucously flapped their wings, taking flight against the backdrop of the setting sun. It was a spectacular view of tens of thousands of pigeons on ledges, on roof tops, feeding off the grounds and reaching for the skies as the busy sounds of the city came alive again.

Maya stood still and soaked in the moment of being. The temple bells were ringing and the aazaan from the mosque rose above the noise, lending an element of purity to the smoky dusk. People in colourful attires walked hurriedly across the streets, the horns from scooters and cars became louder as people with wearing patience returned home after a long day at work.

The vendors hawked from the sidewalk, selling coconut and peanuts. Groups of men huddled around the tea stalls, as they sat in a squat, bodies balanced on their feet, chit-chatting and sipping on tea, catching up over the day's events.

Maya was in the middle of motion, yet within her was a gentle calm that radiated through her body. Maya closed her eyes, stretched her arms out, opened her heart, and smiled softly. Ananda acknowledged with a nod.

'Thank you, Ananda, for sharing these thoughts,' expressed Maya. 'I know exactly what he means, strange as this might sound but his words seem to echo my own sentiments. I could never describe it as aptly but I've had a deep vague longing for it all along,' said Maya as she pulled out her phone. 'This was something I wrote few months ago, here, let me write this down for you...let your Hukum know I offer my thanks and share my sentiments in relation to his thoughts.'

'Memsahib, I will surely share your words with Hukum, he will certainly read into these better than I can.' A smile briefly touched upon Maya's lips before fluttering away like an elusive colourful butterfly as she scribbled:

'Just what would I give to have a day of my life...a day undivided between conflicting parts and not split among numerous roles...a quiet unimportant day of idleness where aimless wanderings of the heart are unquestioningly followed by nimble footsteps...a moment where even the incessantly rational mind surrenders to the soul...without a care of the time gone by or yet to come...to be...alone yet not lonely...me and myself delighting in each other's company...a moment when I breathe and am aware of my breathing...where I see the blue sky and feel my heart beating...where I listen to chirping birds at leisure

and saunter through the green fields...unhurried...unrushed...
feeling the gentle glow of the warm sun...where I sing a song
and chase the wind... I sit... I smile and I whisper...there are
days that are lived and days spent alive...and what would I give
for an unimportant day of my life...'

On her way back to the hotel, Baba and Hukum's words kept
playing on repeat in Maya's mind, like having listened to those
once was enough to etch them permanently in her memory.
As she reflected upon the words, suddenly her mind jumped to
the contact on the email, 'Did it read VPS@dreamsinpink.com?'

Yes, she was quite sure that was what the email read. Maya
promptly googled 'Dreams In Pink' on her phone.

A website called 'Dreams in Pink Charitable Foundation–
Jaipur Chapter' popped up. The header read 'Connecting people
with their dreams.'

She scrolled through stories of empowerment, courage,
events, fundraisers but not quite what she was looking for. She
clicked on 'About us'. No specific contacts were listed. It was
a generic section about 'US'—the enablers and the achievers.

Based upon his response which reflected a deeper outlook on
life and human behaviour, Maya had an uneasy suspicion that if
he wasn't an extraordinary Guru but an ordinary human being,
then probability was that like her, Hukum, strange as this name
was, might turn out to be a psychiatrist. Immediately, red flags
of caution started to pop up in her practical head. What if this
turned out to be someone she knows through her professional
network? In that case, she might want to think about the kind
of information and personal details she would want shared with
him. It could jeopardize her career, after all, that was the only
lifeline that seemed to have remained stable through all else

in her life. She wanted to stop Ananda but had no means of contacting him. The arrow had already left the bow.

Maya went into a panic mode and argued her own thoughts for a while before resting her eyes to a close. The panic started to give way to comfort as the words 'trust', 'grace' and 'malang' softly danced in her mind's eye and the visions of colours, taxi driver, laughter, letters and pigeon's flight wove a mosaic of hope. Maya paused restfully, she was ready to let go of control and greet what was coming her way with open arms...with trust and grace.

A Walk Down Memory Lane

'Nothing fixes a thing so intensely in the memory as the wish to forget it.'

–Michel de Montaigne

THE TAXI PULLED INTO THE grand circular driveway as young fountains of water gushed upwards to reach for the parched summer sky. The peacocks strolled around leisurely and tiny birds chirped incessantly.

The taxi halted to the bowing of the guards followed by the quintessential 'Khamma Ghani Padharo' (We welcome your arrival). Maya walked up the marble stairway sprinkled with rose petals as a sari-clad young girl came forward to greet her. She held a golden plate in her hand which contained an earthen lamp, incense and vermillion. Maya watched closely as she dipped her finger in the tiny tumbler and smeared the vermillion on Maya's forehead in a gentle upward stroke, mumbling some sacred chants all along. Maya didn't quite understand the significance of this ritual but somehow felt safe, as if the red mark was a talisman that would bring her good luck and protect her from harm.

The lobby was fragrant with jasmine. Maya picked up a wet towel and a tender bunch of fresh white mogra still moist with delicate droplets of water, tucking it casually in her hair as she made her way past the lobby. She caught sight of the resplendent lights, dancing in an ecstatic engagement with the musical fountains as the doors of the elevator slowly closed to shut the world outside.

Maya observed her reflection in the elevator mirror; the flowers in her hair and the brightness in her eyes conveyed an image of a forgotten repose. She entered her room, flung her bags and dropped on the heavenly bed with an intense wave of relief. 'YESSSS!' she whispered, feeling reassured that everything wasn't quite over yet.

It was close to 9 p.m. as Maya walked out into the open gardens. Part of her wanted to revisit the performance just to make a point of her comeback, yet a part of her shied away. She figured she'd had a long eventful day and a quiet dinner was all she cared for. She headed over to the Steam Lounge, a beautiful steam engine, recreated as a restaurant that impeccably conveyed the good old Victorian charm. Maya felt right at home with her favourite comfort foods. She ordered herself a glass of wine, house green salad and rich breads and pasta. She felt composed as she looked out the window of her compartment over at the regal structure. She enjoyed the stillness and softly closed her eyes to savour the first sip of wine.

Just then, her phone rang. It was her mom. Maya answered, 'Hi Mom.' Just the sound of Maya's voice was enough to let her mom know how she was feeling. She never quite felt the need to ask her how she was doing. Based on how Maya answered her phone, her mom would jump to 'what's wrong' or simply state 'I'm glad to hear you're doing well.' Tonight, it was the latter with a huge sigh of relief. She had been extremely worried about her beautiful, talented and loving daughter. Knowing she had nearly lost her had half-drained her own life. She believed that somehow her own life hinged on Maya's well-being.

Maya's reassuring voice wasn't pretentious. She told her all about Ananda and the day out in town, the scrumptious lassi meal and the interesting taxi driver. 'And Mom, there is even a tech-savvy mystical sage who writes emails of wisdom!' she laughed and giggled. 'Hang on, let me FaceTime you,' she said excitedly. And there she was, looking as brilliant as she sounded. She showed off her new avatar—dressed in harem pants and colourful bangles.

Her mom was besides herself with joy and promptly said, 'Be sure to apply a little black mark somewhere behind your ear, just to ward off the evil eye. Or better still, buy a bag of dried red chillies. Move seven of these around your head exactly seven times and request a chef to throw these on a hot griddle.'

'Really Mom, you want me to ask the chef to do that? Throw seven random chillies on a hot griddle? And then what? Watch it go up in smoke, smile and say thank you as that should be spicy enough to send my evil-wishers running for cover!' she said jokingly.

'Alright, never mind,' said her mom, a little embarrassed and very protective of her new-found smile. 'But be sure to apply the black mark, no one will even notice.'

Maya laughed receptively and said, 'OK Mom, if that makes you happy. My food is here and I'm starving, I'll talk to you soon.' Before Maya could hang up, her mom questioned, 'Do you recall anything of the city at all?' Maya answered casually,

'No, not really, it seems like my first time here and it's beautiful. OK I love you, now stop worrying and take care,' she said as she hung up the phone.

She stepped out of her train compartment after enjoying a richly indulgent hot chocolate fudge. The night was still. After an action-packed day, Maya finally had a brush with her own thoughts that, for a change, seemed equally at rest and right there with her in the moment as she sat on the platform bench. The server interrupted, 'Madam, this is a must,' extending a platter lined up with an assortment of paans. 'Try the sweet one,' he politely offered, 'if you would rather not experiment much.'

Paan was delicious and Maya was cherishing every minute of the open skies, warm summer nights, cool breeze and the silence. Somehow, something felt amiss. She had a very strong urge to smoke. Maya smoked occasionally—either when she wanted to feel in control or when she wanted to soothe her frazzled nerves. She pulled a box of Marlboro Lights out of her black sling bag and held it in her hand. The pack that had appeared as her confidant and her support all this while seemed like a coward now, inviting her to hold on to her dependence. To Maya today, it seemed as a chain linked to her dark past that had held her captive all along. Today, the association reminded her of the stressful, not-so-pleasant pleasant times instead of the infused sense of confidence.

She held the pack and stared at it for a while. She knew she was facing a new direction in her life. She had to redefine the rules, rewrite the script, redo the play and dictate the end. An end that would be worth finishing off. An end that wouldn't leave her begging for another chance. This was the chance, and she had to make it count.

Slowly, she walked away, tossing the cigarette pack in the trash can.

'That is a brave move,' came a voice from behind a newspaper.

It was a middle-aged man smoking a cigarette and browsing through the newspaper at this hour of the night. 'I noticed you contemplating this packet of cigarette—the duality of its two faces. I was betting you will give in to the temptation, given just the sheer setting for a smoke but you surprised me. Well done!' he said.

'I do believe that every conflict lies within us,' he said as he folded the paper and dropped it on the bench. 'The battleground, the fights, the limitations, the failure and the victory are all in our mind. The reality simply confirms and reaffirms. After all,' he added, 'what lies within cannot be resolved outside.' Maya looked at him with an unwelcoming glare. It was offensive to her that someone should be observing her in her private moments. She did not quite trust his appearance or his intention.

He stepped forward adjusting his glasses, extended his hand and said, 'Chetan, I write for *The Economist*.' His heavy voice was further muffled by his thick moustache. Maya politely responded, 'Good to meet you.' Chetan added, 'Sorry if that offended you but observation is part of my job. I read into things and form my judgement based upon that. People value my opinions, and my opinions are what pay my bills. Long story short, I'm expected to be in the know of the past, in control of the present and to a certain degree, a reasonable predictor of the future. And I often pretend I am. Sometimes I even believe it.

'I try to convince myself that my word and my mind are mightier than my emotions. But I also realize that while the battles may be won in the mind, winning the war also requires true healing. And healing only happens within the heart. The wound can be treated on the outside. You can apply a bandage on the surface, you can nurse the wound but you can't make it heal. Healing is a process that happens internally, one day at a time.

'In case you are wondering why I am saying this to you again, I observe what I see and I state what I know.'

'What do you see?' questioned Maya, a little self-conscious and inquisitive.

'I see myself in you. You remind me of my own struggle,' expressed Chetan.

'And what was your struggle against?' Maya probed.

'At a certain point in my life, I was dealt a huge personal loss. I survived, not everyone did. Those were some very rough and turbulent times. I woke up each morning and repeated to myself—I'm a man. A man does not shed tears, he stands up and fights with life. So, I fought with life and life fought me back just as forcefully, until I realized I could not win this war. I could neither suppress it nor defeat it by power, I could only transcend it by allowing it to make its way past me, through me, around me or over me but I had to make way for it. I had to make peace.

'Often pain and emotions must be fully experienced and deeply realized to be overcome. Denial does not make the pain go away, noise does not drown it, reason does not convince otherwise...what hurts must be confronted, acknowledged, felt and made peace with before it can be truly transcended—what feels its way in, must feel its way out.

'Food for thought, perhaps a piece of advice that might save you some unnecessary fighting.' With this, he stubbed out his cigarette, started to whistle and disappeared into the night. Maya reflected on his words that were power-packed with experience and brutal honesty.

After a restful night, Maya woke up feeling refreshed. Unlike the previous day, this day did not have the same fire to get Maya going. Yet there was a calm, a reassuring feeling within that everything would be just fine. She wrapped herself in the fluffy oversized white gown and wore her hair up in a knot. She picked up the newspaper from outside the door and ordered herself a pot of Indian tea 'with lots of ginger'.

For everything else about Maya being as American as it got, the love for Indian tea was what she had inherited from her mom. Her mom always had an excuse for a cup of tea. Whether you were sleepy or you couldn't sleep, you had a headache or a stomach ache, you were hungry or you had eaten too much, there was nothing to do or simply too much to be done—tea was the ultimate remedy. Her mom's, and now Maya's, life revolved around that perfect cup of 'cooked'—yes—'not brewed, but cooked' tea, and anything was a reason good enough.

Maya cuddled up by the huge bay window overlooking the gardens. The sun-kissed golden hair, the big brown eyes and the pearl-like skin made Maya look divine. She was in no hurry and browsed through the paper until she read of an accident in 'Ambabari'. The name rang a bell. What was it about this name? She had heard it before. Was this the location of some famous monument? She strained to remember and finally gave up. After finishing her tea, she put the paper down and headed to the shower.

As she brushed her teeth, suddenly, out of nowhere, while

she wasn't thinking, strangely flashed—'SD-52 Ambabari Jaipur'. She was startled, that's exactly how she recited her address. That was where she lived. It became more vivid, she heard the tiny voice, 'Where do you live? SD-52 Ambabari Jaipur.' Along with that came flashes of her playing in the front lawn under the soft glow of the sun and spring flowers in the yard. She sank to the floor as the reel started to play a flashback in her mind. She remembered the little doll her mom had gifted her, and, in a caring attempt to make her hair grow longer, how she had oiled and ruined it. And the happy bright red and pink flowers she had painted after getting her hands on her mom's lipsticks. She laughed recalling it while tears rolled down her pale cheeks. It was like a live viewing on a projector that showed the past, and she watched motionlessly.

This had been a part of Maya's life that she had managed to store in a deep dark attic in her heart. Her mom and Maya had moved to the US after losing her father in a car accident. They never talked about that life again although they carried deep-seated emotions—the understanding of a timeless, unceasing, unconditional love that stands beside one through each turmoil and every struggle. A love that sees you through, that even without a physical presence, somehow always delivers. Hazy reflections of her dad walking her on his shoulders started to appear, slowly growing clearer.

She recalled the summer lunches on the front patio, the bucket of mangoes filled with chilled water and floating ice cubes—the sweet fruity smell was still tangible. How her dad would dotingly watch her go through dozens in one sitting. It kept playing on. Life—when it was all too simple and days all too long.

Maya felt sharp pangs of nostalgia and decided to revisit her childhood home. She called the concierge and requested a car service to Ambabari. 'Right away, Ma'am,' came the response. Maya hurriedly stepped into the shower. She felt as if the floodgates of memories had been opened to this uncontrollable overflow. The images kept reeling in her mind, becoming more vivid with each step she took into it. She saw the small brick steps and the midway landing covered with bed sheets to create her playhouse. The tiny cups and platters with little pink roses. And the rooftop. She remembered lying next to her dad on crisp white sheets on cool summer nights, watching the stars and listening to her favourite stories. How she longed to touch the stars and couldn't ever understand why they were so far away from her reach. She distinctly remembered the backdrop humming of the table fan and flailing of bed sheets as waves of air tickled her face with each half-rotation while she stared into the open sky.

She remembered the impatient awaiting of the large pitcher of rose-flavoured milk chilled with ice, and quietly listening to the footsteps as her mom walked up with it. She could easily tell where her mom was at any given point of time by the jingling of the bunch of keys that she carried in a huge silver keychain that resembled an anklet with tiny hanging trinkets. She could see it so vividly that she was sure she could touch it if she just reached out.

Her parents were the epitome of love. Her dad wrote poetry for her mom, and she cooked him hearty meals. Maya recalled singing, dancing and catching butterflies. She also remembered being woken up in the predawn hours to the soft melody of religious hymns, peaceful glow of an earthen lamp and the peculiar fragrance of sandal incense. The breakfast table was her morning workshop, where she would paint 'The Starry Night' and 'Good Night Moon' themed artwork, reflecting images her heart had captured on the rooftop the previous night. It was proudly displayed on the Gem refrigerator that was situated in the main dining area with the sign of a glittering diamond next to its name.

The mornings were pious, days were blissful and the evenings took her on adventurous journeys to faraway lands, and for the climax, fireflies put up a magical show just like the grand finale of Fourth of July fireworks. Maya, as the little girl, secretly believed that these fireflies were just as much an audience and they applauded the ending by putting up a light show.

Saturdays were spent exploring the town. Rain or shine didn't matter nor did the mode of transport. They were as happy riding on their Vespa in the rain as they were singing in the back of their Volkswagen.

Sunday was the big day. It started with the sacrosanct head bath ritual. Hours were spent on outdoor daybeds, reading books while drying hair in the gorgeous natural sunlight. Lunch was a special treat, mostly dosas.

And then followed Sunday Part 2.

Right around 3 p.m., people would slowly start emerging on their terraces with colourful patangs (kites) and manjas (strings) for a colony-wise session of patangbaazi (kite flying). Gradually, the sky would turn into a colourful portrait, a collage of vivid colours and shapes as the entire town turned into one giant interactive playing field. People yelled, shouted, cursed, competed and, most of all, entertained each other. Maya jumped up and down to cheer for her dad who often asked her to pick a kite to engage her. Maya would pick the most colourful, in-your-face kind that appeared to brag in the sky or the humble one that belonged to her next door 'enemy friend' or 'frenemy' as she might have referred to. The sky was a vibrant battlefield. The fighter kites would engage one another relentlessly until one of them was cut loose and softly drifted away.

Children ran, following the drifting kite as they jumped over ditches and dashed across homes to catch the prized kite. The winner returned home like a victorious and valiant soldier who had just captured enemy territory and was returning home with a souvenir of victory held in his hand.

Maya's dad was one of the better kite flyers of the neighbourhood. After losing their own kites, the neighbours would gladly team up to join and cheer them on SD-52 rooftop.

The game usually wound up in time for the evening tea and hot pakoras as everyone settled down for the much-awaited movie of the week. It started sharp at 5.30 p.m. on DD National network better known as Doordarshan. DD's signature tune and the spiral visual seemed permanently imprinted in her memory as were the words from its logo, 'Satyam Shivam Sundaram', which she often reflected upon but could rarely make sense of.

If she knew it all so well, if she could even recall the logo, how did she not remember any of it—all those years?

Maya wanted to question, but she wanted something more than her answers, she wanted to keep walking further down the memory lane. Bewildered, confused, an Alice who may have found her Wonderland and was living a lifetime in a matter of minutes.

For most households, the ritual was the same and the movie

show, an event in itself. Often, a few families would get together to watch these in huge family rooms—adults and children, masters and helpers. It was the quintessential convergence of something everyone enjoyed in common regardless of age or class. There was pin-drop silence during the viewing followed by loud chatter and hustled trips to the kitchen back and forth during the interval. Maya recalled setting up her very first business right there. She used to stack a table and pull out snacks from the kitchen pantry to operate a snack bar where family and friends could 'buy' and munch on goodies without leaving the 'theatre'.

As much as Maya was a part of those memories, she was also a distant observer. She could watch but she could not be... she could see but she could not touch...it was there, and yet it wasn't. She had finally found something precious that she had lost years ago.

Maya felt hesitant stepping into the taxi. She didn't quite know what to expect. Would it be the same, or would it be different? Her thoughts seemed to run through her mind faster and louder than the sights and sounds through the window of the speeding taxi. Her mouth felt dry and her stomach felt a strong unease, a churning—an unsure nervousness, anxiety and questioning as though she was secretly going to meet an old lover. Maya firmly pushed her hand against her stomach in a feeble attempt to soothe her gut but she could feel the tangible throbbing. Suddenly, she glanced at a familiar looking water tank. This could not be the same water tank she looked up to, wondered Maya. She was small then and the tower reached to the sky. Today it seemed neither tall nor commanding, just one among the many ordinary structures that stood in a complex maze. Perhaps the tiny eyes were lost in the past, or the once tall structure paled in comparison to bigger and better designs or maybe she was simply mistaken.

She scouted the surroundings with desperate eyes but too much had changed for her to gain a reasonable perspective until she saw an old tea stall vendor in his makeshift tent. Yes, she was right! This was the tank and the tea vendor she called Baba. He looked perhaps a little older but he had been old ever since she had known him. Maya waved at him enthusiastically with a hearty smile and glittering eyes as she held the taxi's door tightly with her other hand as if in an attempt to hold herself back. He looked at her with the eyes of a stranger and went right back to his work.

Soon, the taxi came to a halt in the middle of a busy street. 'You have arrived,' he said. Maya insisted, 'No this is not it. I'm looking for SD-52 Ambabari.' He spoke, pointing towards the black marble nameplate that hung below the mailbox, 'You see that?' She stared long and hard trying to recognize the place as the driver interjected, 'Madam, don't waste my time. I have brought you to your destination, now I need to get back to work.' He was rather rude as he stepped out and opened the door making way for her to leave. Maya paid him. 'Keep the change,' she said, not as a token of appreciation but rather as an instruction for him to leave.

Maya stared at the house. This was not it, it appeared nowhere close to what she recalled. Was her mind playing tricks on her? Was it all a lie? The house stood there estranged and withdrawn while Maya eagerly awaited a sign of acknowledgement. She stood there silently staring at the aloof structure when she suddenly noticed the intricate work on the ledge near the window and her heart leapt in delight. 'YES. This is it!' Maya was besides herself with joy.

She recalled that her dad had invited some local artists to create this ledge with intricate jaali work, reminiscent of old-world charm. People travelled from distances to see this creation. It seemed that the new owner had changed everything about the house other than this small structural piece of art. She wanted to go and lay her hands on it.

'Yes, can I help you?' came the shrill voice of a rather short and bulky woman wearing blue rubber slippers, her sparse hair tied in a neatly oiled braid. 'Why are you here and what are you looking at?' she questioned with raised eyebrows and a loud voice. Maya, very politely, mentioned, 'We lived here many years ago and I just came by to see the house.' She asked if she could come inside but the lady slammed the gate saying, 'We don't let strangers in the house.' She walked away, shaking her head and mumbling loud enough for Maya to hear, 'Lived here! Like anyone who ever lived here owns a piece of this house forever. Show up when you feel like and expect us to welcome you anytime. Next thing I know is the past owners will be occupying this house while we would be waiting at the door.' As she opened the door to her house, she looked back angrily one more time, 'You are still here girl...shall I send my son to deal with you?'

Maya ran away barely holding her tears back. She ran until she came to a dusty dead end where stood a kind old mulberry tree. Maya instantly recognized it. Its branches were once the playful arms that Maya climbed and sat upon and today they were the arms that opened in embrace. Maya hugged the tree and sobbed. As strange as it was, she felt a connection, like the old tree recognized her from the little girl she once was... it understood her playfulness then and it understood her pain today. Maya sobbed, unsure if it was the woman's rudeness or the pain of reliving the old memories that was making her weep. She cried her heart out.

As the minutes passed, the loud sobs transformed into shallow sighs and the flood of tears slowed down to a trickle. Maya started to feel better, overcome by a feeling of peace cradled in the arms and shelter of the tree that now seemed like a gentle grandparent.

She pulled out a pen and paper and wrote...

You walked me high above the crowd on your shoulder...
because I was too little to see...
You showed me the moon and the stars at night and told
me where I could be
Your hands that clapped in sheer delight to see my first step
in joy
The arms that held me when I felt weak and renewed my
strength somehow
You placed those hands beneath my feet so won't hurt me
the sun or sand
You cried and you smiled...you held back and you gave...
for destiny wasn't in your hands
I went away to start my life anew and to learn to walk alone...
I stopped in doubt many a times but you waved me to carry on
Patiently you stood there always...as a rock so reassuring
Knowing your hands will contain somehow...every sorrow
and each turning
And then you went so far away...I no longer see those hands
or stars

I stumble and I stand...I long and I pine but my true anchor seems afar
What's a daughter truly...without her dad... But a tree without a shade...
A garden in all its glory...yet every blossom fades. I miss you, Papa!

Maya sat there for a while neither thinking nor reflecting. She just watched the neighbourhood buzzing, children shouting and running, mothers walking with bags of groceries, postman delivering mail on a black Atlas bicycle. So much had changed and yet so much was still the same. It was all so alive and throbbing within her soul, yet no traces of it were to be found in the physical manifestation anymore.

The shadows of her past, the laughter of the little girl and the memoirs of her life were lost somewhere in this sprawling urban jungle. A rapidly expanding forest that seems to have submerged and trampled the fleeting footsteps of the tiny birds that briefly halted on their migratory journey through this once open land.

Maya slowly gathered herself and stood up to look at the tree. Her heart whispered notes of love that the kind tree acknowledged with its sweeping leaves. She quietly walked away without looking back.

Like for a weary traveller who has lost his luggage, the journey seemed long and the destination far...

Simple Abundance

'Not what we have but what we enjoy,
constitutes our abundance.'

–Epicurus

 ACK AT THE HOTEL, MAYA spent the rest of the day in her
dimly lit room. She couldn't quite put her finger down on what
it was, but she was overcome by a deep dull pain, a melancholy.
She recollected Chetan's words, 'Battles may be conquered in
the mind but wars are won in the heart, where true healing
happens. You can't fight pain, you must transcend it.'

She felt a few cold tears dampening her pillow before passing
into a lonely sleep. She was woken up by a knock on the door.
'Good evening Madam, may I come in? I have some tea and
a letter for you.'

Maya did not pay much attention to the mention of the
letter but the cup of tea was what she truly needed. She pulled
aside the curtain to let in some light and looked out over the
evening smog, chirping birds and a few flickering lights amid
the dimming sunlight. It must have been close to 7 p.m. She

finished her tea and noticed the letter placed next to the teapot, it was a beautiful red envelope tied with an orange thread. She reached out and opened it casually, expecting it to be an invitation to some hotel exhibition. The cover read, 'You are invited. She flipped it open and read the words 'To our home.'

Maya was taken aback. 'Could it mean that the woman possibly changed her mind? No!' Maya quickly dismissed her own thoughts with reason. 'That could not be. Why would she invite me back after sending me away like she did? Besides, she would not know where to find me,' she contemplated. Maya turned the card over to read 'Atithi Devo Bhava'. Of course, she smiled! Ananda it was, yet again!

Maya knew exactly where to find him. She ran over to the poolside and found him skipping rocks as usual. As he saw her approaching, Ananda yelled. 'These rocks tell me that your life is about to change,' he proclaimed in a happy, certain voice. Maya responded with a faint smile as she walked towards him, wearing a white silk shirt and green pants, hair casually tousled, and her bare brown eyes a little swollen and puffy. She held the red card in her hand, as Ananda started to explain without being asked.

'I told my mother about you and she insisted we invite you to visit our home and village. Who can argue with mothers? Despite all my protests and reasoning on how you are used to living in comfort, she insisted that the greatest comfort is found in hearts filled with love, not rooms filled with luxuries. She asked me to state this to you exactly like that—we welcome you to be our guest, and allow us this opportunity to serve our god.' Maya bit on her lip in an attempt to keep her tears in check. She choked and silently nodded her head.

Ananda said, 'So come on, let's go!' Maya questioned, 'Now?' sounding a little surprised. Ananda replied, 'Now, why not?'

'...But I need time to pack and plan,' said Maya.

'Plan for what?' said Ananda. 'Memsahib, you plan too much and live too little. What I mean is...well, I will let Hukum explain this, he does a better job. I sent him an email sharing your thoughts and he responded back with this,' said Ananda, handing her another printout.

Maya eagerly grabbed it from his hands. Somewhere, she had been looking forward to this response. Back in New York, Maya had coffee friends, book club friends, Broadway friends, movie friends, travel friends, and gala friends but never before had Maya opened up her heart to bare her innermost feelings to someone. No one had read her personal thoughts, no one had commented on those, partly because she wasn't sure anyone would get it, but this was different. She knew without a doubt that in those hands, her words would find both their meaning and their reason. Whoever this person was, he seemed to have gained Maya's respect with his unconventional outlook on life. He seemed so very right. Maya read the words carefully again.

'Ananda, thank you for sharing the beautiful prose. The words about days spent living and days spent alive convey a yearning of a life half-lived, like a flower waiting for the spring, a nightingale aching to sing and a bird longing to fly. It conveys a sense of someone who is torn and conflicted between her heart and her mind, her demands and her desires, her life and her dreams. It is the price which every dreamer pays to live in this world which sells it a tomorrow that doesn't exist.

'Unfortunately, it is all too easy to get seduced by the logical whisperings of our mind that prefers to live everywhere but in the "now". There will never be that one day when all our work is done and we can finally engage with life on our own terms. We must be prepared and ready to seize the moment when it presents itself. We must learn to ignore the ticking of the clock and recognize the beating of our hearts. We must live it by our inner rhythm, the yearning as it emerges in our hearts.

'The desire or longing must be quenched when it arises, just as we would drink water when we are thirsty as opposed to drinking because it is time to drink.

'Also tell your Memsahib, that after many years, when she looks back over her shoulders and tries to recognize her life, it would not be the well-managed hours or the efficiently executed plans but the handful of timeless experiences which she will steal out of time to carve a beautiful memory, that will still be standing there. In her own words, it's not the days spent living but the days spent alive that count.

'Important things can wait, but life can't. Flow with it!

'My best wishes.'

'Need I say more?' questioned Ananda innocently.

'After reading this email Memsahib, I suggest you adopt this piece of advice. Quickly pack some clothes and get set for another adventure. I can't promise it will be comfortable but I can promise it will be worth it.'

Maya needed no further convincing. Quickly buying into Ananda's suggestion, Maya exclaimed, 'Give me 20 minutes.' She excitedly tied her hair up in a knot and said, 'I will be right back. And convey my heartfelt appreciation to Hukum for his time and kindness.'

Maya was secretly grateful that she would not need to spend the night alone. Time and again, little Ananda was proving to be quite the angel she had needed. And this Hukum guy was impressive to say the least. His words certainly seemed to have a therapeutic effect on Maya, easing her constricted nerves and releasing her unyielding stress. It was no less than a deep tissue massage therapy and a counselling session delivered in a compact five-minute letter-exchange ritual. She was also rediscovering the lost art of letter writing and messenger deliveries. It held a greater charm than instant and incessant texting.

While she was aching to know more about him, she also did not want to know. He could be an old grandfather, or a family man, he could be someone she already knew or someone she would never care to have known. She did not want to ruin it. Right now, it was a black hole that she could neither see nor reach, which acted as a repository of her unrestrained emotions and fears.

Maya had always found comfort and consolation in one of her own theories—a perfectly imagined fantasy was far better to live with than a flawed reality. She had always been a dreamer at heart and a hopeless believer in fairy tales and happy endings.

Maya was gone for a little over 20 minutes. She returned dressed in jeans and a long white kurta with a colourful tie-dye scarf casually wrapped around her neck. The lessons of Bapu Bazaar were not yet forgotten. Ananda's father soon arrived, a tall lean man still dressed in his traditional hotel uniform. The deep folds of his wrinkled face contained untold stories of his toil and strife, yet his kind and loving eyes spoke volumes of gratitude, gratefulness to existence and a complete acceptance of the role assigned. Ananda proceeded to bow down and touch his feet. His father lovingly blessed him and together they walked up to Maya.

Maya, a little unsure of the greeting norm, folded her hands and vaguely nodded her head. He smiled and with an indication of his hand, asked her to lead.

There was an uncomfortable silence as the three of them walked together through a rough, nearly two-and-a-half-mile stretch of narrow roads and filthy streets. Maya placed her steps gingerly, avoiding pungent heaps of trash and scattered filth as if she was navigating a landmine territory. She looked around to observe dimly lit passages blaring various radio and TV stations, barking dogs, loud kids playing recklessly in the middle of these streets, shouts, screams and seemingly unending chaos.

Maya was already beginning to doubt her decision. 'Sure Ananda is a good boy and means well and perhaps things were going to get better but am I being too naive, too impulsive perhaps?' She questioned herself and her rationality in taking this decision. There was no arguing the fact that they belonged to different spheres of life. All her life she had been taught not to trust strangers, and the idea of trusting people she knew little about and that too in an unknown land didn't seem very prudent. 'Am I overstepping my own boundaries?' she questioned. 'And even if it is not so dangerous, is there really any common ground? Is it really rational, logical, smart?'

She was snapped out of her self-absorption by the noise of a squabble. She noticed two middle-aged, short and heavy women standing by the water tap. Their hair tied up in tight buns, sarees pulled above the ankles and tucked slightly around the waist, they were fighting bitterly over their turn to fill the bucket first. They were surrounded by some obviously amused spectators.

Ananda spoke, 'Don't look so surprised, these women

are not really fighting, they are simply trying to create some entertainment around their lives. I mean…literally! They have been having this argument for years, and quite interestingly, there is another tap just 50 metres away. But what good would life be if they had nothing to argue about? Imagine each one going to a different tap, filling their buckets with water and returning home. That would be unbearable,' he laughed sarcastically, 'I can't imagine!'

Maya did not respond to the comment obviously aimed to strike her as funny. Ananda quickly responded to her sombre look by confirming, 'We are almost home.'

Maya walked quietly along, lifting the scarf just a little to cover her nose and avoid the dust and pungent smell. As they walked along, gradually the dullness and noise of the village started to fade away and was replaced by the silent brilliance of the moon and the stars. Before she knew it, all she could see was the infinitely vast sea of coarse brown sand, and the cool silver moonlight kissing the ground before shattering itself into a million scattered jewels.

At a distance arose a soft glow from what seemed like a small grouping of mud houses and the warm smoke from burning wood stoves. 'This is our "Dhaani",' said Ananda pointing towards the group of huts. 'We are all one big family here—aunts, uncles, brothers, sisters, cousins and relatives. We have some common ancestral property a little distance away that we take turns cultivating. Regardless of who actually cultivates the field, it is considered a collective effort and we share the produce equally among everyone.'

Maya was relieved at this sight and her racing mind started to relax just a little. Soon they arrived at a slightly elevated doorstep. A mud-plastered wall ran around the boundary providing an enclosure to their modest home. Ananda gently knocked on the door which was promptly answered by a lady in a veil. Ananda reached forward to touch her feet and said 'Maya Memsahib is here.' He made a quick introduction, 'Memsahib, this is my Amma.' Maya muttered 'namaste' under her breath as she stepped forward.

The door closed behind them and Amma lifted her veil, resting it in a fold on her head. She was simple and beautiful with an absolutely heart-warming smile. She wore a large red bindi on her forehead, and bright red sindoor adorned the parting of her hair. Amma's jingling bangles and chiming silver anklets added melody to her movements as she walked to and fro, clad in her traditional attire that somewhat resembled a flowing ankle-length skirt paired with a buttoned shirt and a muslin chunnari. 'Khamma ghani Memsahib,' said Amma. Maya interjected, 'Call me Maya please.' Amma offered a reluctant smile as she remarked, 'Memsahib, I mean Maya, my apologies for any inconvenience. Our homes here do have light bulbs but we rarely get electricity, so for most part of the evenings we rely on traditional lanterns and good old earthen lamps. Hope that will not be too bothersome. One of our distant relatives owns a generator, and I have requested him to send it over but I'm not sure how long it might take.'

Maya looked at the golden glow of the earthen lamps resting in little crannies of the courtyard wall, the peaceful moonlight sweeping the floor. She felt the soft breeze and heard chirping crickets. Maya exclaimed, 'Amma, this is beautiful just as it is.'

Beautiful it was, and even in the soft glow of earthen lights, the intricate white painted designs on the walls and the entrance stood out. The courtyard was clean and sparse and showcased in the middle was a beautiful tulsi plant resting in a large white rectangular pot. On one side of the yard was a small structure sectioned off to a side and at the other end of the courtyard stood a humble hut with wooden doors, thatched roof and a plastered verandah.

Maya's concerns about her decision started to melt away as she was overcome by a feeling of inspiration that arose from the simplistic beauty of what stood in front of her. Amma hastened her pace as she prepared to serve dinner. 'I'm sure this has been a long day for all of you, I will bring the food right out.' Ananda quickly rolled out three woven mats, multisectioned steel thaalis and large steel glasses. With a quick sideways nod and rapid eye movement, Amma indicated for Ananda to replace those with shinier, brighter, newer looking plates and glasses. Maya insisted this was perfectly fine but Ananda shrugged his shoulders, 'Amma says so, therefore it must be done.' Amma started laughing, 'Memsahib, I hope Ananda hasn't exhausted you with his big talk. The villagers have an idiom to describe his old soul. They claim "Iske Pait Main Daari Hai", which means, "he has beard growing in his stomach."' Maya burst into laughter, 'That is a very funny expression, I have not heard that one before. What does it even mean?' Ananda jumped in, 'It means to have an old head on young shoulders,' and they all laughed together.

Maya, Ananda and his father sat down to eat while Amma served steaming lentils, fresh vegetables and perfectly round baajra rotis. Maya insisted that she eat with them, but for Amma the joy of a good meal lay in her loving service and fulfilled smiles. She kept bringing more food and Maya devoured this light cooking with peculiar spices and fresh ingredients. 'This by far has been the most satisfying meal I have eaten over the entire trip. I am so full that I don't know if I will be able to eat for another week,' she said. 'You eat better when you eat together,' said Amma as she adjusted the scarf over her head and smiled.

Amma showed Maya to her room which was a sparsely furnished open space, with a low-lying platform bed and two large windows directly across from each other. The only accents in the room besides the bed, a utility box and a mirror were the exposed beams and a wooden ledge with a space to rest the lamps, decorated underneath with similar paint art.

Pointing towards the box, Amma suggested, 'Maya Memsahib.' 'Maya please,' she corrected Amma. 'Yes, of course. Maya, you may use this to store your belongings. I have placed a glass of water by your bedside, please get some rest, you must be very tired.' Maya sat down on the edge of the bed. The sheets were clean and crisp white, the room was neat and outside the window, danced waves of crops in the small mustard field. The light and clean notes of mogra infused the air with sweetness. It was drop dead quiet and absolutely gorgeous.

She pulled the phone out of her bag with a desire to tweet about this little Zen-like oasis she had discovered, but of course—she looked down at the 'No service' signal and smiled. Slowly but surely, each habit and every dependence was falling by the wayside. It was time for her to stand on her own...to live, to experience, to attain...all for its own sake...freedom in its true sense and form. 'Oh well, so be it!' she said as she put her phone away, not regretting for a minute this loss and soon passed into a deep restful sleep.

There was a nip in the air and Maya wanted to snuggle under the covers just a little longer. It was barely 5 a.m. but seemed as though it was well into the day. The courtyard was buzzing with activity. Maya stepped out on to the narrow verandah.

Day was just breaking in, the deep dark orange hue slowly fusing into the gentle blue of the night. A light mist enveloped the barely visible trees and a thick blanket of fog rested on the fields that still seemed fast asleep. The cuckoo sang its happy song perched on the branches of a mango tree, as a pot of tea boiled atop the clay stove powered by burning logs. The smell and smoke of burning wood reminded Maya of her favourite fireplace back home. It was a perfectly cozy morning.

They huddled together next to the stove as Amma poured tea in small handleless terracotta cups that she called kulhars. The earthy aroma of terracotta seeped into the spiced tea and gave it an unusual flavour comparable to the hint of oak in a bottle of well-aged wine. Maya reached out to hold Amma's hand and said, 'Thank you Amma.' Ananda's father silently looked with an approving smile and affectionate eyes, content with the abundance and simplicity of this life.

Maya and Ananda followed Amma for most part of the morning. They took turns feeding chaff into the 'toka', the fodder from which was then contained in large piles of loosely tied muslin rags. Maya carefully balanced the pile over her head while cautiously taking tiny steps as the three of them made their way over to the cows. The large piles that appeared a lot heavier than they actually weighed left a telltale trail both behind and beneath. By the time they arrived, Maya was covered in hay with tiny pieces scattered all over her hair and clothes. 'Memsahib, you look like a scarecrow; look, even the birds are flying away,' said Ananda with a boisterous laugh. Maya and Amma followed suit.

Maya derived quite a thrill out of this adventure. She secretly also enjoyed the fact that she was being treated as though she belonged there, as if she was one of them. The cows came running up as they walked in with food and followed them right into the barn. Maya watched Amma in awe as her hands transformed into a mechanical instrument with precise motion and timing as she swiftly filled bucket after bucket. Ananda entertained Maya all this while with a name and story for each one of the cows. At the moment she was milking 'Kamli'. Her name was Kamla but since she was a little strange in her behaviour, he lovingly called her Kamli (crazy). Occasionally, Amma directed a stream aimed straight towards Ananda's mouth.

Maya was delighted. She believed this was the coolest thing ever. She recalled how arrogantly 'natural' she had felt walking down the organic unpasteurized aisle at her favourite farmers market but this was beyond comparison!

Amma got busy preparing meals and cleaning the house as Ananda and Maya lounged in silence on a charpoy (string bed) under the shade of the large kikar tree. Maya brushed her hand across the coarse ropes woven in a delicate pattern as she sat at the edge of the charpoy staring motionlessly into the vast openness. Country chicken ran freely around and the flies created a consistent hum.

Maya projected a hazy vision of herself perched on her dad's shoulder as they sauntered across the open vistas. Ananda noticed her crystal gaze but chose to remain quiet. In a sombre voice, Maya muttered, 'I must call her. I need to speak to my mom.'

'Sure, why not?' offered Ananda reassuringly.

'It will take us a while to get back to the city for your phone to find a network connection, however, back in the small town that we crossed last night, there is a public telephone booth. Would you like me to take you there?'

Maya nodded her head and stood up, her gaze still intently fixed onto the vast openness. She walked quietly beside Ananda until they arrived in the midst of civilization once again. The town wore a different character during the day with the peculiar paints and coloured doors. Of course, shabbily dressed happy kids still ran down alleys yelling and calling each other and the shops bustled with business, but the colour added a new dimension—an uplifting vibrant backdrop.

Ananda pointed towards a man standing next to a chair and table placed under a tree. 'That right there,' he indicated in an attempt to gain Maya's attention, 'is my haircut salon.' Maya noticed a man sitting comfortably in a fragile chair with wobbly legs that she was sure would crumple if she so much as blew at it. He appeared rather relaxed in the hair-covered smock tied around his neck. He smoked and blew perfect circles through the lathered shaving foam, immensely enjoying this open air shave as an old boxy radio suspended from one of the tree branches blared Bollywood songs.

A young boy delivered small glasses of steaming tea in a manner that could more precisely be described as dancing rather than walking. Maya observed just how happy everyone seemed, everyone except her. She walked on, trying harder than ever to conceal her emotions. The sun was strong and the sand beneath her feet radiated heat.

'How much longer to the phone booth?' she enquired

impatiently, breaking the long spell of silence. Ananda halted and responded in a kind voice, 'We are here.' They stood in the middle of the bustling bazaar and Maya could see everything but what she was looking for. Ananda asked Maya to follow him as he stepped through the door onto an unwelcoming and dark flight of narrow and high steps. Maya's heart began to pound faster and tiny droplets of sweat appeared on her brow. She could not tell if this was anxiety or claustrophobia.

At the top of the steps was a small room with an old desk, a stool and a phone. Behind the desk, slept a man in his vest, his feet rested on the table and a handkerchief covered his face. Behind him was a small window with thick iron bars that made it appear more like a cage than a window. Each wall was painted with prominent STD, ISD and PCO signage in yellow and black. Ananda cleared his throat—synonymous with 'Excuse me'—and the man without moving his feet or removing his handkerchief, responded lazily, 'Phone is on the table, dial the number and make your call.' Maya sat on the plastic stool and stared at his dirty feet and then back at the plastic encased phone right next to it. She hesitated for a moment, feeling unsure.

The voice spoke again, a little louder this time 'The phone is on the table, dial the number and make your call.' Maya was a little frustrated yet this prompted an impulsive response. She quickly picked up the phone and dialled her mother's number as if not allowing herself a chance to question. There was a shrill beep and the man finally uncovered his face and turned around to stare at the meter display that now showed the time and charges as they jumped by the second.

Maya held the phone. She heard her mom's voice, 'Hello, yes, who is this? Hello... hello...' Maya remained quiet. The man was now staring her in the face with an expression that clearly read, 'Have you lost it? The meter is jumping lady, talk now and think later!' Maya did not want any observers, interpreters or intruders through her emotional journey.

Slowly, Maya spoke in a soft voice, 'Mom, it's me...' her mother asked, 'Is everything okay?' Maya instantly changed her tone and probably her decision as she exclaimed in a high-pitched happy sounding voice, 'Oh yes, it's all very good,' she said with tears welling in her eyes as she recalled yesterday's visit. 'I just wanted to let you know that I'm with Ananda's family for a few days, there is no cell phone coverage there so my phone will not work in case you try. I did not want you to get worried so I thought I would let you know. Don't worry, I'm having a great time Mom, and I will call you soon. I love you.' Maya hung up before her mom had a chance to respond. She settled the bill and left hurriedly. Their silent shadows grew longer and darker as they walked back home.

Later that evening, as the family gathered together for tea, Maya enquired, 'Is Ananda back? He had mentioned he was going into town for some work but it's been a few hours.'

Just then, Ananda walked in and announced, 'Amma, I am taking Memsahib to see the Purana Kila (The old fort).'

Maya resisted, 'Ananda, we will do this another day.' Amma laughed, 'You will not win this one Maya. I do not know what connection Ananda has with that place. I often try asking him why he goes there. He repeats the same reasoning. "When I can't find myself anywhere, I find myself there," he says. He is a little hard to comprehend sometimes.'

Maya's faint smile paid her the first visit that day. Ananda was pleased to see that.

Ananda led Maya along a stretch of rocky barren land that seemed to grow increasingly arid as they progressed. The path was covered with sand, dust and rocks, with occasional patches of wild vegetation and small thorny bushes. The sun was still strong and the sand bright.

Ananda pointed upwards and said, 'You see that Memsahib; we are going to the top of that hill.' Maya looked up in exhaustion. Ananda comforted her, 'Don't worry Memsahib, it seems a lot harder than it actually is. Baba tells me you can focus on the distance or on the destination. He says if you look at the distance, the road will appear to be separating you from your destination, but if you look at the destination, the road appears to emanate from it. What separates also connects. Besides, something good awaits you there and you're going to like it,' indicated Ananda with his signature twinkle in his eyes.

A sceptical Maya trudged through the winding path making occasional pit stops for water. As they approached the top of the hill, Ananda cautioned, 'From here on, I am required to follow strict instructions so please do as you are directed.'

'Are the instructions a part of some posted warning?' asked Maya wondering about safety concerns that she needed to be aware of. 'Oh no,' chuckled Ananda, 'these guidelines came in an email from Hukum.'

'Hukum?' Maya felt better at the very mention of his name, as if a dark cloud had just appeared in the scorching sky, shielding her from the harsh heat and offering her a promise of relief. She almost looked forward to these counselling sessions with this mysterious angel.

Finally in her life she had found the opportunity to be on the other side of the table, where instead of analyzing others' problems, she was reflecting on her own. She felt free to express her emotions without fear, hesitation or judgement. This was because Hukum belonged in a reality that did not overlap with her world. He was as much as he wasn't and she liked it. It gave her the freedom to be herself unabashedly. For in a space free of baggage, with no image to live up to, no expectations to meet, no motives to achieve, and no destination to reach, we begin to unfold our petals and reveal our true colours.

'Now stop asking questions Memsahib, you will miss the very reason we are here,' reiterated Ananda. 'Close your eyes, and keep them closed, move forward, keep coming, to the left and now stop.' He led her a few steps forward and adjusted her angle. 'Now,' he said, 'you may slowly open your eyes.'

Maya opened her eyes and stood speechless. From what appeared to be ruins of an old fort with broken walls and rundown structures, the panorama was simply spectacular.

In front of her stretched a horizon that seemed to unite the brilliant sky with the sweeping views of the vast city into one unified canvas suspended in a dimension beyond time. Maya was exhilarated.

After a few moments of silence, Ananda took out a letter.

'This one is for you.'

'For me?' she asked, sounding a little baffled.

'Yes, fresh off the printer at 1.45 p.m. What do you think I was doing in town?'

Maya smiled as she impatiently read on.

'Khamma ghani. I send you my greetings!

'Hope you are enjoying the beauty and splendour of this place.

'In my growing up years, I would often come to this place and I greatly encourage Ananda to do the same. He may not fully realize the significance of why I ask him to do that, but one day when he grows up and might be dealing with one of life's challenges as all of us do from time to time, this place will speak to him, it will offer him a shift of perspective.

'Ananda is a special boy and I have been somewhat of a godfather to him.'

'Godfather,' Maya paused to read the word again.

Maya looked at Ananda with an element of unpleasant surprise blended with a tad bit of disappointment, 'So...is he your godfather?'

'I don't know about that but in India we have a custom called "Gudti"—ceremonial first feeding of honey to a newborn. The family chooses a person they hold in high esteem and desire for their child to model after. In my case it was Hukum. So yes, maybe he is my godfather because other than Baba, he's always been there for me,' replied Ananda.

Maya felt a little disconcerted but shrugged the feeling to read on.

'Ananda called me today. He tells me you are dealing with certain problems in your life.

'First off, may I humbly suggest that there is an inherent problem with the term "problem" itself. When we call something a problem, we are already judging it by using this label. I prefer to call it a "situation". And every situation can be observed in multiple ways, and each observation has a specific sequence attached to it. What we perceive then defines what we process, which determines how we judge and the label we place—"good or bad", "positive or negative"—that we start to believe as the factual reality. Our judgement triggers a chain of emotions, responses and reactions which essentially align our situation with our judgement.

'In essence, it isn't truly the "problem" that matters but our response to it. The events in themselves are objective; it is our interpretation that colours them in a positive or negative light. It is our judgement against our own expectations that induces delight or disappointment, and further causes joy or pain.

'Remember, a flame is brilliant against the dark night but insignificant in broad daylight. A line on a blank wall cannot be defined as long or short, thick or thin. It is only the comparison, the reference, the judgement that allows it to be defined as such.

'Then essentially what we experience is not what is but what we make of it. Circumstances may arise but they do not bring with them the experience—that sphere belongs to us. When Ananda called me today, he sounded deeply concerned. He stated that he sensed an emotional turmoil raging in your heart, and a constant struggle to cope with this upheaval. That you wanted to suppress it, to somehow quieten it, to bury it somewhere deep and dark.

'Remember, a volcano erupts and causes all the destruction because it cannot find an outlet. The repression builds up and eventually it must escape. If it waits too long, it becomes corrosive and destructive but when it finds an opening, the lava gently flows out.

'We must face our situations. Running away, hiding or denying them is never the way out. Yes, we can run from them but wherever we go, we will find them right there waiting for us.

'Coming back to where we started, you might ask why I chose this specific place to have my message delivered. Well, in our typical world, we stand right at the centre of our universe. Self-absorbed with a self-centric approach, we remain forever preoccupied with our problems, our situations, our wants and our desires. This myopic vision starts to dominate our view and our whole life.

'I come here when I want to feel insignificant, like a speck in eternity. And interestingly, when "I" shrink, "MY" problems disappear as well.

'This vast open space that you see in front of you is unique. The sky above stretches into a glorious eternity and the sprawling town below holds millions of stories in the folds of its heart. Hundreds of homes and thousands of people, each one fighting his own war—some against hunger, others against disease, some against misfortune. Each has an "I" story, yet the sun rises and sets, the stars keep shining, flowers keep blooming, the seasons come and go and yes, life goes on...and we go on with it.

'This vastness of life serves as a reminder that in the overall scheme of things you aren't exactly as important as you think.'

Maya became quiet, giving herself time to digest what he was trying to convey. Maya paused to look up and stared into the horizon as the sun's orange and pink hues faded away, paving the way to unveil millions of scattered jewels adorning the night sky, flickering in sync with its heartbeat. Twinkling above and glittering below, the visions of the town faded away slowly, replaced by the scattered stardust of lights.

The closing note read, 'If you are facing the ruins, remember you have your back turned towards all the splendour that holds the promise of a beautiful tomorrow.

'A great poet of our country once noted, "If you shed tears when you miss the sun, you also miss the stars."

'The stars are not afraid to appear small. They shine so they can give, so they may live. These giants stand disguised as tiny specks in the vast sky and look at the beauty they create! Au revoir!'

The Carnival

> 'Wherever you go,
> go with all your heart.'
>
> —Confucius

*M*AYA STARED OUT OF HER bedroom window at the patch of fields that quivered in the silence of the night's gentle embrace, like the morning dew trembling upon the lips of a young flower. She looked up at the stars that now appeared brighter and more distant. Maya recalled the words, 'These stars aren't afraid to appear small. They shine so they can give, so they may live. These giants stand disguised as tiny specks in the vast sky and look at the beauty they create!' as she peacefully drifted off to sleep.

She was startled awake by a piercing melody that grew louder and closer. It was the sound of an eternal song, a cry of love, a deep longing. Maya looked out her window and gauged it was still the dead of night. She saw nothing but darkness, yet, this song carried on. The music was compelling. Maya felt strangely drawn towards it, like it was calling her. It was a melody that stirred her soul, that pierced her heart, that tore her apart and then faded into the nothingness of the night.

'What was this strange pull?' Maya spent the rest of the night tossing and turning and much to Maya's relief, the soft light of the morning sky greeted her again. Maya grabbed her shawl and ran out to where Amma and Ananda sat and blurted out, 'Who sings at night? I heard...a song...a beautiful melody...a painful yearning, a strange familiar song that my heart knew... I could not understand the words and I know it wasn't a dream. I heard someone singing in the middle of the night.' Maya looked flustered as she breathlessly blabbered trying to make sense of something so utterly unbelievable.

Amma casually remarked, 'That must be Leela.'

'Leela?' questioned Maya in relief, feeling consoled that she hadn't completely lost her mind yet.

'Who is Leela and why was she singing so late at night and the pain in her voice—what was that about?'

'Memsahib, Leela is a strange woman, an enigma of sorts, a legend of the desert, a mystery as deep as the sea. For now, it is best that you simply understand that she cannot be understood. Don't waste your time thinking about her. Treat it like it was a dream,' Amma replied.

'But it wasn't,' insisted Maya. 'It felt more familiar and more real than anything I've ever known. The sound was coming from her, but it echoed a song that belonged within me. It drew me to itself, I felt helpless.

'Do me a favour Amma, please tell me where she lives. I must meet her before I return. Just tell me where I can find her,' persisted Maya.

'No one knows where she lives. She has no home, no

whereabouts. She is free like the wind that chooses her path, that follows its heart…no one ever finds her…she finds them—the chosen few.'

Maya felt a little disappointed at the vagueness of Amma's response. 'There must be a way,' she pleaded. 'Or a time,' Amma offered compassionately. 'What is meant to be, will be. Just when and exactly how it is meant to be. There is a time, place and a reason that we can't question. Trust Memsahib…and let go. She's a fragrance that can't be captured and a season that can't be timed… These can only be enjoyed while they last and relived in our minds when we desire.'

Having observed Maya's emotional state over the past few days, Ananda could understand her desperation to find Leela more than Amma could. As Ananda and Maya sat outside on the woven bed having chai, Ananda suggested, 'Come Memsahib, let me show you father's workshop.' Maya was surprised to hear that. All she had known of his job was as a darbaan back at the hotel.

She followed Ananda to the enclosed shed on the left side of the courtyard. It was a dark, dusty room which looked more like a storage shed than a workshop. Ananda opened the windows and removed the protective sheets to reveal stunning wooden sculptures in all shapes and forms. Maya was awestruck. Some were contemporary, almost abstract art and the others more traditional sculptures of gods and goddesses. Each exquisite piece of art deserved to be showcased in a gallery rather than lay hidden under covers.

'These are incredible, absolutely magnificent!' she exclaimed. 'I had no idea Baba is such an artist. Is he even aware of how brilliant he is? He could make a fortune if he practised this as a profession.'

Ananda laughed, 'Father is a simple man, he has no desire for recognition or fame. In fact, he would not even take credit for any of his creations, he believes that these creations appear through him but do not belong to him. He works when the inspiration arises, and when it does, nothing else matters. It could be the middle of the night or the scorching summer heat. It does not matter if it takes hours or weeks, he gives himself to it completely and totally.'

'Doesn't he get tired carving through nights and working through days?'

'Actually speaking Memsahib, on the contrary, these are the moments, that I see him most content, rested and even energized. Baba insists that all great works of art, inventions, or creations were never a result of hard work or long hours, but immense love, passion and surrender.

'For these creators, the creations are not separate from their sense of self...but an extension of their own being. Rather than creation, Baba prefers to call it "expression or manifestation" of that which already exists within them. Baba maintains that the most important, in fact the only lesson I need to learn in life is to find my passion before my ambition for this is the true road to fulfilment and success.'

'And he says,' laughed Ananda, "don't let yourself get in your own way," whatever that means!'

Maya's entire being was infused with a deep sense of respect for this humble unassuming artist. She quickly internalized and compared this philosophy with what modern-day progressive society teaches us day in and day out. It's all about the fame, the success, the sweat, the cut-throat ambition and the vain recognition. We are driven by all the external factors to an end result that people do manage to achieve but in the end it costs too much and means too little.

As extreme as this philosophy sounded, it was so much more holistic, flowing inwards-out rather than outwards-in.

An understanding of that passion was its own purpose and its greatest joy.

Ananda spoke after a moment of silence.

'Diverging from father's philosophy, I brought you here for a different reason today. Remember Hukum's words, "Experience is the greatest teacher in life."'

'Yes, of course,' confirmed Maya.

'He certainly has a bias towards action, and in accordance with that, he suggests a practical lesson for today.' Ananda announced. 'Follow me this way,' he said, as he headed towards the other end of the room, basking in the pride of a top-secret mission, it appeared.

'Sergeant ready for the mission!' exclaimed Maya, eagerly anticipating her mystery session. As she followed Ananda, Maya accidentally stumbled upon a block of wood and stubbed her toe.

With a sudden outburst of emotions, she said, 'All bad things happen to me. If something can go wrong, it will.'

Ananda quickly ran over and asked, 'Memsahib, are you alright?'

'Yes I am,' said Maya in a bitter tone as she held on tight to both her toe and her frown.

'Seems like you are in pain Memsahib, shall I call Amma?'

'No Ananda, I'm fine, I can handle this on my own,' dismissed Maya, as her breathing became shallow.

'Excuse me Memsahib, it may seem like big words coming

from a small mouth but I notice something unusual about your reactions.'

'Unusual? Like?' questioned Maya.

'Like you inherently distrust life and judge it at every instance, like it is always secretly conspiring to hurt you. We do not think like that here, things go wrong for many of us, all too often. We simply call these "accidents" or "god's will" and move on in acceptance. It's an integral part of life. But in your case, it almost appears as if you bear a huge burden of an unreal notion that life is meant to be happy, that nothing must ever go wrong, that we are never meant to meet pain or hurt or disappointments. Life must be a series of joy to joy, success to success.

'Memsahib, Baba says pain is a good thing. It carries potential within its wings; if you spot it, it will lift you up and take you along its flight; if you miss it, it will leave behind the gift of wisdom, a token for you to remember it by after it's gone.'

Maya was stunned to hear these profound words coming from a boy who was yet to meet life. He certainly seemed more equipped to deal with it than Maya had ever been.

'Ananda,' she responded sounding calmer, 'I'm waiting for my lesson.'

'Oh yes, the lesson! Well, Hukum suggests you need to learn how to carve.'

Maya laughed, 'Really, this was the great profound practical lesson that I had to learn in order to transform my life?'

Ananda chuckled as he walked over to the workstation, 'Yes, quite so! Take a look!' he said as he picked up an ornate chisel, 'Watch how both my hands work together yet against each other for the most precise carving. During my first carving lesson, Baba introduced me to this basic idea that much like our lives, it is the yin and the yang, the high and the low, the forward and the backward that lend the perfect balance to this art. Here, now you try what you have just learned. They say each piece of wood contains a secret within its heart.'

Maya scraped the surface of the wood in a semicircular pattern and stated, 'This piece of wood contains a smile I just revealed. Here, take a look Ananda.'

Ananda exclaimed 'Yes, it does. Good work Memsahib, you've got it...almost!'

'How about carving a smile on this piece of wood?' he implored.

'Why not?' responded Maya, already feeling like a pro. She applied the same technique but the entire block of wood fell apart. Maya looked towards Ananda and he encouraged her to try again, this time Maya was more careful and precise, yet, she failed.

'Memsahib, Hukum suggested this exercise to bring home the observation of the age-old saying, "Rotten wood cannot be carved."'

Ananda held out another piece of paper, 'Here you go. Another one for you.'

Maya read on.

'Greetings.

'A short one today. I requested Ananda's assistance in introducing you to a lesson that I believe you are ready for.

'Please remember that before we embark on carving our masterpiece, we must heal ourselves. You are still raw with emotions that you prefer to suppress with vengeance than release with forgiveness and grace.

'Make peace with yourself—with your past and your present. Accept your life.'

Maya read on, 'By no means am I suggesting that acceptance amounts to asserting that everything is perfect and life is great, it simply means facing it, reconciling—giving up the fight. It's about knowing somewhere in your heart that everything is unfolding according to a greater plan, and what you have and where you are is all you need and precisely where you should be.

'Only if we're at peace can we move on to the bigger and better things that life has to offer. Focusing on inadequacies or deviations from our desires creates resentment, it keeps us tangled just where we are. It holds us from looking ahead. We're so busy trying to figure out what we haven't been that we fail to look at all we're capable of being.

'We haven't met and I know little about your situation. From the few lines you sent me the other day, I sense a quiet desperation. You are longing for life yet resenting it, you are chasing hope as you cut through the fog of despair, it is all brewing whether you acknowledge it or not. I will not ask you the reason for any of this, but I will ask you for one realization. Life is too short and too beautiful to waste away. Open your heart and open your mind, be like the river that flows through the highs and lows, that recognizes that the very edges that constrain it are also the edges that push it forward to meet its ultimate fulfilment.

'Celebrate the joy that surrounds you and the happiness you are seeking will come rushing into your life.

'So long, until next time.'

Maya folded the letter and took a deep breath. She almost felt compelled to defend herself, 'Ananda, do you really think

I want to be unhappy? Do I want to be sad? I'm longing to live and laugh and smile, I'm trying, you know,' said Maya in exasperation.

Ananda nodded, 'As Hukum says, we must learn to take one step and one day at a time. And all you need to do is believe.'

'Memsahib,' exclaimed Ananda with a sudden excitement in his voice, 'you came here at the most opportune time. A large fair in Pushkar starts tomorrow. This one comes before the world-renowned fair in November but you still get the entire experience. It is absolutely worth the visit. Let it mark the beginning of an all new journey.'

Maya was up earlier than Amma or Ananda. She somehow had grown to love these silent blue mornings. Ananda was buzzing with an energy and enthusiasm that was contagious. Maya allowed it to rub off on her as they excitedly double-checked their belongings. Ananda remarked teasingly, 'I don't think you are dressed very appropriately, what happened to your jeans and the fancy blouse?' They burst into laughter, a validation of Maya's secret resolve that she would laugh and live and dream again.

'How far is Pushkar Ananda, and are we taking a taxi or a bus?'

Ananda responded, 'Pushkar is approximately 150 km from here, we could use a taxi to get there but that would reduce your experience dramatically. I suggest we take a bus, the real way it's done.' Maya said without the least bit of hesitation, 'OK then, let us do it the way it is done!'

They arrived at the bus stand which was an enormous sea of people. Mothers held the hands of their little ones as they speared through the swarming crowd. Old and young, each passing other by, arriving in a flash and leaving in an instant—the dynamic collage was electrifying. Maya recalled the busyness of Grand Central train station. One of her most favourite things to do in New York had been to sit and observe the waves of commuters stepping hastily in every direction. The commotion itself lent to a certain degree of order.

Of course, that was Grand Central where doors were held and courtesies of distance were observed. This, on the other hand was Jaipur bus depot, where doors were slammed and someone could always be found stepping on your toes or breathing down your neck—of course, apologies were entirely optional. Maya could not thank her good sense enough for her decision to wear her canvas Toms over sandals. After being stepped on and shoved aside a few times, Maya and Ananda made it to the ticket window. Men whistled and commented, some made strange gestures, but Ananda prompted, 'Breathe and ignore...believe for the day you are deaf, dumb and blind... you don't see, you don't hear and you don't speak.' Maya did exactly that and it worked like a charm.

Maya noticed peanut shells and beedi stubs strewn casually around the floor and prominent red stain marks along the corners of the white walls from spitting of tobacco. She was slowly starting to recognize the face of India beyond the sterile five-star hotels and was gradually getting accustomed to it as well. Good or bad was hard to say today after the 'no judgement lesson', so she generously termed it as 'different'. And yes, Hukum was right, 'different' did not kick up a storm of outrage or disappointment as 'bad' or 'dirty' or 'terrible' or 'uncomfortable' would have done. The magic of non-judgement was working even at the level of a softer verdict.

Ananda asked Maya to pick a seat at the very back of the 'air-conditioned video coach'. Ananda clarified, 'Just like everything else, this comes equipped with air-conditioning, should the need ever arise.' Maya shook her head in disbelief.

'Don't worry Memsahib, you will get to see much more of "this happens only in India."'

She sat by the window. Hawkers came around pushing the baskets they carried on their heads, as close to her face as possible and yelling in a peculiar pitch, tone and lingo—a unique art they seemed to have mastered.

'What is he selling?' inquired Maya casually.

'This is a dry roasted snack called bhujiya, but don't feel obliged to say "no, thanks". Remember for the duration of this journey, you do not see, talk or hear.'

'Got it,' she nodded.

People stormed the bus in hoards and within a matter of minutes, the bus was filled to capacity. She then noticed, as she looked out her window, men climbing up the back ladder with overstuffed bundles as they secured a place for the journey on top of the bus. No one looked surprised. Ananda explained, 'This is how our double-decker buses work in India. The top deck accommodates luggage along with its accompanying passengers. Of course, just like luggage, they make do without seats, seat belts or guard rails, but they seem to have nailed it. It is the quintessential open air ride, a true Indian adventure sport,' he chuckled.

Soon after, the conductor yelled what sounded like Pushkar in a repetitive and progressively rapid sound, 'Pushkar, Pushkar, Pushkar, Pushkar, Pushkaaaaar'. Soon, the bus made its way out of the bus stand and meandered through the city streets.

It was still early and Maya noticed people preparing for the day ahead. Some were watering and sweeping the area in front of their shops while others lit incense and prayed at the entrance to their business.

'These shopkeepers and businessmen are a fairly religious community,' added Ananda. 'This is how they start their typical day at work. Interestingly, there is a subculture of "boni", where they look for their first sale of the day to establish precedence for the remaining day of business. Usually, they would offer you an attractive deal for a good first sale. Of course, that also means they frown upon and are greatly offended by any returns or exchanges before the hour of noon.'

'Oh really? Good to know!' said Maya.

Soon the bus was out of the city limits, on to a beautiful countryside landscape—miles of open fields, grazing cows and breathtaking scenery set against sunny vistas. Little children walked in small groups independently to school, shouldering backpacks that seemed twice as heavy as their tiny selves. Herds of cattle walked leisurely across the highway amid blaring horns.

Maya had been up early, her eyelids started to grow heavy. She leaned her head against her bag and drifted off to sleep.

She woke up to the sound of loud brakes and barking dogs. Passengers were deboarding. 'Are we already here?' asked Maya. 'No this is a rest stop for passengers to use the facilities, eat, drink or just stretch out,' explained Ananda.

Maya followed Ananda out of the bus and noticed a little mud-like structure with a thatched roof and an open air kitchen. The sun was bright and the morning was pleasant. Red and white plastic chairs were stacked up against the benches and a charpoy stood under the shade of the trees. Maya headed straight for it.

The resting stop was unusual, situated amidst the sand as far as the eye could see. Ananda invited her to try their dum chai, that he claimed could possibly keep her awake for two days. It was strong, sweet and loaded with ginger. Maya was thrilled and ordered another one. Getting used to the small teacups and tiny glasses after gallon-sized coffee mugs had been a challenge. She ordered a small Indian breakfast plate that she shared with a few friendly looking frail dogs. The conductor soon blew the whistle and it was time to go. 'Memsahib, a chilled Coke to go?' asked Ananda as he rushed to settle the bill. 'How about a Thums Up? Going local all the way!' she said sticking her thumb up with a smile.

Within an hour, they arrived at Pushkar. It was a warm day, Maya generously applied sunscreen, put on her sunglasses and threw on a hat. 'All set for Pushkar,' she announced with a huge smile.

Out of the bus stop, they boarded the great Indian shared autorickshaw. This was Maya's first experience on this strange green and yellow three-wheeler. There was a wooden plank across from the main seat and a stand at the back. Pink hearts with arrows were painted on the sides and a tiny handset played FM radio. All in all, this miniscule three-wheeler managed to load seven passengers in addition to the driver. It was a nice and bumpy ten-minute ride that Maya thoroughly enjoyed.

She could have seen herself doing the undoable bungee jumping in New Zealand or skydiving somewhere perhaps, but riding on a shared autorickshaw was beyond her wildest dreams. The auto dropped them off a short five-minute walk from the fair.

They proceeded with their conversation and journey at an easy-going pace, soaking in the landscape and its raw appeal. They treaded up the rocky mountain trail and then down over to the spectacular view of this holy land, nestled among the majestic Aravalli mountain ranges.

Pushkar lake sat regally surrounded by extending ghats, busy city streets and on this end, the spectacular fair. Maya was entrenched in the vitality of this place. Women, children and men, all adorned with vibrant colours of life—red, yellow, orange, dresses and stoles, anklets and bangles. Camels were dressed in colours and jewels as well. Some even had make-up on. The energy was electrifying.

The landscape was dominated by the two large Ferris wheels reaching high into the sky, loaded with cheerful riders and amused bystanders. The beeline of tiny tents sold small goodies and trinkets—slippers, dolls, bangles and more. Maya felt like a little child in a vast toy store—excited, happy and overwhelmed, not knowing where to start. She decided to get red bangles and an orange scarf that enhanced her brown eyes and light skin. She stood in line for the Ferris wheel that spun to disco lights and Bollywood songs.

This felt like a clichéd mela scene straight out of a dramatic Hindi movie, the kind where siblings got separated to meet at a later time based upon that quintessential family song or the legendry tattoo discovered during a climactic fight.

As she reached the very top, Maya felt a strange sense of connectedness—like it was all a huge continuity. Somehow the fair, the people, the sun, the mountains stretched out from one direction into infinity—a point where everything seemed to merge.

'I'm glad we came here,' said Maya, as they headed over to the caravan of camels. They patted the animals and listened to some interesting stories about their names, behaviour and characteristics.

Ananda remarked, 'You know what would be really interesting?'

'What?' asked Maya.

'A camel safari,' proposed Ananda.

'That sounds thrilling, let's do it!' exclaimed Maya.

They signed up for a ride that was to start in an hour. After quickly wrapping up their visit to the Brahma temple, Maya sought some shade to rest until it was time for their safari. They proceeded through the bazaar and out towards the ghats. The crowds were thinning and the ambient sounds were now more audible. At a distance, Maya noticed a man in green garb sitting under the shaded tree with a long grey beard and a scarf tied around his head. He was rocking gently from side to side in a fluid movement. Suddenly, he pointed out towards Maya and proclaimed, '...she's here...she's here... I knew she had to come back... She is here...look...look she is here...' He then went into a trance-like state shaking uncontrollably and rocking his head.

Maya was petrified and asked Ananda, 'Is he a madman?'

Ananda responded, 'He's a mystic. He has a deeper connection with life. He can often hear and tell things ahead of time.'

The man in the green garb rolled his eyes and walked up to Maya and proclaimed with great authority, '...you are here...

that's a good thing, now go, there are others waiting for you. Find them and let them take you home. Go home, go find them, they are near, they are here. Go find your home. And when you lose her you will find her...and when you lose her you will find her... when you find her you will lose her...' he blabbered on and on.

Maya was too scared to respond or react. She was stunned by this experience. The man turned his back and started to walk away. People folded their hands and bowed their heads respectfully as the crowd parted to make way as he walked through. Maya watched him fade away, leaving a resounding echo of his dramatic prediction behind. Ananda tugged, 'Let's go...come on!'

Ananda explained, 'Look, a phenomenon like this is not unheard of. It happens from time to time. These are holy lands full of holy men, some real and some not so much, who knows? We can't believe everything we see and hear.' But Maya was sure he had recognized her, there was something he knew and something he conveyed. 'Go home, people waiting for you...' he was clearly talking to her in her terms. Undoubtedly, he knew something.

Ananda pulled her away towards the town and said, 'We really need to go, the safari will leave without us.' Maya walked along slowly, looking visibly disconcerted by this experience.

The sun had started to descend a little and the caravan was ready, waiting for them to arrive. Ananda ran forth to greet them. 'Sorry,' he said apologetically, 'it took us a little while.' The group, primarily composed of easy-going Europeans in a holiday mode, seemed quite relaxed, much to Ananda's relief.

By now, Maya too had regained her composure. The

operator introduced the camel. 'His name is Jonny Cash.' Maya couldn't help laughing, looking at the decorated and beautifully dressed Johnny Cash as images of the icon ran through her mind.

'How did you name him that?' she asked inquisitively. 'Well, his name is Jonny but then one day an American tourist rode him. He said that this was the best experience of his life and left some extra cash for the camel and told me to call him Jonny Cash. I figured that it was a little trick he had shared with me to bring lots of it. So here I have Johnny Cash, Jackie Cash, Ramu Cash and Sonu Cash.' Maya broke into a wild laughter, while the innocent overtanned operator with huge silver moustaches wore a very puzzled look. She said, 'Nice!' and moved on to making herself comfortable on the saddle.

She adjusted herself forward and sideway a few times before finding her spot. With a little kick and a little tug, the camel stood up, almost throwing Maya back and forward until it was fully upright and they were towering way over everything else around them. They passed through the villages looking at children playing on the streets, and women who walked with veils down to their waist carrying multiple pitchers on top of their heads, and a few in their hands. Maya was moved by the difficulty of life but having stayed with Ananda's family, she could faintly recognize the sweet simplicity of it.

They moved on to the thinning vegetation and finally the enormity of the great Thar Desert. They crossed beautiful dunes and miles of sand amidst the jingling of camel bells. Soon they arrived at the tents, just in time to watch the splendid sunset over the majestic sand dunes. It was breathtakingly beautiful.

This was followed by light refreshments and a folk performance. Ananda prompted, 'They are enacting the ballad of our legendry lovers from Rajasthan—Dhola, Maaru and their flying camel that finally helped reunite them. In fact, based on this legend, most love songs of Rajasthan till date refer to the lover or husband as "Dhola",' narrated Ananda.

Maya was enchanted as she picked up the handout containing the legend of Dhola-Maaru, and a postcard with a descriptive image that was a visual tribute to a glorious tradition interlaced with the universal notion of an eternal love that continues to live on for centuries beyond itself.

Finally it was time for Maya and Ananda to take the bus home. They walked away into the darkness of the night carrying the sunset, the desert, a love story and a few questions within their hearts…

Aagaman–The Homecoming

'Lovers don't finally meet somewhere;
they are in each other all along.'

–Rumi

*M*AYA REQUESTED ANANDA TO ACCOMPANY her to the town to make a call back home. She appeared relaxed. The rest and the travel seemed to have refreshed her. The town wore a brighter and happier character today and the difference wasn't just the colours but the state of her mind. *Really*, thought Maya, *reality can be quite subjective, much more than one gives it credit for.*

Maya observed men and women hustling, coordinating and putting together some temporary structures. 'Is some festival coming up?' Maya enquired. 'Sort of,' answered Ananda vaguely.

Maya told her mom all about her Pushkar adventure, the camel safari and even the Sufi's prediction. Her mom chuckled, 'Since when did you start believing in such predictions?'

'No Mom,' she insisted, 'he had this strange energy around him. I could feel it.' Her mom laughed harder, 'And are you sure it wasn't the heat that got to you,' she giggled. Maya responded with a laugh, 'Whatever!' she said, 'I totally see all the fun you are going to have at my expense. Okay Mom, I have work to do here. Gotta go now. I love you,' she said as she turned around, beaming with joy.

She felt content knowing that she had managed to deliver to her mother what was dearest to her—her own happiness.

That evening Maya dug out a book from her backpack and immersed herself in it. In this deeply relaxed state of mind she seemed to be enjoying her once favourite pastime yet again. She was known to be a huge bookworm, the kind that snuck flashlight under covers to get through that one chapter. It enabled, Maya reflected, to transport her to new worlds and surround herself with new people and exciting adventures. Just like that!

She gathered a few rather raw household candles for her 'special effect'. The soft glow was always comforting. Comforting it was, even with the plain white frail candles that were frequently used as a backup when electricity went out. Neither scented nor contained in colourful fancy jars, they delivered their purpose nonetheless.

It must have been close to midnight when Maya once again heard the melody. Still distant and deep. Maya's mind instantly went back to the Sufi's words. She was certain that this belonged somewhere in the mystery he had hinted at.

She changed quickly and quietly slipped out through the front door, running fast into the deep blue night. Maya followed her footsteps as they led her in the direction of the song. However, the further she ran, the more distant the voice seemed, as if what she was hearing was an echo, misleading her in a different direction.

Getting a grip over the situation, she stopped and dropped

to her knees, struggling to catch her breath. She was surrounded by a dark motionless desert. Maya felt concerned to find herself alone in the middle of this great vastness, with no one and not a house in sight. Instantly, her rational mind took over, making her feel utterly stupid and nudging her to return to Ananda's home.

As much as she wanted to give up her search and return to safety, she also felt desperate to seek Leela out. As usual, Maya was caught between her head and her heart. She looked up towards the sky in disappointment, staring into the darkness, looking for an answer. There was none.

As she slowly turned around to head back, something caught her attention. She believed she might have just seen the first glimmer of sunlight from the corner of her eye. But how? It was still the dead of night. She quickly flipped around and narrowed her focus, straining harder to look at the glow that emanated from a distance.

Miles of bare desert, dark expanse of the night sky and the strange glow. Maya quickly dropped her rational hesitation and ran again, like her life depended upon it. She ran as fast as she could and arrived breathless.

Finally, there it was—the enormous raging bonfire crackling in fury, and a woman seated next to it. The woman who sat facing the fire seemed oblivious to the world as she poured her heart into her song and swayed to its melody.

With soft steps, Maya slowly started to proceed in her direction. Just as she came close enough behind her, the singing abruptly stopped.

'Welcome Maya, I have been expecting you here,' the voice stated in a commanding tone.

Maya was frozen with fear, her face became pale and her lips turned blue. This was uncomfortable, supernatural, paranormal even. She struggled to continue breathing as she gasped for air.

'Don't be afraid,' said the woman, 'you have come to the right place. I called for you.' There were a few long moments of silence that felt like an eternity. Slowly, she stood up and turned around, revealing her face in the soft glow of the blazing fire, 'Welcome to Leela's world,' she declared in a commanding thunderous voice that seemed to radiate far.

At about five feet two inches, with a broad frame, olive complexion and clear skin, her personality contradicted the norm. Covered from head to toe in silver jewellery, she jingled with every move as she walked towards her, clad in an all-black shirt, flowing skirt and a black linen scarf pinned on top of her head. Even her breathing seemed to make music with her trinkets. The triangular dots tattooed on her chin and her temples adorned her beautiful face like an ancient script on a pious textbook. The deep kohl in her hazel eyes seemed potently capable of hypnotic powers. Maya composed herself and remained quiet until her breathing normalized. She instinctively reached out to fix her hair so she looked half-presentable.

Leela hummed a tune and closed her eyes as she circled Maya. Maya collected her courage and muttered, 'How do you know my name...and why were you expecting me here?

'Is this some magic or a miracle?'

'Depends on how you view it,' said Leela, opening her eyes again, 'in one sense, there are no miracles in life and in another sense, life is nothing but a miracle. And magic is everywhere, as long as you believe in it.

'For now, you are here because you have questions and I

have the answers. You walk around chained to the yoke of an oppressive past, and I hold the key to set you free. In short, you are no good without me.'

Maya was taken aback by this rather curt display of arrogance but she chose not to make it evident.

'Come sit beside me,' prompted Leela as she sang louder than ever. The depth of her emotions radiated into the stillness of the desert night.

And then she stopped.

The sky was silent. The sand glittered. The stars twinkled. And Maya's heart beat louder and faster—each beat audible, each rhythm tangible.

The look on Leela's face intensified as she stared into the fire, 'I see a thirsty fish surrounded by water and desperately longing for water. And I see darkness, immense darkness, both inside and outside. But wait, I also see hope. I see hope,' she repeated as she closed her eyes.

Turning towards Maya, Leela stated, 'The deepest realizations and true awakenings emerge from our darkest moments and greatest challenges. Just as each sorrow contains the promise of a joy, each breakdown holds the potential for a great transformation.

'Where you stand today Maya, you have two distinct choices. Fight with the darkness and keep searching for the light or find your light and believe that darkness will disappear on its own.'

'Not an easy situation. It's hard to fight with darkness, for darkness is not a thing by itself...it's a state, merely the absence of light,' Maya said.

'You must give up your fight, go find your light, you must go...alone...you must go...far, when you go far enough, you will end up where you started. Your home awaits you.'

Leela lifted her hands to the sky and bowed her head. The first glimmer of sunlight peeked through and Maya came face-to-face with her mentor. 'You must go now,' insisted Leela, 'and I must return as well.'

Maya questioned impatiently, trying to prolong the abrupt ending that was no more helpful than the Sufi's prediction '… but… but wait how will I meet you again?' Leela continued to walk away. 'We shall meet again, Maya.' She kept walking without looking back. 'I will call you…you will come just like you did today…you must…'

This was a lot for Maya to absorb. She did not quite know if this was happening for real or was a compelling hallucination. Maya pinched herself. This was undeniable. Something told her she was in the right place, she just had to hang in there and keep believing until the rest unfolded.

Maya narrated the encounter to Ananda and Amma and they did not seem the least bit concerned. Amma placed her hand on Maya's head and gently patted her, 'You have been blessed.'

'How strange is life?' whispered Maya. 'Back home, where I had everything anyone could ever want, friends, family, work and luxuries, I felt lonely and incomplete and I travel to this strange faraway land with nothing at all, where in fact, I should be lonely, trying to figure it all out, and there everything seems perfectly orchestrated. As if everyone here is secretly conspiring to make it all better for me… Stranger than life are its ways.'

That afternoon, Maya decided to go for a walk. She needed some time alone to collect her thoughts and brace herself for all that was coming her way. She strolled along quietly trying not to analyze, conclude or even think about it. She was simply looking for some space where all the dots would start to connect. She looked around at the fields, the grazing cattle and the men of the village who as usual sat under the shade of a tree, playing cards.

However, Maya also noticed something different. People were dressed a lot nicer—the whites were a little whiter and the reds a little brighter. As she walked further towards the bazaar, a crowd started to converge. Maya moved over and stepped on to an elevated concrete sidewalk. The crowds lined up the street with men holding dholaks and kamaichas, while women held large decorated thalis with flowers and aarti elements.

It appeared that they were waiting for someone important to arrive. Women and children also gathered in their balconies and on their rooftops. Within minutes, the bazaar was completely swept over by a sea of villagers. It was like a congregation of many villages and the crowd kept swelling by the minute. She looked behind at the approaching families, carrying children on the shoulders and babies around their waist, just holding hands and marching along, as if on a mission. Old men and frail women, taking deliberate slow steps that kept inching forward. All eyes remained fixed on the road, and the silence felt like the lull before the storm.

Soon, a faint image appeared at the top of the hill, gradually drawing closer. Maya noticed it was a boy who appeared to be running downhill towards the crowd, a messenger of sorts. He waved a flag and Maya could hear a distant call, 'They are here... Lo and behold, they have arrived!'

Maya arched her heels to peek over the crowd. A convoy of four black cars emerged on the horizon, over the hill and on to the deserted road that made its way directly to this gathering.

The dust settled and the cars came to a halt. Maya saw a tall man, wearing a sharp Italian suit, emerge from the Bentley. He stood there humbly with folded hands. She could not quite see his face but she did notice a graceful older woman, wearing a white saree that elegantly covered her grey hair, standing next to him and his conspicuous tan shoes. She leaped up to catch another glance but felt like a tiny grain of sand on a seashore attempting to catch a glimpse of the sunrise.

The whole village broke out in cheer. Instantly, the instruments started playing and there was a shower of rose petals. Women ran up to him and surrounded him with thalis, chanting prayers as the older women hugged and blessed him.

Maya was taken by surprise. Who was this man? Never in her life had she seen a man receive such reverence and adulation. Yes, she had heard of the Mandelas and Gandhis, but here was a real life phenomenon that this village seemed to know very closely. Maya was absolutely enchanted. She tried to move ahead to take a closer look at the man but could not make her way through the deadlock of people. Just then, she was tapped on her shoulder. It was Ananda, of course!

'Remember you had asked me if there was a festival approaching? Well, here is our festival, our Man, one and only, Hukum,' said Ananda.

'Hukum, the...same Hukum?' questioned Maya, pointing towards him in a state of complete daze.

'Yes, the same Hukum,' confirmed Ananda.

'But...this is Hukum? Wasn't he your godfather or something?'

'Yes, but how does that matter, he still is Hukum.'

'Who is he? And what's with all this celebration upon his

arrival, is he some political figure?' asked Maya, completely blown away. All along, she had carefully and deliberately avoided seeking his identity but today, she wanted to know everything about him…and some more. This was unreal.

'It's a long story,' said Ananda, as the man and the saree-clad lady started to walk away, the swarm of men and women followed, singing songs and playing instruments. Maya and Ananda proceeded as well. Each time Maya tried to make her way forward, she found herself shoved further behind the exuberantly celebrating crowd. After a few miserably failed attempts, she gave up. Ananda laughed, 'Don't worry Memsahib, we will get plenty of opportunities to see him. Hukum is here for six weeks, just follow the crowd home. Besides, he himself expressed the desire to meet you while he is here.'

Maya's stomach churned with an uneasy anxious apprehension and a starry-eyed enchantment.

'He wants to meet me?'

'Yes, that's what he said. Why do you appear so surprised?'

'Forget that,' she snapped. 'What did you tell him about me? Does he know who I am?' asked Maya thinking quickly about the impression she had cast.

'He knows you as Memsahib from New York. That's all.'

'Breathe Maya, breathe…that's better,' she mumbled to herself.

After a good twenty minutes of tense curiosity following what was grander than the greatest wedding procession Maya had seen, they found themselves in the middle of the desert. The man turned around, folded his hands and bowed to the crowd. The crowd showered him with cheers and blessings and watched him walk away into the huge gated mansion that was majestically nestled among the sandy hills of the boundless beige expanse. Still standing on her toes for that elusive glimpse, Maya soaked in the dizzying elegance and class of this place. She had seen outrageous beach mansions and sprawling Italian villas but this was beyond comparison.

The long road through the giant gates led to a circular driveway which looped around a fountain made of Italian marble. Behind that, stood a building wrapped in soft pink sandstone that could easily have been a famous palace.

Maya was now aching to find out more about this man and she could list every reason for it. She had been floored by his intelligence, touched by his compassion, impressed with his wisdom and was grateful for his concern. If that wasn't enough, she was now witnessing his widespread fervour, reverence, grandness, style, stature and humility. At this moment, he certainly appeared larger than life but what made him this special to these people?

'Ananda,' asked Maya, pretending her best to conceal her inquisitiveness, 'so what makes Hukum so popular? What is it with this "festival"?'

Ananda answered, 'Hukum is what we fondly call him. His actual name is Veer Pratap Singh or "Veer" (The brave, fearless and strong).'

'Thank god, much better!' mumbled Maya.

'Sorry Memsahib, you said something?'

'Nope, nothing, carry on.'

'This lady with him is his grandmother Sadhana Devi. His father was a very successful industrialist in London. Unfortunately, at the tender age of 18 months, his parents were killed in an ill-fated plane crash.

'His grandmother brought him back to India where he was given the finest education along with a deep foundation of Indian culture and values. It is said that as a little boy, every time he left his mansion, he questioned why people lived in such poverty, why there was pain in this world, and wondered how he could change it. His grandmother tried to shield him from the harsh realities but he seemed more and more drawn to them. In fact, he was well-known for giving away to anyone in need—money, food, anything at all.

'One day, it is said that he saw a man out on the roadside sleeping without a cover, and he instantly removed his clothes and covered this man with his tiny clothes. He was severely admonished. This made his grandmother very worried and she sent him to London for his further education and better influences.

Ananda added, 'His great-grandfather and predecessors were wealthy landlords of this place. They greatly cared about the residents and constantly strived to create employment, education, infrastructure and social justice. Personally, their lifestyles were filled with extravagant luxuries—grand parties, expensive vacations and pursuit of fine arts like poetry, painting and drama.

'Veer's grandfather had a deep philosophical inclination along with an aesthetic appreciation. His grandmother, a very strong lady, raised her only son, Veer's father, in great protection from the potential trap of vanity. While he was introduced to the fine tastes of life, the higher motive was education and self-reliance. He spent his childhood in the company of the most brilliant minds and went on to become a very successful entrepreneur. Unfortunately, his life was cut short by the tragic air crash. He was only 34 when he died, shortly after losing his own father to cardiac arrest.'

'That must have been so rough,' said Maya, '18 months is a very tender age.'

'Yes, it was,' replied Ananda.

'Veer being the only child and without parents, would often get lonely. His grandmother found him a best friend—this huge library, which was created to fill his life with ageless wisdom and wonderful fantasy. The rest as they say is history.'

'Veer it seems got the best of all worlds. While his heritage gave him security and finesse, his grandfather gave him a dimension of philosophy and his father, the gift of intelligence and ambition.'

Ananda continued, 'In England, Veer went on to study at Oxford and was recognized as a pure genius. His pool of knowledge was too vast and people often jokingly referred to him as the "encyclopedia". While people his age were busy making friends and living life up, he was always restless, in search of a greater meaning. He enjoyed deep conversations and sought out the brightest minds in science, business and social sciences. He joined associations and charities for social welfare.

'Eventually, education could not hold him long enough. He dropped out of college to start his real estate fund. At this age, he is independently worth a few hundred million and is single-handedly responsible for much of the development across this region. He established schools and libraries for young minds. He introduced vocational colleges, evening colleges and training institutes to promote self-reliance among the youth. He also established one-of-a-kind technology that brings computer, Internet and social media at our fingertips. Veer believes people must never have to worry about medical care. He opened state-of-the-art hospitals with visiting volunteer faculty from all over the globe. He also donated land and money to create parks and playgrounds for a quality of life that everyone deserves.'

Ananda added, 'You know Memsahib, there are many people out there who feel fortunate and want to give back a part of their success in life, but there are very few who give back not in kind but in person. He can often be seen sitting down with the villagers, sipping on tea in tiny glasses, as they discuss events and plans, or at times you will find him on the soccer field kicking the ball with 10-year-olds screaming and celebrating a goal. He speaks with women and inspires them with the impact they are having world over.

'He runs in our blood, he speaks in our minds, he beats in our hearts. This is our man, our son, our soul. Words are not enough to describe him. He's a rare gem, I don't even know if another one like this exists in this entire world. He's special, very special.'

Maya was spellbound and could not get Veer out of her mind. She felt compulsively and intensely drawn towards this charming and charismatic Veer. She felt strange butterflies in her stomach, an elation in her heart and a surge of joy that swept over her like a raging tsunami. Gosh! She was nearly in love with a man she had not yet seen, how ridiculously bizarre!

She snapped herself out of the feel-good emotions. 'It's really just the fairy tale of a prince charming who lived in an enchanted palace doing the damage here,' she mumbled dismissively. 'He does fit right into the mould! Well, I can't afford this frivolous indulgence of emotions, after all I'm on a quest to find myself, not lose my sleep over love again.'

That night was long, so very long. Maya was restless. Sleep fluttered around her bedside and kissed her eyelashes, leaving a few dreams and distant faces. Maya tossed and turned. She shut her eyes, she practised deep breathing, she counted sheep and she dug her face in the pillow, none of which worked!

She took a deep sigh and muttered under her breath, 'I'm in a distant land far far away...I haven't spoken with an interesting man in over four weeks. Perhaps, it is my mind enslaved to seeking attention that is trying hard to convince me. Let me tell my mind loud and clear that I know what it is up to and nope, I will not let it throw me off track.'

Maya felt better at this declaration, a little empowered and a tad bit in command. She hugged her pillow and hummed a sweet melody. Slowly, the humming faded away and Maya passed into deep stupor.

A Distant Voice from the Past

*'The world breaks everyone, and afterward, many are
strong at the broken places.'*

–Ernest Hemingway

*M*AYA SAT ACROSS FROM LEELA on the cool desert sand, awash
by the silver radiance of a full moon that looked upon them
peacefully. Leela's ornamented camel sat serenely next to her.
'She is a beauty,' exclaimed Maya.

'Yes, today she is,' said Leela, as she tenderly stroked her
camel, 'six months ago was a different story though.'

'What do you mean Leela?' asked Maya.

'Maaru is a survivor, one among those eighty-seven camels
who lived through a horrifying nightmare stretching along a
journey of 1,327 kms from Rajasthan to Ranga Reddy district
in Telangana. Covered in bleeding wounds and cracked hoofs,
with minimal food and water, she walked day and night for
months, to reach her gruesome destination—a convenient
slaughter location.

'This inhumane journey would have ended in an even

greater tragedy, had it not been for the timely rescue by an animal rights group called People for Animals (PFA).'

Leela added, 'At the time of rescue, most camels were severely malnourished, critically injured and deeply wounded. Fortunately, this group not only rescued them but also raised money to transport the camels back home.'

'Such an atrocious act of cruelty. What could possibly prompt someone to do this?' questioned Maya, enraged at what she had just heard.

Leela answered 'Maya, the camel is not categorized as meat product in India, consequently, slaughterhouses are not equipped to handle an animal of this size. However, given the soaring popularity of camel meat, now considered a delicacy, camels continue to be slaughtered illegally, often in the open, with inadequate equipment, in ways that can only be described as severely brutal to downright inhumane. Oftentimes, unable to slaughter these large creatures completely, butchers simply leave them to die slow painful deaths.'

'Look at Maaru's feet,' Leela pointed out. 'Do you see this cushion-like padding that connects the toes? Well, nature intended for this animal to walk freely as the king of the desert. This webbing spreads open and widens when they stand to make it easier for them to walk on the soft sand. However, when exposed to the rough tar and concrete, they damage their feet with each step they take, often getting ripped and wounded by sharp rocks, glass and metal objects. The hard surface of the roads also results in severe injuries to their knees and bellies from the impact of abrupt landing on the harsh surface again and again.'

'But why would people sell their camels to those who treat

them like this in the first place?' protested Maya.

Leela explained, 'Camel population has been dwindling over the recent years and in an attempt to stabilize it, camel was recently adopted as the state animal by the government of Rajasthan. This came with certain restrictions on selling camel milk and related products in the market.

'This led to a decline in income from the traditional sources for the camel-rearing community. The illegal market for camel meat on the other hand has been becoming more and more lucrative, earning anywhere between ₹250 to ₹450 per kg. Desperate for money to sustain their families, these communities resort to the tough choice of selling their livestock which is then smuggled off to southern states or even neighbouring countries for slaughter.

'Maaru was unusually fortunate, but each year, hundreds of camels who fail to get spotted or rescued continue to die day by day...wound by wound.'

'Leela, this makes me so sad, what can we do to make sure what happened to Maaru does not happen to other camels?' questioned Maya.

'The ban on camel slaughter has obviously done little to stop the killing. Some suggest supporting an active market for camel milk and products which might motivate these communities to rear camels rather than distress sell them.

'However, even that will do little unless we, the people, stand up for the rights of creatures that can't stand up for themselves. Remember, economics derives its power from the demand that shifts based on the underlying values and principles of the market that it operates in. When you and I say "No", we become a part of a revolution that will shift this economic equation. Every revolution begins in the heart before it spreads into the world.

'Bapu said the greatness of a nation and its moral progress can be judged by the way its animals are treated.

'Sadly, this makes me question if we are really progressing as a nation despite the great space missions, technology breakthroughs and infrastructure explosion. Perhaps we need to remind our people that greatness doesn't just lie in attaining the skies that glitter above, it also lies in embracing the steady ground that stands below.'

'Anyhow,' said Leela, as she patted Maaru, 'what brings you to this desert, Maya? Of course, this desert chooses who walks upon its sands. The winds act like messengers conveying to me the arrival of a visitor. I also know what it is you came in search of. But explain to me what you think brings you here.'

Leela had just turned on a strobe light directed at Maya. She felt unprepared and caught on the spot. There wasn't anything specific she had to say after all. She answered, '...uh...um...well...let me say I'm looking for happiness.'

Leela laughed, 'Good attempt. Well, why do you think you will find it here and not anywhere else?'

Maya found herself cornered again, 'Because where I was and among all the things I had, I could never find it. Maybe now that I am no longer there and I have nothing left, I just might find it.'

'Very well, carry on,' said Leela. Maya sighed as she lowered her gaze to stare at the sand and started to speak.

'We lived right here in Jaipur where life was uncomplicated. Time and pace had a rhythm that was both melodious and soft.

Life was happy, we were happy, it was all perfect. And then one fine day, the dream came to an end with a harsh reality nothing could have prepared me for. My father left this world. He was gone in an instant, leaving behind a void that could never be filled and forever changed the world as we knew it.

'My mother proved to be stronger than I could have ever imagined. She knew her life was over but mine was just beginning. We moved to the US. With some assistance from her brother, she managed to get me into a good school and provided a platform for me to start my life over again. I went through medical school and graduated as a psychiatrist. Soon after, I started my own practice in New York and thankfully, it flourished.

'As I climbed this ladder of success, I took each step obediently, following society's recipe for happiness. If I had a good career, made lots of money, lived in a fancy apartment, had many friends, I was guaranteed to be successful and happy.

'With a stellar career that was the envy of many, a stunning apartment overlooking Central Park, a good-looking partner who ran a successful hedge fund, I truly did have more than I could ask for. I believed I must have arrived, secretly I longed to trust that I had.

'Our summer home in the Hamptons and jet-setting global vacations were the topic of hot discussions at most social events. Everything was picture perfect. I received lavish compliments for my beauty but they gave me little fulfilment. Everyone who knew me felt I had every reason to consider myself to be a very fortunate woman and here I was, feeling completely empty inside—stifled, suffocated and choked. What made matters worse was the fact that I could neither find a reason to blame it on nor an excuse to hide behind. And trust me, I tried hard to find one.

'I started to blame and question myself. I should be happy. I must be happy. And the biggest fear in life started to haunt me louder than ever. If all this doesn't make me happy, perhaps nothing ever will.

'I came face-to-face with this glaring fact of life—when you have much lacking in your life, you also have much hope. A hope that somehow when the vacuum is filled there will be happiness, so you keep chasing the rainbow for the elusive pot of gold. But it's truly when you have most of what you could desire that hope becomes weak and fulfilment feels elusive. After all, there wasn't truly much I could point towards what was missing in my life or the one thing that would take my life to the next level.

'I was shattered, and no one including myself could figure out this counter-intuitive paradox. A seemingly perfect life, no pressures of survival crumbling me down, yet, little by little I was falling apart. Antidepressants became the glue that was keeping my life together. I had family and friends, hobbies and entertainment but there was something amiss.

'With each milestone, the degree, the job, the private practice, the huge apartment, the engagement to a super successful entrepreneur, the fog surrounding me became thicker and thicker. I felt congested, claustrophobic, confined, enslaved. I had forgotten to laugh, forgotten to live and no longer recognized the person who greeted me in the mirror each morning. What remained of me was a notion of Maya, while I was dying each moment.

'Beyond my own pain, the pressure of keeping up with

hollow appearances and social duties day after day was wearing me down—the glamorous vacations, fancy cars, designer clothing trendy bags, looking fabulous, being the ultimate couple and living it up. It was demanding—everything had to be perfect, each time and all the time. Leela, I was living perfection, not a life.

'At the peak of my juggling, at the very summit, my superficially plastered life developed a crack, and everything came gushing through like the torrent of July monsoon.

'I guess I invited it in many ways, but my fairytale romance landed on a bumpy ground. My fiancée started taking my unhappiness personally and it hurt his ego very much. The fights we had started to intensify with each passing day. What started as another argument one night led me to my worst. He left the house in a fit of rage, and in a bout of depression, I slit my wrist.

'There was a pool of blood on the floor and the scene around me started to blur. Somehow, strange as it may sound, I was overcome by this feeling of peace and I settled into surrender. I started to hear a faint melody—the lullaby my father used to sing as he would put me to sleep while rocking me gently in his strong arms. I heard my unrestrained laughter, and I saw the sunlight streaming through the trees in my childhood backyard. I saw flowers and bees; I saw my mom and dad and my life flashed before my eyes. I saw my happiness, I saw my pain and I saw my end...the end though stirred something within me.

'I realized that this was not an end worth finishing at and this was not worthy of being called a life. I crawled over and with trembling hands, I picked up the phone and dialled my mom's phone number. I whispered, "This wasn't the life and this should not be the end. I want to live, I want to rewrite my story and direct my ending. I want another chance, I want to do it over again. Mom, help me."

'What followed was the police, the ambulance, hospital, rehab, counselling and questions. I had managed to hit rock-bottom at my very peak. After many days and nights spent sleeping on pills, I realized that the ladder I had been climbing all along was leaning against the wrong wall.

'I had questions but no answers. I knew that could not be the end but I didn't quite know where the beginning was.

'In the midst of my quandary, I started having a strange recurrent dream. I saw glimpses of a little girl running barefoot through narrow cobbled alleys, surrounded by towering brick walls and hot glimmering sand. The sand glistening in the light of the bright sun. There was absolute silence, the whole place awash in tender hues of yellow and gold under the clear blue sky. She laughed with a resounding echo of joy. A laughter that reverberated in every direction. A laughter that claimed to understand happiness. At the end of the alley, the little girl stopped by an old blue door, sketched a house on the sand and whispered, "Come home."

'It was a strange dream that repeated over and over and always ended right outside a blue door I was being invited to come through. This dream tugged at the strings of my heart, like it was drawing me towards itself. But where was it? In my mind or somewhere out in this big wide world? There was a door I had never seen, a girl I had never met, alleys I had never visited, how was I to explain what I was searching for?

'The only other home I ever knew of was right here in Jaipur where I had spent two years of my childhood. I was drowning in the sorrow of my emptiness, and this dream gave me hope. I made a conscious decision to get away from the "life" I knew and everything that defined it.

'I embarked upon a journey into the unknown—back to my roots, to this "Pink City" of Jaipur. At this point, I trusted that dream more than I trusted my reality. With that determined, I was on a plane with a suitcase and a hotel reservation.'

There was a moment of silence and then Leela spoke, 'You explained it well Maya. You were honest. But remember words are but mere crutches for your emotions that can carry them along, but with effort and pain.

'Henceforth, drop the crutches, give your emotions wings. Let them stir you and make you dance to express you are happy, make you cry to lessen your pain, make you giggle to bring you joy and sing to celebrate rain.

'Maya, it's time to release your shackles and step into the truth of every feeling, every emotion without restraint. Let the floodgates open, let the water rush and flood, eventually it will find both its direction and its level.'

Maya felt a sense of relief knowing that she had just bared her soul to a stranger who wasn't already judging her as an ungrateful spoilt brat. She seemed to have recognized both the agony and the irony of an unfulfilled perfect life.

Leela looked up at the glittering sky, 'Now let me tell you a story Maya, listen very carefully.'

'Of course,' said Maya.

'Once upon a time in an enchanted land lived a princess. One day, while chasing butterflies by the stream, she lost her most treasured object—her crown. She looked for it everywhere but it was nowhere to be found. It hurt tremendously, for without that crown, she wasn't special—her life and her identity were lost along with it. Life seemed to have cruelly snatched it away from her tender hands. She was heartbroken. The princess could not bear the pain of this loss so she sealed her heart in an iron cage where she would not hear its cries and pain. The heart called out for her but she kept walking away from it, afraid that if she returned, the heart would remind her of her loss again. She distrusted life and wandered off alone and lonely, far away to a place where no one recognized her, not even herself. Without a heart, the princess floated along the stream of life—anchorless and unhappy.

'The mind convinced her that it was enough to live by. It promised her a way to happiness. "Achieve so much in life that its riches far exceed the glory of your lost jewel," it told her. "Come on step onto this fast-moving track and see the places you'll go." The princess obediently followed but she was a simple girl and this shallow materialistic life began to choke her.

'One day, moving through this fast-paced life, she met with an accident and in that instant, her heart cried out, "Are you alright my dear?" The princess begged, "No, I'm not alright. I have lived these years but I haven't been alive. Where are you my heart, I want you back." The heart whispered, "I'm still at home, right where you left me and I've been calling you every day, ever since." She cried, "But I don't remember how to get home anymore." It patiently answered, "Don't worry, just follow my calling, I will guide your steps. When you come back, you must unchain me, there will be pain that is caught within, just weep with it and bid it goodbye...and beneath the pain, you will find me alive and beating...and together we shall be forever free... Once you are home, you will be happy..."'

'How did you like the story Maya?' asked Leela. 'Don't they say home is where the heart is?' she added, observing her reaction.

Maya fell silent, 'I understand it Leela. I understand.'

'Maya, such is life,' reiterated Leela.

'But why is it so complicated, why couldn't it be simpler? Why can't we just be happy?' questioned Maya.

Leela responded, 'Happiness is based on one fundamental understanding that life is a constant duality—the love and the pain, happiness and sorrow, laughter and tears, day and night. The two sides of the same coin—when we invite one in, the other waits by the door.

'Besides, the very reason one is so appealing is because it is seen against the context of the other—white on white means nothing, it is the black against the white that writes an epic, the hunger that gives food its meaning, it is the tears that enhance the laughter. It is the space between the notes that creates music, the valleys around the mountains that give it the identity.

'What I mean is that what appears contradictory may just be complementary. It is a continuum. One single note key constantly pushed down does not create music, it only creates noise.

'If we had everything we ever wanted, life would be meaningless. Give a child everything he wants, act on his every whim and fancy, and you will give him the gift of unhappiness.

'Problems are inevitable. But they are there for a reason. When you are put under pressure, Maya, you crack open and the potential within you is revealed. Only a hot iron gets forged. Situations are created with your highest interest in mind.

'I'm from the Kalebelia tribe of gypsies. Traditionally, we

are snake charmers. There is a saying that I know well, Maya, "It's not the bite but the venom that kills a man." Situations happen, but what you allow to enter and circulate in your system is what truly kills you. We can't always control what comes our way, but we can certainly make the best of it. What do they say? When life hands you lemons, make lemonade,' said Leela.

'Or as my best friend says, grab tequila and salt!' smiled Maya softly.

The Seven Beads

'You are not a drop in the ocean.
You are the entire ocean in a drop.'

–Rumi

*B*ACK AT THE HOTEL, MAYA held a note in her hand that read:
'Meet me at sunset by the clock tower,

Leela.'

Maya arrived well ahead of time. The marketplace was busy
and Maya wandered aimlessly around, browsing through stacks
of heaped spices in red, yellow and brown. She felt impatient
and anxious as she aimlessly paced up and down. Just then,
Leela emerged through the crowd against the perfect backdrop
of the setting sun. She wore a black cape that partially covered
her face. You could tell her distinctly apart from the throng of
villagers. There was a certain charisma even in the way she
walked.

Maya eagerly started to head in her direction but Leela was
rather dismissive. It appeared that she was either in a hurry

or wanted to avoid being recognized. She indicated for Maya to follow her, and hastily led her away from the main square towards a secluded corner. Leela finally pulled her cape back and sat down on a bench overlooking the barren terrain.

She did not ask Maya how she had been or indulge in small talk about the weather. She meant business and cut right down to the chase. She questioned in a forthright voice, 'Maya, do you know why you are here?' Maya, a little bewildered, answered, 'No, not really.'

'I don't mean here at this place but here in this state of your life,' clarified Leela. Maya nodded her head again, looking clueless.

'Look at the sun,' suggested Leela. 'It is the same sun that ruled the sky when rishis lived and kings reigned. It has been around since times unknown and will continue to be until time unstated. It emerges each day, bringing with it the light, hope and a brand new promise—day after day, month over month, for years and centuries. It is just as new each day as it is timelessly old.

'Similarly, some things keep changing yet remain the same. It is also the story of the great spirit and its desire for itself manifested as your heart's desire. Let me explain this in simpler words.

'Life isn't just black or white Maya, it's composed of the entire spectrum of colours. The artwork of our life depends upon the colours we choose—basically, our own thoughts and beliefs. While we create them, we also get created by them.

'Each new day that greets us offers us a blank canvas. Every colour is equally available on our palette, eagerly waiting to be picked, brush held steady in our own hand, and the possibilities, as you can imagine, are endless.

'But each day, we repeat the same worn-out patterns, the known and familiar strokes. We are disappointed by the scenery of a life that we paint with our own hands.

'The deeper problem is not the picture we see but the picture we somewhere wish to see, that makes us unhappy. A picture that resonates our truth. Unhappiness in life is not caused so much by what we're doing, as it is caused by what we know we should be doing and we aren't.

'Pain is the result of the song that we hear but don't sing, the beauty that we see but we don't paint, the truth that we are but we don't become. It's caused by running through life, glancing at our dreams on the sidelines...still waiting to see the light of the day.

'But it's never too late to make a different choice. You can continue complaining, or start reclaiming.'

'Reclaiming how?' questioned Maya.

'Reclaiming is an act of surrender and trust. You must unlearn your fears. You must forget that you do not know.

'This truth is crystal clear but only to your heart, the safekeeper of this secret, that protects it like a pearl in an oyster. Our goal in life then, is to dive deep into the depths of our heart in search of this precious pearl, to bring it from the darkest depths of the ocean and hold it up to the brilliance of the sun.

'No one knows of it, no one can access it, but you,' said Leela.

'So Leela, what you're saying is that there is a reason for my existence that is known only to me?'

'Well, it is known to your heart, Maya, and every road will lead you to it, but it is a journey that you must consciously undertake.'

'Where does this journey begin though?' asked Maya, inquisitively.

'Your journey has started. You have already taken the first step on this path,' answered Leela.

Maya seemed surprised. 'I have? And what is this first step, Leela?'

'Recognizing the very faint but consistent knocking of your heart, its restlessness, its desperate longing to unburden itself of the secret it guards.

'Your heart is in every place that your truth is and it keeps bringing you back to it—somehow. This is the same force of the unknown—the pull that made you fly across oceans in search of a dream.'

'You mean my truth is here?' said Maya.

'I don't know, only you do...remember the story of the princess and just follow your heart along as you have done so far. It will guide you. You know Maya, believing in your truth is an act of tremendous faith.

'Look at a seed. It contains within it the purpose to become an oak tree. A seed is just a seed today and it does not know where it may end up tomorrow. It neither understands destination, nor ambition. It simply surrenders to the all-knowing process. It does not struggle to be something it's not, it does not pretend to know what is best for it, it just allows itself to stay true to its nature and be revealed.

'This it achieves by submitting to all that is around it, working together to enable manifestation of its potential—the sun, the soil, the water, the gardener. It does not for a moment assume it stands alone and is thereby solely responsible for its fate. It does not compare and agonize over not being enough.

It understands one truth—that it contains within itself all that it is meant to be—and patiently waits in knowing.

'Do not judge yourself based on what you appear to be today...wait, surrender and most of all, listen to your heart.'

There was a short pause that was broken by the passage of a bullock cart. Women in colourful attire sitting in the back swinging their dangling legs as they chewed on long sugarcanes, giggled and waved their hands. Maya waved back instinctively before returning to the conversation.

'What if you can't hear your heart?' questioned Maya.

'The heart is relentless, Maya, it will never stop speaking to you. If you can't hear it, it simply means that its tiny voice is buried beneath the rubble of our daily grind. Just dust aside the debris and blow away the dust, this tiny voice will reach out to you with a resounding echo.

'Consciousness created you to manifest its own dream and it cries blood for each teardrop of helplessness you shed. It celebrates its triumph when you stand up for your dreams and it soars in ecstasy when you start walking towards it. But when the gifts that you are born with simply wither away and die in a deep dungeon of your heart, this universe becomes a little less—forever.

'Enabling life to express its glory through yourself then is the highest service to humanity and the greatest religion. In attainment of our purpose, the universe rejoices, the glory of consciousness is revealed and this desire of the universe for itself becomes the wind beneath our wings that sends us soaring into the unchartered and limitless skies—free and fulfilled. Like a majestic eagle, we open our wings and take flight.'

Leela handed Maya seven wooden beads and a string. 'Here,

keep these with you,' she said as she picked one back up.

Maya's mind instantly went into a rapid-fire rush to analyze the significance of seven beads. Seven suggested mystical and mysterious—seven days, seven continents, seven lives, seven days of earth's creation, seven Egyptian paths to heaven, she could have enlisted these forever but impulsively she questioned.

'Why seven?'

'Six for the number of truths you will encounter and the seventh one to bring them all together,' stated Leela.

'Maya, lessons await you. But be aware of the opportunity when it makes its appearance. Your teachers may not be teachers in the strict sense of the word so keep your mind open. Think of opportunity as a beautiful woman that always comes disguised; she wears a fold around her eyes and has wings beneath her feet. She knocks, but only once. She neither sees the time nor cares about the situation, but when she knocks, you must both recognize and invite her into your life. If you get caught up in doubts and questions, or hesitate for a better time, she will fly away, never to return.

'Each time that you translate an opportunity into a lesson, string one of these beads into the bracelet. Come back to see me with six of these to earn the seventh and the last one.

I leave you here Maya, may the Spirit be with you.'

'Leela, I'm not sure if I'm ready,' stated Maya.

'You will be fine, remember to listen, trust and accept.'

Maya knew she could neither make Leela stay nor could she make her come back. After all she was free like the wind that blew of her own accord, and in her own time.

With this, she turned her back towards Maya and walked away affirming, 'And don't be afraid to make mistakes. Follow the reason but allow your bliss...unreasonable...perhaps, uncertain...maybe, but engage the magic of life. Wish upon a star...let your heart skip a beat...break into a dance...laugh, live and most of all, love, love, love...'

At the entrance to the bazaar, Maya hailed a taxi and stepped in. Her heart wanted some space and a good cup of tea—and that she heard loud and clear. 'Take me some place away from the city, perhaps a truck stop that sells dum chai,' requested Maya. The taxi driver seemed a little sceptical of her vagueness and quickly scanned her bag, watch, earrings and shoes. Almost reassured of her ability to pay him, he invited her to take a seat.

Suddenly, Maya's phone rang. 'Oh wow, I do have coverage for a change,' exclaimed Maya. It was her mom, 'Maya, guess who called me today! Your friend from college, Pia.'

'Oh really Mom, wow, it's been ages,' said Maya.

'Yes,' said her mom, 'and the very interesting thing is that she is with her family right there in Rajasthan, in Jodhpur. I spoke to her mom, Kothari Aunty, and they were delighted to know that you are in Jaipur. Although it seems like they do know about your incident, so I wasn't exactly sure how you would feel about meeting them. I did not give them your number but I took theirs. See if you would like to talk to them and plan a visit. Perhaps some family time and old company might be good for you. No pressure though beta, see how you feel about it.'

'Okay Mom, I will do that.'

Maya and Pia had been best friends in college. Unlike Maya, Pia had short hair, wore torn jeans, was loud, rambunctious, drove motorbikes, and hung out only with boys. She was everything Maya wasn't. She strictly avoided hanging out with girls since she could not handle 'drama', she claimed arrogantly.

Maya and Pia had also been roommates.

Maya dialled her number and said, 'Hello' apprehensively, almost ready to introduce herself. 'MAAAAYA', screamed a shrill voice on the other side.

'Where are you and how are you? Who cares, wherever you are in India, get your ass over right now.'

It felt as if the last eleven years had collapsed into a blink, they hit it off right where they had left. Maya was equally excited and said, 'Send me your address, I will see you tomorrow.'

Maya left a quick note for Ananda at the front desk, 'Leaving for the weekend, will be back soon,' and left with the first light of the day.

She recollected the wonderful moments they had shared in college and looked forward to seeing her after all this while as the taxi made its way out on the open highway. 'Madam,' interrupted the driver, 'if it is okay with you, we could stop for breakfast at Ajmer.' Maya was starting to feel hungry and exclaimed, 'Great suggestion, I could certainly use some food.'

Before long, she found herself sitting on a long wooden bench, if it could be called that. It was more of a wooden plank perched precariously above an open drain. 'Try the bread pakoras, Madam. They are a specialty here,' the driver suggested. A sizzling platter of bread pakoras dripping in stale oil made its way over to her. Entangled between shooing flies and soaking the oil using flimsy paper napkins, Maya failed to respond to the driver's request. 'Madam,' came the voice again. 'Sorry to disturb you, but would you be kind enough to wait for a few minutes?'

The typically patient Maya's endurance had already been pushed to the limit by the swarm of flies. 'Why?' she asked instinctively, borderline intruding in his personal affairs. 'I just wanted to pay a quick visit to the dargah,' he said. Ready to do anything to not have to wait on top of the open sewer, Maya grabbed her purse and stood up, 'Sure, I will come with you!' The driver simply nodded his head with a confused blank expression on his face.

Once out of the breakfast street, Maya regained her composure and took a deep breath. As she walked next to the driver, Maya spoke again, 'Did you say you wanted to visit the dargah?'

'Yes Madam, that's right, it's called Ajmer Sharif.'

'I don't mean to overstep but I can't help asking, what is your religious affiliation? And it's perfectly fine if you choose not to discuss or disclose it but I'm just curious. I saw these pictures and figurines of Ganesha and Shiva all over your car. I assumed you are a Hindu.'

'Madam, you are absolutely right. I am a Hindu by birth and religion but Ajmer Sharif is not about a certain religion, this is the home of the living spirit of peace and harmony where everyone is equally welcome. It's the dargah of Hazrat Khwaja Moinuddin Hasan Chishti, popularly known as Khwaja Gharib Nawaz, who occupies a prominent place among the spiritual healers of the world. For your reference, he established the Chisti order of Sufi saints and till date, people come from all parts of the world to have their wishes granted.

'It is an age-old belief that people who visit Ajmer Sharif and pray with a pure heart free their souls. People tie these threads of mannat to have their wishes granted and no one ever returns empty-handed from here,' he said as they walked along.

'Could I come inside the dargah as well? I've never been

to one and I am not exactly familiar with the customs of this culture.'

'Madam, you need not worry about it. This place is a convergence pot for all cultures and religions. In fact, many of the customs followed here stem from the Hindu religion. For example, wearing red and yellow threads around the neck or wrists of devotees, pasting sandal at the mazaar, cracking coconuts at the doorsteps of the dargah, and the lighting ceremony at dusk are all derived from Hindu influence. Of course, they have their own order of sama-qawalli which has led to the spiritual awakening for many.

'If you could, I highly recommend that you experience the fervour of it one day in your life. It draws you into an ecstatic trance. As you probably know, music has always played a prominent part in the spiritual traditions of India from bhajans to kirtans. Khawaja Sahib took this singing to a Sufistic style that was well-suited to this culture's temperament, customs and traditions, the reason why it remains popular to this day.'

Maya quietly followed the driver as he bought a chaddar and a basket of crimson rose petals and fresh mogra. Maya requested a repeat order. The streets became progressively narrow and vibrant green colour seemed to dominate the bazaar. There was a distinct fragrance of rose petals, blended with an intense aroma of tea and sohan halwa. The strong scent of attar was also peculiar.

Maya admired the exquisite Mughal architecture as she walked through the commanding Buland Darwaza. The driver noted, 'Great Mughal emperors Akbar, Jahangir and Shah Jahan were his ardent devotees. It is said that Akbar invoked the blessings of the saint by a vow that he would travel on foot from Agra to Ajmer if he was blessed with a baby boy.'

'Really?' said Maya, sounding very interested as she stepped inside the Dargah.

Maya was in midst of offering her prayers when she heard an old gentle voice, 'Beti, go tie a mannat, your wish will be granted.' Maya whispered, 'What if I do not have a wish?' The man nodded his head and smiled as he said, 'Very good, in that case, you are making the job easier. A wish will be granted nonetheless, the Spirit's wish for you and for itself.'

The old man said, 'Let me tell you an interesting story. 'Once Alamgir Aurangzeb came to pay reverence at the glorious shrine of Hazrat Khwaja Gharib Nawaz. Along his path, right outside the dargah, he found a blind beggar who was crying out for mercy, "Ya Khwaja Gharib Nawaz! Restore my sight. Allow me to see this beautiful world of yours." He stopped and asked this beggar, "Baba! Since how long have you been begging for your vision?" He said, "It has been ages but my wish remains unfulfilled." Aurangzeb said, "I shall return after paying homage at the holy shrine, in the meantime, if your eyes regain their vision, very well, otherwise I will have you killed." The King called for the guards to keep an eye on the beggar, and went inside to pay his respect. The beggar started regretting his story and wept woefully, "Khwaja! Earlier it was my eyes only but now it is my life, show mercy my lord or I will be killed." When the King returned, the old man ran to greet him, "A miracle has occurred, a miracle from my lord, my eyes had acquired vision and my life has been spared. How did this happen after all these years?"

'The King smiled and said, "Until now you wished with mere words so your wishes remained unfulfilled, and now because your life depended upon it, for the very first time, you reached him from your heart and he heard you right away.'"

Maya paused to think about Leela's message about heart and the connection to the great spirit and how it orchestrates the events. *What a coincidence that she should end up in Ajmer to hear this story,* Maya contemplated.

'That was a beautiful story, thank you for sharing it,' said Maya as she walked out onto the white marble courtyard.

The man humbly responded, 'It is his razaa, the dictates of a higher order, we are mere messengers, what can we take credit for?'

He placed his hand on Maya's head in blessing and said, 'My child, I can see in your eyes that you are on a quest to find his order for you. I can also see that your journey will be fulfilling.'

'How did you learn about my journey?'

The old man answered 'This universe starts and ends with the wholeness of life, those who know of it can recognize those who come searching for it.'

'I call this the Whole Truth of life.'

'My child, we are far greater than what we appear to be. It's the process of disengagement from the greater self—the all-inclusive—that lies at the root of our suffering. When eyes of the soul and the voice of the heart are forgotten, our entity becomes a hollow effigy of falsehood that wanders adrift and anchorless. But our existence is neither random nor isolated.

'This eternal spirit, this essence and the expansiveness, gives birth to itself as individual consciousness. It lends itself an identity, breathes life into it, forges it with the fire of its passion and places it at its own altar.'

'I'm not sure I understand, could you simplify this?' asked Maya.

'Yes. Look at the ocean, it consists of numerous waves and all that the ocean is, each wave is, and all that the tiniest wave is, the vast ocean is. It evolves out of and dissolves back into itself.'

Maya was fully engaged and eager to respond. 'Oh, now I get it!' Rumi states this beautifully when he says, 'You are not a drop in the ocean. You are the entire ocean in a drop.'

'Exactly, right!' said the old man, as he handed her some rose petals.

'As long as the wave understands its essence, there is perfect harmony. It rises and surrenders, it contains and is contained. However, once it forgets its greater truth, it becomes blind to its own power.

'Sadly, in forgetting, even eternity looks for more time, the ocean thirsts for water, the sun searches for some light, and the flower cries for beauty.

'Remember, an eclipse merely casts a shadow, it only makes the moon appear smaller, it does not make it small. As the light of awareness spreads, the shadows regress and the totality reveals itself.'

'Interesting,' said Maya.

'This forgotten truth of our own greatness is what we seek all our lives. We look for it in the next person, or the next achievement. These can only offer temporary relief and fleeting distraction. These can neither complete us nor fulfill us. For fulfilment does not reside in attainment but in a simple fundamentally empowering realization, that we already are what we seek. Our completion then becomes a matter of recognition not acquisition. I send you off here, my child, with my blessings, and a few lessons from Ajmer.

'Always remember, there are no mistakes, no coincidences and no disconnects in the universe…only perfection, order and complete harmony. Seasons come and go, trees shed their leaves, winds blow them away, day follows the night, earth spins around the sun, acorn grows into an oak, sun keeps rising, birds fly home…our hearts keep on beating and with that our lives keep unfolding in perfection.'

With this, the old man turned around and said, 'It is time for my prayers, may you be blessed my child.'

Maya folded her hands and took leave as she counted her first bead. It was well past noon as they set out on their onward journey.

About an hour past Ajmer, just short of Beawar, the car started to swerve. The driver pulled over to a side, ran a quick scan and announced, 'Madam, it's a flat tyre, which is a good thing. I mean, it could have been worse. This should not take too long to change.'

He placed Maya's luggage by the roadside and pulled out the spare tyre. Maya took her Nikon D-5 out of the case and stepped onto the sand to click pictures of the beautiful arid landscape. She particularly had a thing for capturing images of sand and cactus. It depicted inspiration in the middle of the emptiness and was also a symbol of endurance that withstood harsh elements and the test of time. Perhaps, she owed her strange affiliation to a few summers she spent with her relatives at Flagstaff, Arizona, where she would spend hours exploring the desert vegetation.

The driver turned around as he undid the bolts on the tyre, 'Madam, nature is quite the miracle—as mysterious as it is enchanting. If you enjoy capturing the sights of a desert, imagine capturing the sounds of it.'

'Sounds of the desert? What do you mean by sounds of the desert?' asked Maya.

'Well, in Rajasthan's Barmer district, is situated a village called Setrau, where a unique phenomenon makes the desert sing.'

'How?' questioned Maya.

'There is a particular sand dune in that village whose sand is quite similar to all else around it but when it is struck by anything, the sand emanates a musical sound, similar to a percussion instrument called Bhapang. This sand dune has been making music for over half a century now. When you walk on the sand or collide with it, it breaks into a timeless melody of longing and union. Many teams of scientists and geologists have visited the site but the mystery remains unanswered. What is also interesting is that it is the desert that makes the sand sing. Samples of this sand that were taken back for research to Delhi stopped producing this sound after three days. Really, this colourful land of ours is a miracle, a wonder and a strange mystery.'

Maya thought about that for a while, 'Sounds of the desert, enchanting!'

It was mostly hot and quiet except for an occasional car which came that way and slowed down just enough to curiously observe and go along its merry way. Maya paid little attention.

Then, through the lens of her camera, Maya noticed another black car, except, it wasn't just another black car, it was a black Bentley proceeding in their direction. Her pulse raced and her mouth felt like the sand she stood upon. The car zipped past by in a flash and she let out a deep breath, perhaps a little too soon. The car came to a screeching halt and reversed back up to the broken taxi. The dark windows rolled down first and then the door opened. From the car emerged an alluring man, about six feet tall, with hypnotic brown eyes and an enchanting smile. Maya recognized those tan Ferragamos in an instant. In his dark denims and linen shirt, to call him handsome would be a gross understatement. Maya was entranced and mumbled as she watched him proceed in her direction, 'This can't be true! He can't be real... Please, for heaven's sake, don't tell me he's also this good-looking, and the brown eyes and the sharp nose and the smile...just as I had always dreamed. Send me a saving grace. Something, anything to keep me from falling into this abyss.'

'May I help you?' he said in a deep voice that penetrated Maya's being. The echo of which felt like a half-drawn arrow plunged in Maya's heart.

Maya nervously uttered, 'Oh no, thank you, I don't take help from strangers.'

'So, do you have a problem with taking help or do you have a problem with strangers?' he questioned, confusing her further.

Bewildered, Maya snapped without thinking, 'Both actually!' and quickly caught herself falling in a trap. She meant to correct herself, 'What I really mean is that...' Much to Maya's relief, the driver interrupted, precisely in time. 'Madam, we are ready.' He could not have picked a better moment. Maya had been desperately looking for an oxygen mask to drop from the sky, but this statement was just about as good. She took a shallow breath as she abruptly reached for her suitcase.

The man stepped graciously forward beating Maya to it.

'Allow me,' he said as he held the bag, not giving her a chance to protest further. He glanced over sideways and smiled, lifting the black Tumi bag as effortlessly as a feather. He placed it carefully in the trunk of the car and added, 'Don't worry, Miss, your principles remain uncompromised. The great Irish poet William Butler Yeats said, "There are no strangers here; only friends you haven't met," and what I just did with your bag wasn't "help", but a "gentleman tradition". That's what we do!'

Maya just stood there and stared at him, unable to utter another word as Veer held the door of the car. 'Safe travels,' he added.

Friends Forever

> 'Tis the privilege of friendship to talk nonsense,
> and to have her nonsense respected.'
>
> —Charles Lamb

*T*HE CAR MEANDERED DOWN THE roads as it made its way towards the city. Maya could still not get over the embarrassment of her pathetic reaction. She decided to breathe and shake it off knowing it was behind her, for good.

As they approached the city limits, dark clouds took over the sky and before long, the car was engulfed in a sandstorm. The visibility was low and Maya asked the driver to pull over and wait for the storm to pass. 'It's alright madam,' he insisted, 'this will pass quickly.' The storm was followed by a few drops of light rain. Children and adults rushed out on to the streets wearing joyful expressions. They looked at the sky with hopeful eyes and another strong gust of wind blew and whistled as if to fan their emotions. They rejoiced in cheer and broke into rain songs and happy dances. Maya laughed. The taxi driver responded, 'Madam, this is a very auspicious sign. Rain is a good omen for your arrival. Rajasthan, as you know, is a desert and for many months now, we have been eagerly awaiting a sign of rain. This year in particular, we were hit with an especially brutal draught. If you look at the news reports, they even talked about people cooking eggs and rice on hot sand!' he chuckled.

'These thick clouds hold a great promise of relief from the sweltering heat. I must say you are indeed very lucky for this place, Madam. There must be some connection that such a rare phenomenon came to greet you upon arrival.'

This indeed was a refreshing welcome as Maya looked around to absorb the city amidst the pleasant petrichor that emanated from the land and the unusual stir caused by the sparse drops of rain. She pulled out her phone and reconfirmed the address. Within a few minutes, they pulled up in front of a tall wrought iron gate supported by brick pillars and ornate lamps. The guard asked them to sign a register and log in their entry. He then made a quick phone call and opened the gate. Maya was already impressed. 'Are we at the right address?' she inquired, seeming a little unsure.

Pia had been the most unassuming girl at school. Neither her clothing nor her conversations spoke anything of the heritage that she came from. The garden was neatly landscaped and the long stone driveway led to the Italian marble fountain, which now felt like a standard feature of the typical Indian mansion.

Pia dashed out the main door and almost knocked Maya off her feet as she locked her in a tight embrace. Maya was stunned and dazed as she questioned with gaping wide eyes, 'Whatever happened to you, Pia?'

Pia giggled, 'I know, don't I look different? I finally decided to grow up and become a lady,' she laughed.

Ladylike she sure looked with her light skin, bright complexion, perfectly blown-out long hair and the giant teardrop emeralds that complimented her white outfit. She even wore a pink lipstick!

The steps from the front door led to the grand foyer that staged a beautiful piano. A Murano chandelier hung above it and a grand display of cheetah skins, stuffed animals and family portraits accented the room. Maya was bedazzled by the glory of the place.

Kothari Aunty walked in looking graceful in her pink saree that covered her short grey hair ever so elegantly. 'Maya, I'm so glad you could join us for Pia's engagement,' said Aunty.

'What?' Maya's jaw dropped. 'Pia is getting engaged?'

Pia almost blushed, 'I know, a lot has changed Maya.'

'A lot is an understatement, Pia, how and when did this happen? I guess we have some serious catching up to do,' said Maya as she was led by Pia to her room.

Pia's room was comfortably modern and Zen-like with every shade of white accentuated by rare, fresh and abundant greenery. Pia extended another warm hug and said reassuringly, 'Everything will be just fine.'

'I'm sure it will be' said Maya.

Neither Pia questioned, nor Maya explained, but they both understood nonetheless. The beauty of an amazing friendship always is that questions are unnecessary, and reassurances mandatory.

'Why don't you freshen up Maya, we will talk over a good glass of wine, and some great food. Not many people will understand our appreciation for good food after the four traumatic years of eating campus meals and instant noodles.

Ah! The occasional luxury of ordering in burger and fries. I wonder how we even survived!

'And remember how often I raided the food supplies of the always well-stocked and super organized sisters next door! Wow, we did live those days on a survival mode! Never quite thought that life would really begin on the other side of those years,' said Pia.

Maya interjected, 'So with all this here, why did you harbour insecurities about money and career and standing on your own two feet? Your family would have supported you in any venture.'

'That was exactly what I did not want. As a little girl, my life flashed crystal clear in front of my eyes. I would grow into a fine young lady, who played piano, sipped on tea out of her splendid collection of tea sets, wore fancy hats and bet on horses. I would be an accessory to a man who would take me on expensive vacations and buy me jewels. I did not want to be dead while living.

'I turned into a rebel who wanted to live by her own rules. I wanted to hear my heart beat each moment. I wanted to see life beyond the attention, outside my comfort zone where I was nobody other than myself. I chopped my hair, took to dressing that did not resemble a lady remotely, stayed away from fancy cars and all the men who wanted to court me. I did everything in my life, checked everything on my bucket list—skydiving to scuba diving, drugs to meditation. I worked minimum wage jobs and bought myself that second-hand bike. I did it all. I experimented with myself to know what I truly wanted.

'Turns out that what I wanted evolved with my understanding of life. The greatest failure in life, Maya, is to be closed to the mystery and adventure that life holds out. We must remain open to just about everything. Interestingly, it ends up that I'm still doing what I might have done in the first place but I came full circle. The life I lead now is full of gratitude and appreciation rather than retaliation and resentment.'

'Pia, you make accepting luxuries sound like an act of martyrdom,' said Maya.

'It's not easy you know,' responded Pia, and they both giggled.

They sat in the open air restaurant overlooking the beautifully lit Mehrangarh fort. The crisp white table covers, the white flowers, beautiful candles and the chilled glass of sparkling rosé tingled Maya's senses. 'I'm so glad we met, Pia.'

'Yes, and I'm so happy you will be a part of my engagement ceremony. In India, there is a very famous saying which suggests that each grain of food and every drop of water—daana-paani—has your name written on it. Well, this piece of bread and this glass of wine called you louder than I did,' laughed Pia.

'The more I get to know this country and its people, the more fascinating it becomes,' said Maya. 'They have so much wisdom and grounding.'

'They do Maya, but its presence does not guarantee its understanding.'

'I am learning that Pia and learning that the hard way.'

'Well, life cannot be taken too seriously. Lighten up, whether you laugh through the process or cry through the pain, you will end up nearly at the same place but with entirely different experiences. They say, "A good traveller has no fixed plans, and is not intent on arriving," it's the journey that truly matters. Cheers to that.

'So, I can't wait until you meet Abhay. It will be so much fun. He knows about all our escapades, the long bicycle rides, wading through streams, collecting wild flowers and star gazing in the park.'

'Does he know about the day you beat up that guy who tried mixing drugs in your drinks and was caught red-handed?'

'What do you expect Maya, it was Betmaar inspired!' Pia laughed.

'Betmaar?' repeated Maya.

'Yes, to woman power and man beating,' giggled Pia.

'Really?'

'Remember, I'm not only a Rajasthani girl, I'm also from Jodhpur. Interestingly, Jodhpur is the only city in the world where they celebrate a festival called Betmaar or Dhinga Gavar where women dress up in disguises, from devis to dacoits, from actresses to police inspectors, and parade the city roads at night holding sticks in their hands. If any man happens to come in their way, he's in for the beating of his life. It runs in my culture. More power to women!' said Pia as she winked and raised a toast again.

'Pia, it is nice to see you so content. Honestly, while we were growing up, I believed myself to be the wise one. The one who did everything by the book. I went to a medical school, invested in myself and my career, dated successful men, connected in the right social circles. I thought I was set for life and I was worried for you. You were completely lost, clueless about your future, couldn't care to plan or think. You always lived just for the day, never for the distant future and see how grounded you are while I'm still finding my feet.'

'Maya, if you live each day to its best possibility, you increase your chances of living the following day and when you look back upon life, it is a series of moments and days well spent.

'I don't sit here preaching like I could see the future back then and arrived here by design. I didn't know what I wanted either Maya, all I knew was that I was starting from an unusual place of knowing what I did *not* want. Perhaps, the only right thing I did was allowed my heart to talk to me often. I did what I wanted and asked my heart for feedback. Sometimes, I felt calm and composed and other times, I was restless and anxious. I trusted my feelings to guide me in the right direction.

'Maya, I led my life attempting to discover my outer happiness in order to trace back to my inner joy. I don't blame you at all. Having spent the years in fast-paced New York, I understand how we become accustomed to living by the norms, clocks and the commitments while we know perfectly well what needs to be accomplished or achieved. Still, we have no sense of where our joy stems from. We go compulsively from task to task, equating achievement and productivity with happiness and success.

'At each step, I simply paused for a moment to ask myself if I had all the freedom to choose, no constraints to hold me back, no voices of concern drowning me with advice, what would I be doing? At each step, I had to cut the net of society's collective thinking. I broke the rules, looked beyond the known, threw practicality to the wind and dived deep into possibility. I must say I did surprise myself, Maya.'

'That's quite a reflective statement,' said Maya.

'Honestly,' said Pia, 'up until that point, somewhere deep inside, I was nagged by a belief that it was utterly selfish to think about what made me happy while people were busy working for a great life and a real cause. But honestly, it is far from being selfish, it's the first step towards selflessness, it's the very basis of abundance and happiness. In reaching for the source of your happiness, you step into the process of receiving happiness rather than begging for it or striving to create it.

'And don't try to justify your goals based upon a rational judgement of what is important, possible, achievable, or even worth it—base it purely upon the love, the joy and the experience of it.

'Create a handy list, I have mine on my iPhone. A list of things that make your heart sing...that strike a chord, that stir your soul. Slowly you will realize that for everything that you do, moments when you experience true happiness are the moments when you felt closest to your real self. Maya in her purest form—unadulterated, unfiltered, unprocessed.'

'Is it even possible to experience such moments?' asked Maya.

'Such moments often just happen. These are neither grand nor meticulously planned, they emerge from the moments of truth, moments of complete harmony where the split between what is and what has become disappears.

'Life right after the final year was crazy with intense pressures of surviving in the real world and I, of all, was completely unprepared and unequipped to deal with it. I knew I couldn't go any faster so I slowed down,' Pia giggled, nodding her head. 'That fast mechanical life totally sucked.'

Maya interrupted, 'Pia!'

'Yes yes! I know I should choose better words, but come on, Maya turn on your filters, for now let me express it the way I can best describe it. It did suck. I couldn't give it up and return home a failure so I gradually started to introduce some simple pleasures back into my life. I created a music list, baked new recipes, went for long walks, I signed up for a dance class. Yes, me! The one who could not lift a foot without falling down. I read books—yes, considering I read my first book at the age of 25 as I recovered from a surgery. I watched the rain, spent weekends watching movies in my pyjamas, volunteered at the soup kitchen, planted a garden. And in the evenings, I sat on my deck wrapped in a blanket enjoying a glass of fine wine with a bowl of my garden tomato salad, soulful music, cool summer breeze, chirping crickets and dancing fireflies.

'These simple acts were not aimed at some great discovery but uncovered small joys that gave a sense of balance and well-being. It gave me the contentment that a wardrobe full of fancy shoes could not. I realized that happiness becomes a bottomless pit when you try to fill it externally and overflows abundantly when you pause to smell a rose.

'Interestingly, this process also made me realize that I had lived my life so far without so much as trying half the things I absolutely loved and if I hadn't explored far enough, I would have never discovered this aspect of me. It was as though I had found a source of live wire in these little things that included, as bizarre as it may sound, a long shower and a pair of fresh socks. I felt energized, my eyes found their twinkle, my lips their smile, my heart its music and life was good.

'Maya, it's not that life spared me my share of challenges because I did these things, it just made it easier for me to deal with them. By the way, I not only buy my own jewels, I also design them—Pia jewellery, that's me! I guess those hours spent drinking Starbucks outside Tiffany's weren't such a waste after all.'

The Good Flow

'If music be the food of love, play on.'

–Shakespeare

KOTHARI HOUSE WAS BUZZING WITH laughter as women busily rushed from one end to the other. The agenda was to get one hundred family and friends done with their chais and mithais, selfies and check-ins and ushered into the cars that stood in a beeline, with open doors held by regal turbaned drivers in white gloves.

Kothari Aunty seemed more stressed than happy. 'We need to be there before nine. We can't really be missing at the reception, people. Come on and hurry,' she insisted as she trudged along, fixing her hair and adjusting her saree. 'Relax Mom,' said Pia, 'Abhay will be right there waiting for us even if we show up at 9 a.m. tomorrow.' She shook her head and let out an exasperated breath as she walked away muttering to herself, 'That's exactly what these people need to hear in order to make it there in time. Really, children these days live in a bubble! Come on everyone,' announced Kothari Aunty as she sat down in the car and the engine was started.

Maya simply followed orders as the procession marched at a sluggish pace. The venue was the majestic Umaid Bhawan Palace, downright royal and absolutely magnificent. Maya overheard someone in the crowd utter, 'Why did you check in at home, you should have checked in here, after all this has been named the best hotel in the world.' The chatter continued, 'Wow, impressive, what a place, not a place, it's a palace!' The conversations kept flowing unabated, punctuated with occasional 'oohs' and 'aahs'.

Before long, the groom's family arrived to meet a traditional and grand Rajasthani welcome. Showers of rose petals along with the sound of beating drums, ceremonial tikas, opulent garlands and tinkering sounds of champagne flutes chimed in the air. Oblivious ladies, or at least pretending such, happily gulped down glass after glass of champagne, or 'juice', as it was being referred to.

Family spectators crowded around the front entrance stepping on toes, breathing down necks and rubbing off sweat to catch the elusive first glimpse of 'the boy'. Of course, they knew they would have a million chances to do that over the course of the day, however, at such ceremonies, it is customary to be both over-inquisitive and first to give the verdict. Really, so much depends upon it! One bald old gentleman returned from the doorway with a huge grin and a thumbs up, it was a 'box office hit,' he indicated. Another old relative cheered him on, 'Really, *wah ji, aap to first aa gaye.*' He walked back with an air of arrogance as the lesser relatives who did not quite make it to the door in time crowded around him to hear more about 'the boy'!

The magnitude and the vanity of the gathering was intimidating. Maya felt a little underdressed among the embellished lehngas and ornate jhumars, blinding six-carat earrings and necklaces that appeared more like stocks from medieval times successfully immobilizing these women to some extent. She decided to step away towards the pool for a quick break when she heard Pia's voice, 'Hey Maya, come meet Abhay.'

Maya turned around and there stood Veer, next to Abhay, in all his divine glory, yet again. Maya was part in trance, part in shock and part in heaven. She stood there and just stared. Pia, a little embarrassed, tried to break the awkward moment, 'Ha Maya, didn't we love to play statue! Okay over...' and in the same breath, she grinded her teeth and said 'MAYA, meet ABHAY.'

'Oh yes, of course,' Maya responded, as she stepped forward, following her locked gaze leading up to Veer. She shook his hand and said, 'Pleasure to meet you, Abhay.'

He responded politely with a firm handshake, his signature smile, piercing eyes and a respectful bow. 'The pleasure is all mine despite the fact that Abhay is standing next to me.'

They all broke into a roaring laughter and Maya, looking as dumbfounded as she felt, longed for the earth to crack open so she could sink right in!

Pia brushed it off saying, 'Oh, she did not sleep too well last night,' and turning around to Maya, she whispered, 'I guess we need to talk.'

During the remaining course of the day, Maya purposely avoided Veer at every stage. If he went left, she swung right. If he went in, she slipped out. Hard as she tried, she could not fathom the reason for his omnipotence and her shocking reaction or her inability to keep herself from falling for him hook, line and sinker. She was drawn to him like a helpless moth who clearly sees its fate yet flies right into the flame. However, in this case, Maya was sure the flame was chasing the moth all over the place and no, she restated, 'This was not what she wanted.'

The ceremony was hosted at the beautiful marble Baradari surrounded by lush green gardens and pink bougainvillea. Pia and Abhay looked heavenly together and the rings were exchanged amidst claps and cheers and flowers and champagne. The two families exchanged hugs, and posed happily for photos, perhaps the one time this was going to be done with genuine joy. Sudden onslaught of flashes from the large photo crew felt like a grand lightning. As with typical Indian weddings, there was rich food, top-shelf liquor and plenty of dancing.

There were sassy middle-aged ladies who turned into babydolls and outrageous older gentlemen who mesmerized the crowd with outlandish moves such as a hands-free balancing act of a glass of whisky on their heads. There were others who transformed into serpents and some who looked like dancing ATMs with crisp 2000-rupee notes caught neatly between their teeth. It was quite amusing. The rest of the afternoon was spent diligently watching Veer's every move and strictly avoiding him. Maya was relieved to find out that it was nearly time to go home.

'Lady, all these years, I thought I knew you well enough and I also believed that it would only get better from where I had left you. Goodness gracious,' exclaimed Pia as she continued, 'really Maya? You are so totally, completely, absolutely and hopelessly in love with this man. You were frozen in awe. Could you, for god's sake, tell me what in hell is going on? If only I could show you a mirror with your jaw dropped and eyes popping out like a set of binoculars! I swear, I could even see you drooling.'

'Shut up Pia, today was the first time I have been introduced to this man.'

'You really want me to believe this crap?' retorted Pia.

'Yes, I do, because this is the honest truth and it is also true that I'm in love with him.'

'Seriously Maya? Are we aging or regressing here? You sound like a 14-year-old girl who lived some 50 years ago. What bullshit. Get a grip!'

'Pia, calm down, I admit I've seen him before. My car broke down on the way over and he stopped to offer help but wait, let's go back, it doesn't start there. I fell in love with him before that. In fact, as strange as it may sound, I finally understand love at first sight. Actually speaking, technically it wasn't love at first sight... I did not get to see him... I just saw his shoes and his hair...actually...then he turned around and started to walk away, so I guess, I saw him from the back but maybe it will qualify for first sight...

'Yes, I know it doesn't make a whole lot of sense but there is some weird conspiracy going on. I fell in love with him even before I saw him that day...we exchanged letters and he doesn't know me...but I didn't know him either and then I saw him, even though he didn't see me and ever since the other day when I saw him without actually seeing him, something or the other makes us cross paths over and over.'

Pia's expression turned into horror, 'Are you alright Maya? Sounds like you need help. Do you know what you're saying?'

'Well, I know I'm not doing a good job explaining this but...

'You know Pia, it's not me who is strange, it's him! What gives him the right to be who he is?

'I mean... I grew up dreaming of this man—a man who I created, I designed him to my specifications, I calibrated him to my preferences. It was my vision of my perfection—no one else's. I gave him the height I wanted, I coloured his eyes with my wishes, he smiled for me with those perfect pearl teeth and his style and sophistication were inspired from the blue blood I read about in novels. He was charming, he was successful, he was soft-spoken, polite and cultured but most of all, he was a dream—he was perfect. And neither dreams nor perfection are supposed to exist in reality. And he shows up, he actually shows up. He walks right into my life, just like that and sweeps me off my feet and draws me to himself like a neodymium magnet. This should not be happening; he should not even be. He has no business being who he is. I liked him just enough for his thoughts and then he turned out to be the superstar of the community. He ended up being someone from an elite heritage with killer looks and intelligence par excellence that he utilized to write his own success story. And if that wasn't enough, he then returned his success to the world in a multitude of ways gaining love and affection of all. He's the one who needs help introducing something, at least one thing in his life that's less than spectacular.'

Maya took a deep breath, 'I know I'm ranting here...just trust me, I'm trying. I understand I'm here for something else, Pia, I'm here to find myself, not lose myself to another hopeless love story. I swear, I've avoided him all afternoon, I honestly wish I never see him again. I like the strong, independent, intelligent woman I have been all my life... It's threatening my identity... or whatever little is left of it anyway.

'Pia, on a serious note, I have recovered myself from the

brink of destruction, my life was over and so was my story. I can't afford to repeat the same mistake. I could be honest with you so I am...perhaps more honest than I could be with myself but no, this is not what I want, need or can afford at this point in my life. Please trust me on this.'

Pia gave Maya a tight hug and kissed her forehead. 'You are crazy, but trust life, and everything will be alright. We will navigate this challenge together.'

The morning started with the sound of chants and ringing of bells as Pia stormed into Maya's room. 'Hurry, just wash your face and come downstairs, everyone is gathered for the puja. This is like a ceremonial thanksgiving after a milestone. In case anyone questions, yes, you showered and brushed your teeth this morning.'

During the puja, Maya couldn't help but notice this lady dressed in an elegant white saree with a string of pearls around her neck and a bright red lipstick. Her silver hair seemed to crown her beauty as did the deep-set wrinkles around her mouth and eyes which conveyed a journey of laughter, smiles and happiness. She appeared fabulous, content and fascinating. After puja samaapti, Pia ran over and gave her a tight hug as both of them clapped their hands, gave each other a high five and chimed, 'Yaay, it's over!'

Kothari Aunty nodded her head as if dismissing her two handful daughters.

'Meet Dadi,' Pia screamed, 'a day too late to the celebration.'

'Can I ever be late to a celebration?' Dadi questioned, 'I bring celebration with me. She holds my door and asks, "Shall I begin?"' She laughed in such a hearty manner that the whole house rocked with happiness. Her laughter was contagious.

'Okay,' she said, 'before anything else, go get me my black tea and some biscotti. Your mother insists on performing these pujas on empty stomach like she is going to find god by keeping me hungry. I play along because I'm just too nice,' she continued, 'otherwise I could not care less for it. Well, let me say I care for my food more than I care for a puja and god seems to get it but these trivial people do not.'

Maya was lit up to see her electrifying energy and hunger for life, love and laughter at this age. Pia announced, 'Dadi is planning her milestone birthday bash early next year.'

'Maya,' Dadi declared, 'you have to come. I promise you, you will have the time of your life. It will be beyond your wildest dreams, we will rock it.'

Pia giggled as she exclaimed, 'That's my girl!'

Maya said, 'I'm so glad to be a part of all this. Thank you for having me.' Dadi responded, 'Thank you for being here. I'm so tired of hanging out with all these old and boring ladies like Pia's mother. I like young girls like you—people I can mentally relate to, you know. Pia, you go take care of other relatives, leave me alone with Maya. I would like to get to know her better.'

'So Maya,' said Dadi, 'tell me about yourself. What brings you here? Work, family?'

Maya answered, 'Daana-paani...at least that's what I've learnt so far.'

'Shabaash,' said Dadi, giving her a loud pat on the back that almost knocked her off the edge of the sofa as she continued, 'I already like you a lot. Something tells me we will hit it off big time.'

Maya giggled. 'How cool is your Dadi, Pia. I can see where you get your bubbliness from.'

Pia responded, 'Yes, she practically raised me and was the greatest influence in shaping my thoughts. She told me each night that we were born as stars, to soar, to roam free and shine but this world chains us in the velvet shackles of love, duty and responsibility. You are free to break out and you are free to fly unbounded...you just don't know.

'There is one life, she told me, and it is not just one life to live, it's the one life to love. She asked me to leave my Kothari identity behind and travel far to pursue education, not strictly in the academic sense. She wanted me to learn about myself, to explore my choices, to discover my aspirations and to live out my fantasies...

'She often recited a lullaby:

"Drink to contentment from the well of life...and intoxicated from ecstasy, dance in delight like a whirlwind that catches a storm in her hair and plucks the flowers to create her tiara... spin and be free... Let chaos lead you to clarity. Let the world spin till you become still... Dance till you become a rhythm... carry the love child of passion in your womb...and give birth to a timeless star. Spin till you find your center... Sing till you become a song...""

'Wow, that's incredible Pia. And how did she live her life?'

'Exactly the way she described it. And lived is a wrong word, Maya. She is still living it, and that too, on the edge.'

Pia continued, 'My great-grandfather was a very enterprising man, a native Jodhpuri with humble education but a brilliant mind. He tried his hand at many small ventures before he finally made his fortune in limestone mining. Dadi was a force to reckon with since an early age. As lack of education remained her father's personal handicap and a raw nerve, he wanted to put her through the finest and the best school he could afford.

'She was sent for her higher education to Switzerland. Shortly after a year, much against the wishes of her family, she dropped out of college and enrolled herself in Dalcroze programme for music education. It deeply anguished many, but as she puts it, "it transformed her experience of life forever." She could feel their pain and understand their disappointment but it was her true calling, she says, "which she could neither deny, nor betray."'

'Dalcroze? Sorry Pia if I sound ignorant, but I have never heard of it. What kind of music programme is that?'

'Well, it deeply connects music in its concept and meaning with other forms of arts and human activity through the concept of rhythmic movement. Dalcroze observed that his students displayed subtle, spontaneous movements such as swaying, tapping or swinging as they sang. He started to recognize the fact that our bodies were conscious of life and the movement of music.

'He started to build upon these natural, instinctive responses, encouraging his students to amplify their physical response as they sang or listened to him improvise at the piano. He called this study of music through movement, "eurhythmics", derived from Greek words "eu" and "rythmos", translated as "good flow". He believed that our body is an instrument through which music is created, perceived and comprehended.

'The movements weren't choreographed but rather spontaneously used as a feedback mechanism for the performer himself, essentially creating a circuit of information and response between brain and body, which, with training and experience, continues to rise to higher levels of precision, coordination, and expressive power.'

'How amazing! I'm surprised we haven't heard more about it,' said Maya.

'Yes, it is fascinating. Her father had big dreams for her but her dreams were greater. She dreamt with open eyes that gazed lovingly upon her soul. Her father even travelled to Switzerland but could not convince her otherwise. Music and movement had taken over her life. She was as helpless as they were.

'She met my grandfather during one of her summers back home and stayed for love. Of course, she missed her life in Switzerland but she was the wind that could not be tamed. She heard about a classical dance teacher, a distinguished guru, known to be extremely selective in picking his students. She went to his school and offered herself as his disciple. He was dismissive, assuming she was just another rich woman with much time on her hands, seeking a venue to beat boredom. He declined to take her in and she refused to take no for an answer. She declared that music and dance were food for her soul and she would starve until death at his doorstep if that was what pleased him. She sat there for three days and nights without food and water and on the fourth day, the guru came and blessed her. He was impressed with her devotion, courage and determination. It is said that the rhythm she had learnt to identify with at Dalcroze flourished into electrifying surreal performances.

'She went through some trouble in her own marriage since the high society looked down upon performing arts which was considered purely a means of entertainment, not indulgence. But, she was determined to stay loyal to her chosen path, or the path that had chosen her—unashamed, unwavered. Slowly but surely, that commitment itself earned her respect and regard in the society. She was a fire that was only fuelled by winds and not a weak flame, blown out by the first gust.'

'That must have been so difficult,' said Maya.

'I often ask Dadi how she kept herself together in face of opposition at every step of the journey. Dadi advises me to just protect and keep my spark alive, while it is still young, tender and vulnerable. This path will be filled with doubts, questions, and hesitations. You will need both courage and persistence to persevere. Courage is not the absence of these feelings, it is understanding why you must feel what you're feeling, and step beyond it anyway.

'She often tells me, "Be very protective of the small spark that has just ignited, and each day that it shines within you, it becomes stronger and brighter…and one day it will no longer be a spark…it will become a flame, your beacon of light that sets you free. Questions leave, doubts vanish and the winds only serve to make it bigger. Your fire become your shield and you become invincible."

'She learnt Bharatanatyam, performed all over the world and finally started her own academy right here in Jodhpur. In case you are wondering where she was yesterday, she was chairing her school's annual performance gala. She was behind the stage, clapping and inspiring the girls for the performance of their lives. She called me earlier that day and said, "With hundreds of your guests there, do you need me that much? Because I can tell you, these girls really do."

'I just smiled and said, "Save the wedding date, I will need you for that one!"'

Maya recognized her opportunity had arrived and was knocking on her door to be invited in. Promptly, she planked herself on the floor next to the couch on which Dadi sat, much like a disciple next to his master.

'Dadi, your past is so fascinating, tell me how you see this world with your eyes today and what did it look like from the eyes of a 30-year-old you?'

Dadi laughed, 'Good question! Interestingly, neither the eyes ever change nor the "I", what changes for us with the years is the way we view life—our perspective.'

'So what is your perspective on life today?' questioned Maya.

'You have probably heard all about me from Pia so I will not revisit my life but I will talk to you about life in general as I see it. I like your name. Do you know what "Maya" means?' questioned Dadi.

'Sort of,' stated Maya, 'I believe it means illusion.'

'Correct, and this material world of ours is all but a huge illusion or "Maya" where people mistake shadows for substance, pleasure for happiness and peace and joy are ever elusive. This illusion always holds out the promise but it never delivers, my child.

'Maya is neither true nor untrue. It's a dreamlike state which is real while we're in it. We never question the world of our dreams, do we?' asked Dadi.

'The realization of falseness happens after the dream is over.'

'That's right, very interesting!' said Maya.

'Yes, it indeed is!' exclaimed Dadi.

'It can get complicated fairly quickly so let me begin with the story of "Maya", the reality of our Material Truth. Maya roams this earth playing upon the harp of the observer effect. Each observer, using his individual perspective, chooses a different string on this magical harp and plays a tune which adapts the appearance of reality to the sound of its own music. It is as if each one is watching the world through different glasses and dancing to a different song, the colour and the sound of which originate in his own experience. Some songs are bright and happy, others are dark and gloomy. Some glasses filter the dreams, some stream the fears.

'Maya appears in the light of the projections shed on it by our state of mind. A heart in love finds a sunset beautiful and a gloomy heart finds it hopeless and discouraging. The filters that colour the glasses are unique for each observer, what appears then in front of us is one possible version of reality draped in the hues of individual perspective. In other words, the reality is greatly subjective, true only in relation to time, place and mind.

'The earth is neither flat nor stationary. The brilliant moon has no light of its own and stars are anything but glittering jewels studded in the vast nothingness. What I mean, Maya, is that your version of reality then may not be the ultimate reality but a mere appearance of reality.

'Maya also has a companion or a partner in crime called Trishna—the insatiable desire. Trishna stands there in Maya's shadow with open arms, enticing and inviting like a glittering desert mirage.

'The gullible deer chases this mirage, certain that it has found a water source which can quench its thirst forever. As it runs towards it, the mirage shifts. The faster it runs, the farther it appears, turning this journey into an unending quest with no traces of fulfilment.

'Maya possesses another secret weapon as she tiptoes around

The Good Flow • 151

this world in disguise, her weapon is called deception. Joy might come disguised as obstacles and sorrow often smile smugly behind the veil of pleasure. We often take events, people and situations at face value. In the overall scheme of things, events might be quite contrary. Not all disappointments come to hurt us, some come to prompt us to look in other directions, some to reset our course, and some to teach us valuable lessons. And not every pleasure results in long term happiness.'

'Very profound,' said Maya, 'it does make sense. So then, is desire the real culprit?' she questioned.

'Not always. Desire taken to its opposite extreme give rise to another dimension—aversion, the repelling force that counteracts what life brings our way.

'We spend our life running after what we want—our desires, or away from what we don't want—our aversions. In any case, we are dancing to the tunes played by circumstances pulled and repelled like puppets dictated by play of strings and controlled by powers totally beyond them. Sadly, in this game of chase, we mostly end up unhappy, either for the lack of what we desire or for receiving that which we despise.'

'This is quite a disheartening story, Dadi. I'm starting to feel hopeless,' said Maya.

'You're missing the point Maya, this is not the conclusion of life, this is simply an armour you wear as you proceed through life. You can't fight an enemy in the dark. You have to face it, realize its power, predict its strategy and then work wisely to protect yourself.'

'I guess that's the wiser way to approach it. Practically, it does make sense, carry on, tell me more, Dadi.'

'Okay. So occasionally, Maya will be generous and grant you

your desires. But a word of caution here; with the fulfilment of desire, she sends its messenger—Moh, the attachment to desire. It works as an invisible chain, keeping you secretly bound to Maya. In view of this fleeting life, the ultimate law is, "This too shall pass."

'However, each object carries within it the seeds of its attachment. Our mind registers the joy and pleasure it experiences from a situation or an object and the memory of that pleasure takes on a life of its own. It seeks its own fulfilment over and over. We no longer just desire it, we also desire to possess it.

'And Maya, when we cling too hard or too long to what comes our way, we deprive it of enough room to grow into something beautiful, to evolve. We suffocate it before it has a chance to blossom. We enclose our lives, and bolt the door to the stagnant pleasures. We reel in his grip unaware, as Moh sits contentedly across the room watching us play with shadows while the real joys soar free outside our door. In claiming our possessions, we cling to the shore of a fast moving river.

'Nature rests upon the laws of impermanence. This life is but a ripple in the vast sea of consciousness, it emerges and subsides in the blink of an eye. Don't take it for granted, it will not wait for you to spend it, it spends itself, participation is your prerogative.'

'So then, do we have any powers to deal with these subtle tricks Maya plays on us? Can she be tamed?' questioned Maya.

'The answer is a resounding yes,' responded Dadi. 'Vedas say that our real self and our ego self are like two birds sitting on the branch of a tree, one eats the fruits of this world bitter

and sweet and the other simply watches i
are the Jiva and the Atman, the entangl
within each one of us.'

'How would you define this awareness within us an
does it help?' Maya probed further.

'Awareness is a presence, simply a quality of focus and attention that you bring about to your engagement with life. The minute you are aware that you are dreaming, you are awake, the minute you become aware that you're thinking, you break the chain of thought...

'In awareness, you pierce through the veil of Maya and become an unbiased spectator. Here, life transforms into a stage and you participate in playing out any situation that comes your way. Whether it is happy or sad, humble or grand, you perform to the best of your abilities.

'Maya, when you can observe without getting entangled, when you can want without needing, when you can see without judging, when you can accept without questioning and when you can flow without resisting...you step out of your own way to a place where you allow life to happen.'

'What about her companion, Moh?' added Maya.

'Non-attachment is your weapon against Moh. The art of enjoying what we have while we have it and releasing it with love when the moment of separation arises, like a tree releases a ripe fruit, is very important. When we detach ourselves from possessions and situations, we attach ourselves to our potential, possibility and joy...

'William Blake, in his famous words, expressed, "He who binds to himself a joy, does the winged life destroy. He who kisses the joy as it flies, lives in eternity's sun rise."'

'Wow Dadi, you summarized the entire philosophy of life in 15 minutes.'

'Maya, people can only teach you but learning happens on your own. Remember, as you hear it, you learn it but as you experience it, you own it.'

Maya smiled. She disappeared for a moment and came back with a bead, 'Dadi, would you please honour me by stringing this bead of wisdom in my bracelet? I will name it the bead of material truth.'

Dadi winked and said, 'Absolutely, but you owe me a drink at Zorba the Buddha!'

Walking in My Shoes

'Be yourself; everyone else is already taken.'

–Oscar Wilde

MAYA AND PIA WERE DRESSED to the nines as they were escorted to the glass-themed restaurant on top of the hill. The windy road was lit with torches and splendid flames.

'The food here is to die for,' exclaimed Pia. 'It is actually a culinary institute where they experiment with farm-to-table seasonal produce in a fusion-style cooking. Their sommelier is our absolute favourite, his wine pairings are always spot on.'

Abhay showed up, a thorough gentleman. He observed all the courtesies—held doors and pulled chairs with his favourite 'May I?' Maya was already impressed as she whispered in Pia's ear, 'You did hit a home run with this one Pia, where in the world did you find him?'

'All great things are made in India,' Pia exclaimed and they giggled again.

The laughter took Maya 15 years back in time as she felt her adolescent years had suddenly been resurrected, revitalized by its sound. 'Really Pia, I'm convinced that our essential elements never depart, they might fade, they may be forgotten, but somewhere they remain intact... I haven't laughed so much in ages.'

They soon realized there was a third person at the table who wasn't exactly laughing with them. He just sat across the table with interlocked fingers, smiling and waiting for their attention to return to the company.

'Sorry Abhay,' blurted out Pia, 'it was a private joke.'

'No, you don't have to be sorry, that's how it goes when old friends reunite. You should be sorry if it isn't that way.'

Maya, in an attempt at politeness, enquired, 'So Abhay, what do you do for a living?'

'I enable people to express themselves to the world without words,' came his reply.

'Wow. And how exactly do you do that?'

'Well, they say eyes are the window to the soul and shoes are the window to about everything else. I make shoes.'

'Fascinating!' said Maya.

Pia interrupted, 'He doesn't just make shoes, he is obsessed with shoes, as you will soon find out!'

'But why shoes?' asked Maya.

'Well, it goes back in time to when I first read 'The Elves and the Shoemaker'. I was hooked. All I could think about was shoes and elves. One day, I noticed a cobbler just down the street. When children would gather to play ball in the park, I would plead him to teach me how to make shoes. He was an old disgruntled man with a good heart. He never did allow me to make a shoe but said I could sit and watch him work at his craft. I watched him for many years and I learnt everything about it.

'I also devoured every piece of information I could find around the significance and symbolism of shoes, from them being a statement of status and wealth in old times when the masses could not afford shoes to the present-day understated symbol of power and authority. From the sex appeal of high heels to fashion statement of varied styles. Cinderella's fairy tale reunion owed her fortune to her slippers, and Puss in Boots undertook exciting adventures with these. Van Gogh's famous painting depicted hardships of life through a pair of worn-out shoes and, of course, we are all familiar with the well-known black shoes that hang behind trucks to ward off buri nazar.

'From the stealing of shoes at weddings being symbolic of the power one has over another to tossing the bride's red shoe to seal marital bliss, I know about it all. But my all-time favourite is the handing over of the bride's shoe by her father to the groom as the transfer of her caretaking rights. I am currently working on that one for Pia, made by me, sold to her dad, and earned by me once again, as a certificate of commitment to my two loves—Pia and shoes,' he said with a confident grin.

'Interestingly,' he added, 'shoes do speak a lot about your personality—whether you are aloof, stand-offish, extrovert, loud, couldn't care less, meticulous, ambitious, conservative, smart, tough, confident and the list goes on. In fact, a 2012 study by the University of Kansas found out that people are able to accurately judge 90 per cent of a stranger's personality, including their emotional stability, simply by looking at their most worn pair of shoes.'

Maya quickly paused to look at her own shoes and wondered what it might reveal about her to Abhay.

'So I get it. You do eat, breathe, live and dream shoes,'

reiterated Maya.

'Yes, I discovered it was my calling at a very early age. My family initially laughed at it, then grew concerned, then tried to dissuade me, then shamed me, then tried to control me, but then they gradually became despondent and eventually indifferent. They basically wrote me off,' said Abhay.

'And I certainly don't blame them, it wasn't exactly easy for them to explain to their neighbours and relatives that their capable son wants to make shoes. That must have been hard to deal with.

'It wasn't easy for me either. So many times I walked right to the brink of giving up on my dreams. Yet something gave me strength to believe in my unconventional dream,' he continued.

'How did you manage to accomplish so much without any support?' Maya asked.

'Maya, when you proceed to pursue the plan life has in mind for you, it is green lights all the way. I applied for a small loan and proudly made my first batch of handcrafted shoes. My passion shone through in the quality of my craftsmanship and attention to detail. It was well-received and the rest as they say is history. In a few years, I was able to put myself through an internship programme in Italy. Now, I run a factory that works with some of the top-line design powerhouses across the world but to keep my passion fuelled, I personally design limited edition collections for clients who share my passion in shoes.'

'What an inspiring story of courage and determination. I'm proud of you,' said Maya.

'So is my family…you have to hold on to your dreams… just long enough.'

They talked over mozzarella with melon, spicy corn and

harvest soup. The flavours were abundant. Maya exclaimed, 'The food is just delicious. You know, speaking of Italy, I must say I ate the best Chinese, Thai and Indian food in Italy.

'Now don't look at me like that, I survived on pastas and pizzas for the first one week and then my Asian palate got the better of me. Well, coming back to the point, I think the common link between the amazing flavours across all styles of cooking was the freshness and taste of the ingredients. This experience certainly belongs in the same league. What a medley of flavours and aromas. Thank you for picking this place.'

'You are so very welcome!' added Abhay.

'So Pia, why did you choose Abhay?' asked Maya as she turned towards her.

'Easy! Because he is the man who gave life to his dreams and a man who knows how to do that. He values both his life and his dreams and by extension everything and everyone who is in it. It's a man's character that matters, charisma in this case came as pure bonus—cream on the top,' she said with a grin as she skimmed her bowl of soup.

'You know Pia and Abhay, I have met more interesting people and seen more varied aspects of life up close and personal in the last few weeks than I did living in one of the world's greatest cities over a period spanning more than two decades. The more I learn, I feel the lesser I know. I'm fascinated by the powerhouse of wisdom that seems ingrained in the very fabric of people here. They are somehow in sync. Perfectly put together.'

'Not always so,' clarified Abhay, 'we have our shares of struggles. It just might be a simple turn of fate that has lined up the right people ripe with experience to share just the right lessons with you.'

'If you had met me 15 years ago, I could not have been sure of what I was saying. Now, I am more hopeful, I am wishful. I might have shared my conviction but certainty lies only in hindsight. Who knows what you might be sharing with us in a few years? Possibilities!' They raised a toast to that note.

'Do you know what my lighthouse was through this entire journey, Maya?' said Abhay digging a fork into delicately marinated and perfectly cooked chicken cubes served over lettuce.

'What was it? Your dream?' asked Maya.

'No, it was my understanding that there is a reality of us that has been physically created, inorganically manufactured. I named it The Created Truth.

'Success, to me, is not a degree of achievement but a bridging of the gap between yourself and your potential. Even if you succeed at someone else's dreams, success would come to you as a stranger who is empty-handed and lost. Your own dreams may be small but they are innately yours and the only measure of true success!

'I once read a very simple quote that may not mean much to others but had a very powerful impact on my mind. By Lao Tzu, the great ancient Chinese philosopher, it read, "Let nature renew the sense of direction men undo."

'This well-meaning society and our support structure within it believes that it is their responsibility to offer you an identity, to carve your character, hand you a predefined purpose, introduce you to your likes and dislikes, inform you about the dos and don'ts. In their best intention, they assume that if they do not do this, they are failing at their job. They lay out the entire roadmap for your life, show you the direction and the goal. They set the benchmark, rules for evaluation and the criteria for decision.

'Unfortunately, the best magnet is dormant against the finest wood. The problem is neither the wood nor the magnet, it's the combination that is incorrect. It is, as they say, judging a fish by its ability to climb a tree.

'Remember, right things done for the wrong reasons did not create legends. We cannot be driven by the desire to make others happy, to fit into the crowd, to enable fulfilment of dreams they did not have the courage to pursue.'

'It seems like pursuing your dreams or standing for your truth is akin to waging a war against the entire society and its conventional ways,' wondered Maya

'No, not really,' asserted Abhay.

'Do not fight, do not ask, do not resist or claim. This world has no power either to deliver or to deny. It has no power other than what you assign to it in your own mind. Don't bother debating, convincing or arguing. Simply go ahead and do what you know is right for you, in your eyes.'

'Don't walk in someone else's shadow. Let your own light guide the way. And remember, your persistence is not defiance, nor is it rebellion, it is a consequence of knowing too well and seeing too clearly that not doing is not an option.'

'But what if your instincts are off the mark? What if you do make a mistake?' said Maya.

'There are no mistakes in life except for not trying and not reaching for your dreams, even if you were to fail at them. What we regret at the end of our life is not the mistakes that we made or the scars that we bore but the chances we didn't take and the weary load of unfulfilled dreams that we carried around our backs.

'It's not giving up the safety of the shining cages which we regret but not spreading the wings and taking to the sky. Sure, mistakes happen and it also brings hurt and pain but along with lessons, experiences and growth. In my opinion those who haven't stumbled enough haven't wandered far enough.'

'You are right,' said Maya. 'My mom often recites one of the lines my dad loved to quote, "*Girte hain shahsawaar hi maidaan-e-jung mein, Woh tifl kya giren jo ghutnon ke bal chalen.*" What it means is that a brave warrior mounted on a horse in the open battlefield is prone to falling, not the faint of the heart who prefer to crawl about on their knees.'

'Absolutely spot on,' said Abhay.

'In my case, I knew one thing without a doubt. I'm neither an opinion nor a judgement, neither a shadow nor a reflection. I'd rather live with my own failure than someone else's success. I'd rather lose the dreamed possessions than lose my ability to dream.

'Maya, it's simple—either that is all you want, even if it costs you everything or you do not want it enough. And so I made shoes.'

'Fascinating Abhay! That's incredibly brave,' applauded Maya.

By now the city lights were in full glory. Abhay offered to continue with the desserts on the terrace. They stepped out through the French doors on to the stone patio. The breeze was pleasant and the firepit hit just the right notes. Maya and Pia sat on the edge of the thick stone wall overlooking the city. Abhay handed them the dessert menu and poured some chilled wine. Maya went for the apple strudel while Pia nodded her head even before Abhay could utter 'Chocolate Gateau cake'.

'Abhay,' said Maya, 'I can't get over your story. But how much or in what ways does an ordinary person deal with the repercussions of this created truth?'

'Let me state my personal observations in the light of practical appeal. I will call my first observation the Law of a Fable.'

'We spend our lifetime writing our story and also living by it. At some point in life we actually become the roles we play, burying our real selves so far underneath so much that it suffocates into dormancy. We become the story and the storyteller, the character and the author, the critic and the reader, the hero and the victim.

'This story defines how we act, decides what we do, and determines what we achieve. We strive to fit better and better into the role rather than creating a role that meets us at our core.

'We believe in it to such an extent that we stop trusting our basic instincts. In ignorance, we continue to allow what we've built so far to become the foundation of what we build next. Then, how far we leap becomes anchored upon where we stand today.

'My second observation stems from this—where you stand and who you are today is not who you essentially are but what you have become over time. A mere snapshot of your history thus far. An accumulation. The chisel of time and experience carves and enhances our definition deeper and deeper each day. If we were suddenly to forget the past, we would not know ourselves anymore. We are disoriented and lost without our past reminding us every day of who we are, which is as smart as driving forward based upon the road that appears in the rearview mirror.

'We need to be extremely cognizant of what we leverage in order to define ourselves, for what defines us also defines our limits. It is the invisible web we spend our years weaving and our days trapped living in.

'As a child we do not have a story binding us down. We are free to think, believe and imagine. We never question our ideals by referring to see if they fit well into our story, if our recognized strengths sustain or support it.

'As we grow older, the possibilities do not change. What changes is our belief in our self and our abilities. Longer the story the weaker the belief...and the narrower we spread our reach. Our legends, our heroes were people who believed in the evolution of the story, not the mere repetition of it.'

'True!' reflected Maya as she summed up all that Abhay had stated and captured it in the third bead—the bead of created truth. She was halfway through her journey.

Maya switched the conversation to a lighter note, 'So coming back to yesterday, with that friend of yours. I apologize, I was caught a little off kilter. It was a little strange to have run into the same person two days in a row. My car broke down on the way over here and he was gracious enough to offer help. I guess it was a little strange to find him standing in front of me again the very next day.'

'Come on Maya, no apologies needed here. It's Veer. He's the last person you should be worried about and the coolest person you will ever meet,' exclaimed Abhay.

Pia nudged her a little.

Abhay continued, 'In my 32 years of knowing him—well,

we were born four months apart—I'm yet to see him ruffled or unhinged. Nothing seems to be able to touch him. It's like he isn't even there. Always calm as a Zen Zone. You should get to know him. He can be quite resourceful.'

'Yes Maya, you should get to know him,' reiterated Pia as she chuckled.

'Sure, thanks.'

Pia's phone rang. 'Mom, why are you still up? I told you that you should sleep,' insisted Pia. 'Alright, we will leave soon. I love you too.'

'Okay guys, you know Mom. She won't sleep until we get home "safe and sound"!' Pia smiled, nodding her head, 'For god's sake, we are all adults here. I guess, we grow up from being children to adults but once a mother, always a mother.'

Maya looked out the window at the starlit sky as the soft music played on, drowning Pia and Abhay's conversation. A shooting star streamed across the sky and Maya wished upon it...with a smile. The stars seemed to smile back...

The Catalyst

'Be the change you wish to see in the world.'

–Mahatma Gandhi

'DADI, DID YOU SEE MAYA anywhere?' questioned Pia with concern in her voice. 'I've been looking for a while but I can't seem to find her anywhere. She's not answering her phone either. Where could she have disappeared?'

Dadi, who stood by the window watering the planters that hung over it as she sipped on her black tea, responded, 'There she is, sitting under that tree for the last few hours.' Pia found Maya deeply immersed in the book she was reading as if the world around her had ceased to exist.

She blended right into the surroundings much like a chameleon cleverly preventing itself from being spotted. 'This girl is still the same—a bookworm at best,' muttered Pia. 'Always been this strange. You know Dadi, she would choose to stay home with her books and eat dinner out of a box while her friends were busy painting the town red. Well, it wasn't all bad, in a way it did quite work out since she was always there—

Ms goody two shoes, to take care of hungover buddies, our very own Florence Nightingale.'

'Maya!' yelled Pia from the window. 'You got me worried.'

'Worried? Why?' screamed Maya back. 'I assumed by now you would know this equation by heart. Trees + shade + books = a potent mix that allures and fundamentally alters the elements of Maya. That's my fantasy if you will and I'm living it right here,' she laughed.

'You silly goose!' laughed Pia. 'Wait right there, I will come down.'

'Well, Abhay just called,' said Pia as she walked up to Maya. 'He has tickets to the World Sacred Spirit Festival tomorrow night. More like a Sufi night. Here,' she said, handing her the phone, 'check out the website and event listing and let me know if you are interested. It's not everyone's cup of tea. You have to have an ear for that kind of penetrating and profound, almost philosophical, entertainment.'

'Sure,' said Maya, 'let me check it out.'

She typed in the words 'worldsacredspiritfestival.org'. Instantly, an alluring mystical tune started to play. It enticed her senses and captivated her heart, like it was an extension of Leela's soulful melody. The words started to appear one by one on the screen and she read along:

'Well, a childish dream is a deathless need. And a noble truth is a sacred dream'—Bob Dylan.

Maya paused and looked up with a sparkle in her eyes. 'I wouldn't miss it for anything.'

'Good choice. You will not regret it,' said Dadi as she walked towards her. 'This festival is all about spirituality without borders, love without distinction, a path without direction and a song that springs forth from the eternal fountain of compassion.'

'It is all very interesting Dadi, you know I accidentally ended up visiting the dargah at Ajmer Sharif on my way here,' said Maya.

'Well, nothing is accidental,' said Dadi, 'there is one author that directs every story.'

'I faintly recall that there was some connection between my grandfather and Sufi culture. Of the little I have heard about him from my mother, he went into a trance-like state and danced in ecstasy each time the famous Sufi qawwali 'Mast Qalandar' played,' Maya laughed in amusement.

'Actually speaking, I'm intrigued now, both to understand him, his aspirations, his inclinations and the Sufi philosophy. Maybe I will come to know myself better by understanding him,' said Maya.

Maya's father had been the only son but she knew his grandfather has a sister, her dad's Bhua, who lived in Bikaner.

Maya texted her mom quickly, 'Is Bhua still alive? Please send me her number.'

A notification popped up on Maya's phone within minutes. 'I haven't heard otherwise but we haven't connected in many years either. I send you my love and blessing along with her number. I'm glad you are reconnecting with your roots. I must have done something right despite all the mistakes I made as a parent.'

Maya quickly responded, 'Mothers do not make mistakes, they do their best and sometimes it works and sometimes it doesn't.'

Maya shook her head, thinking about the immense guilt her mother carried despite the great sacrifices she had made to provide Maya a good life. Each time something fell apart, she only looked at herself to see what she could have done better.

Maya promptly called the number. She soon realized that she did not even know her name and so she did not know who to ask for.

'Hello Ji,' answered a voice on the other end. 'Who is this?' inquired Maya. 'Raju,' came the reply, 'Memsahib is in her puja.' Maya let out a sigh of relief. 'Memsahib' was a great umbrella that would shield her from the embarrassment of not even knowing who she was calling for, and that too someone who was related to her by blood.

'Oh wait,' he said in the same breath, 'Memsahib is here.'

'Hello,' said a shaky voice, 'who is calling?' Maya thought for a moment, little unsure if her identity even existed in her life. Maya spoke apprehensively, 'I'm Bikram's granddaughter. Bikram, your brother.'

'Maya?' came the response.

'Yes, Maya.' Before she could question further, Maya asked abruptly, 'Could I come meet you today? I'm in Jodhpur. I can leave now and be there by 3 p.m. Unfortunately, I will need to leave early tomorrow morning.' There were a few moments of complete silence. 'Hello?' said Maya, just confirming if she was still on the line, which of course she was. The lady cleared her throat as if from choking on tears, 'Come beta, I will wait for you.'

Maya had always been impulsive. If something came to her mind, she automatically shifted gears to one track. Unless she went ahead and did exactly what she wanted and exactly right there and then, she felt incapacitated to think or do anything else. She did not know how to wait and she did not know how to divert her thoughts. She now related to herself in moments such as these as obsessive compulsive. Time stopped, the world came to a still, there was nothing else she would rather do, there was nothing that mattered more and all she could care about was how to get there as fast as she could—it had to be instantaneous.

Pia offered to drive her there. But Maya claimed she'd rather spend quality time with her thoughts than listen to her incessant chatter. They had a hearty laugh. Before long, Maya was once again on the road to a destination that was as familiar as unknown.

As they drove through the suburbs, Maya noticed a girl walking briskly with her head bent down, eyes sweeping the road and books held firmly against her chest. Maya asked the driver to slow down, she noticed tears in her eyes and a rambunctious trio on a motorbike throwing obscenities at her. Maya stopped and offered the girl a ride in the car. The girl desperate to breathe again promptly stepped in, shutting the world outside as she closed the door with a look of relief and gratefulness. The obscenities grew louder and louder as they tried to keep up for a while, trying to make gestures through the tinted windows until they finally drove off in another direction. Maya asked for her address, and dropped the girl to her house without exchanging another word. She did not want to add to her humiliation.

Maya fell silent as she looked at the arid landscape and the quiet road. 'Is there hope?' she asked the driver who had witnessed everything and had said nothing so far.

'Yes, madam, there is hope. Change is happening, the evolution is coming and eventually we will restore a place for women in this society that is rightfully theirs. No one should ever have to go through this.'

'But how can we contain this pandemic? How can we change the mentality and thinking?'

'One person at a time, one family at a time, one village at a time, one state at a time and the whole country eventually. Slowly but surely, the change is emerging. It's a revolution that is spreading its roots and will burst forth with flowers soon,' affirmed the driver.

'How can you say this so confidently? By the way, my name is Maya.'

'Myself Pawan, how do you do?' came the reply. Maya smiled and said, 'Good to meet you Pawan, but how can you be so sure?'

'Gandhiji said, "Be the change you wish to see in the world," and we are the change.'

'Meaning?' asked Maya curiously.

'I'm from a small village about three and a half hours south of Jodhpur. It is called Piplantri. In this country where people fear having girls for reasons well understood, including abuse, dowry and others, we welcome and celebrate the birth of our girls. Interestingly, the village plants 111 trees to celebrate the birth of every girl child. Not only that, the villagers collaboratively collect ₹21,000 and with a contribution of ₹10,000 from the father of the girl, set up a twenty-year fixed deposit that will be her financial security when she comes of age. To further protect our daughters and ensure that every girl child receives adequate education, the parents are required to sign an affidavit which restricts them from marrying their daughter off before she attains the legal age for marriage. We teach our daughters from the moment of birth that they are special, we celebrate and empower them.'

'This is incredible. I'm very impressed Pawan. I had no idea that people from small villages can be so progressive in their thinking.'

'Yes, it takes one person to start a movement. In our case, it was our sarpanch who lost his 18-year-old daughter. But instead of spending his life crying over it, he decided to make her live on in ways that he could, so he planted trees for her and then he did it for every daughter of the village.

'A good deed never goes unnoticed by nature, Madam. Look at the power of a single good thought. Now we are an oasis in the heart of the desert covered with sheesham, mango and amla trees that have dramatically improved our water table, and placed our women in a position of respect, and economic and environmental success. Besides, to keep termites from infesting these fruit-bearing trees, villagers planted nearly 2.5 million aloe vera plants around them, which they later discovered could be processed and marketed. We are now known far and wide for our aloe vera juices and gels. It fostered ecofeminism, employment creation and commercial development all from one thought—let us welcome our girl child.'

'Pawan, that is truly remarkable and makes me feel so much better; maybe there really is hope. Maybe the revolution has already begun and they will follow, one and all,' said Maya.

'Yes, Madam, we were once the golden bird of the world,' said Pawan, 'and measured not so much by our treasures as by our values. We are the land of the seers and the sages. Goodness is in our DNA. It may be forgotten but rest assured, somewhere it still lies simmering, waiting for someone to come fan the flames. Our greatness is not extinct, only overshadowed. We will come full circle to it, till then, it's one man, one village, one state and our country behind it.

'By the way, if you have a chance, you should read about this phenomenal movement stirring among the youth of this country. It's called M.A.R.D.—Men against Rape and Discrimination. Mard is the Hindi translation of the word "Man". This organization was conceptualized and founded by our country's superstar Farhan Akhtar in wake of the gruesome incident that happened in 2012. Since then, this organization has worked tirelessly with the youth, with our future, educating, empowering and redefining the image of a "Real Man"—the one who is enough in himself to allow women the respect, freedom and support they deserve as another human being. Maya Memsahib, it's not just you and me and the village of Piplantri, this is a movement that is taking roots across the nation. There are thousands and thousands of men and women who have stepped forward and pledged to fight for women's dignity.'

'But what a sad plight we have managed to get ourselves into. More than anything else, human rights and women empowerment is what we should have modelled after the western world.'

'Not true madam. Essentially, we as a culture have lived what we are fighting for, yet again. During the early Vedic period, women of this great nation commanded an elevated and respectable status. Works of Pitanjali suggest women were educated at par with men. Vedas also indicate they married at a mature age and were free to select their husbands. This nation gave birth to women who were great seers, philosophers, teachers, administrators, rulers, poets and warriors. They were equipped with an education in philosophy, scriptures, martial arts and arms training. We have known the power of Gargi, Maitrye, Razia Sultana, Chand Bibi, Laxmi Bai, Nur Jehan, Jija Bai and Meera. We are also a nation in which women's right to dignity and freedom from discrimination has been secured under the constitution. We have had a woman lead this country as the president and prime minister. We need no introduction to their abilities, we just need an awakening from a nightmare and a step back into the brilliance of our inheritance.'

Maya applauded, 'Well said, Pawan!'

Pawan blushed, 'Ji Madam. Thank you!'

The journey went rather fast, caught up in small talks and big conversations. Pawan pulled off the highway about 30 kms short of Bikaner. 'Madam, if you have 15 minutes to spare, I would highly suggest you make a quick stop at the Karni Mata Mandir better known as the Rat Temple the world over.'

'Oh yes, you are right, I have heard about it, I think it was a documentary I watched a long time ago, but I had no idea this is right here. Sure, let's do this, but this really is a strange phenomenon. Not to offend anyone but—why rats?' asked Maya, sounding inquisitive.

'There is a legend that says one of Karni Mata's sons drowned in a pond while attempting to drink water from it. She implored Yama, the God of Death, to spare him. He failed to revive him but agreed to reincarnate him and all of her sons as rats.

'They are called "Kabbas" or little children and are worshipped as gods. People of the village see all their ancestors in these rats and some even eat, drink and sleep with families.'

Maya said, 'But that could pose a serious health concern. Rats can transmit over 20 different kinds of diseases to humans through just skin, hair and other means.'

'I'm not sure how to explain this, perhaps belief is stronger than disease. There is not even a single documented case of a disease that was contracted through or related to the presence of rats in this temple,' answered Pawan

'Wow,' said Maya, 'that totally beats medicine.'

Maya walked through the temple admiring the Mughal-inspired architecture as she carefully placed her bare feet on the black and white tiled marble floor that appeared more like a chess board than anything else. Over 20,000 rats scurried around climbing steps, drinking milk out of huge containers, enjoying exotic sweets and running over people like they were an obstacle course in an amusement park. Maya clicked a few pictures, paid her respects and despite the regard, could not muster the courage to share a glass of milk and left after merely seeking the blessings of the rat gods.

It was nearing four o'clock as they entered the city of Bikaner. While Maya was eager to meet Bhua, she also did not want to greet her empty-handed and requested Pawan to stop and pick up some sweets along the way. They arrived at Kote Gate and Maya soaked in the old city charm of busy sweet shops, vegetable sellers and bangle vendors. Cows stood in the middle of the congested roads, motionless as decorative sculptures. The roads were populated with scooters beeping consistently as they rambled through the narrow streets.

They arrived at the railroad crossing which was closed down to traffic with a flimsy black and yellow bar called the 'gate'. Barring a few cars, it was interesting to watch people tilt, slide and slip their scooters, motorbikes and bicycles under the stop bar, through the crossing, on to the other bar and across. It seemed to be the norm. It was busier and more chaotic on the crossing with an approaching train than it was on either side of it.

Maya looked a little concerned as she asked, 'Is the gate not working?'

'Madam, it is working as it always does and people are doing what they always do. To pedestrians and people on two-wheelers, the stop gate does not necessarily indicate they must stop. In their minds, it sends an alert—inconvenience, now they must get off and get their two-wheelers across to the other side.'

'That is dangerous though,' said Maya.

'We all know it,' said Pawan, 'but adventure comes in all shapes and forms to an average man. This is his moment to defy the danger and bend the rules.' He laughed, 'They seem to do it more for the sake of doing it rather than a real urgency to get somewhere. Perhaps by doing this, they will arrive five minutes earlier for their much-awaited thirty-minute session of tea drinking and newspaper reading.' He chuckled again.

They drove past a congested section of the town near Mohta Chowk through serpentine roads and sharp corners till they arrived at a narrow street. The alley consisted of houses facing each other, lined up neatly one after the next. 'Madam, after I drop you off here, I will look for a place to park,' said Pawan. Maya found herself standing in front of a massive wooden gate of a red sandstone haveli embellished with intricately carved green jharokhas overlooking the street.

Maya paused for a few moments and then knocked on it. '*Kaun?*' came a male voice from inside. Maya found it easier to question in response than think of an easy answer. 'Is that Raju? I called this morning to talk to Memsahib.'

The answer worked like a charm and after a series of sounds from undoing multiple chains and locks, the door finally opened. Raju quickly grabbed her bag as he wiped his face with the red and white cotton scarf that hung over his left shoulder. His white vest and crisp dhoti appeared damp with sweat.

'Memsahib has been pacing up and down for the last few hours waiting for you. She forgot to take your phone number and had no means of contacting you.'

'Oh really? I'm so sorry,' said Maya feeling bad about all the leisurely detours they had been taking.

Inside the gate was a beautiful open courtyard and many corridors. She was captivated by the antique red sandstone and the tiny jharokhas, some opening onto the courtyard that was awash with abundant sunlight. A wire mesh stretched above the roof, possibly to prevent pigeons and birds from destroying the intricate carvings. Tiers of balconies extended out beyond the rooms. These pillared corridors were decorated with paintings, furniture and large pots.

'Memsahib is waiting for you in Daawatkhana,' announced Raju. Maya followed him to a room which, to say the least, appeared to be poetry written on stone. The ceilings had goldwork on it, paintings that resembled Mughal art. Pillars contained glass mirrors inlaid in marble with colourful flowers and leaves carved around it. She also noticed paintings of Radha and Krishna, peacocks and birds. It was a step back in time. She did not know whether to admire the historic wonderland she had stepped into or pay attention to the reason she was there in the first place.

Raju announced, 'Mata Ji, Maya Memsahib is here.' An old lady dressed in a striking cobalt blue bandhani saree turned around and greeted her with open arms. She looked as colourful and as antique as her surroundings. Her body shook as she stood up and extended her open arms, barely keeping them from flailing. Maya instinctively ran right into them. The old lady hugged her, held her face in her hands and kissed her forehead multiple times.

'My blood, my child, my Maya, this longing to see you never left my heart, but the dream was distant and the land was far. You, my child, have blessed my wishes, my prayers are answered and now in peace I can die. I never thought I would see you or hold you in my arms again.'

Maya was quiet. She held her hand, speechless, experiencing feelings she couldn't describe in words. Her eyes were moist and spoke volumes nonetheless.

'Run Raju, get my daughter something to drink. She must be weary and tired. Come back Raju,' she said in the same breath, as she pulled out a little pouch and handed him a handful of notes, 'Go buy a tokra of ladoos and distribute it in the neighbourhood. My daughter has come home. Also arrange to feed the children and the homeless. Make sure you tell them my daughter has come home.' Maya was overwhelmed and very thankful for her decision to visit her roots as her mother had stated.

It seemed like what the new branches had forgotten, the roots remembered well and at some level, they remained deeply connected.

Raju showed her to her room which was equally beautiful with a four-poster bed, heavy curtains and a light blue Victorian chair. Maya sat down on the chair and noticed the glass-top table in front of her. She gazed at her reflection, looking more beautiful than ever—without any trace of make-up and hair tied back in a ponytail. She had come a long way indeed.

After a refreshing shower, Maya changed into her lounge pants and joined Bhua for the evening tea. 'Here Maya, try the bhujiya and this rasgulla. You can see all the deserts, forts, temples and museums but your visit to Bikaner is incomplete without a taste of this local food.'

'Wow. This is really good. Where did you buy it? I should take some back for Pia.'

'Of course you should. This is from the famous Chhotu Motu Joshi on Station Road, essentially the food street of Bikaner. I will have Raju arrange for some boxes.'

'It's delicious. Thank you so much Bhua, I hope it's okay if I call you that!'

'Of course my child. It's been ages since I heard the sweet sound of that phrase.'

'Bhua,' said Maya. 'I'm here to listen to a story.'

'What kind of story Maya?'

'Our story, the story that connects you and me and everyone else in our lives. Tell me, what was Dada's connection with "Mast Qalandar" song? Perhaps this is the only thing I remember so distinctly about him. I had almost forgotten until I accidentally ended up at the dargah of Ajmer Sharif and was told that sama-qawallis can be transformative and must be experienced once in a lifetime. As chance would have it, someone has tickets for me to attend the Sufi festival tomorrow night. I'm starting to realize how little I know about myself other than myself. Tell me, I'm curious.'

Bhua's eyes lit up as she spoke softly, lifting her gaze to look at the mirror on the wall which seemed to have transported her to the golden era.

'The story starts in Pakistan in the year 1885 in a village called Khara near Kasur. By the way, you may not know but Kasur is better known as the hometown of Bulleh Shah, the great Punjabi philosopher. Your father's great-grandfather or your grandfather's grandfather was a very wealthy landlord. He owned the village with 2,400 acres of land and had every comfort he could wish for in this world. His two wives, who lived like sisters, took great care of him. However, despite his riches, he was a broken man for he did not have a child. He tried all means and finally gave up on his fate. One morning, in pure dismay, he called for his helpers and asked them to bring everything he had earned over the years. It is said that back in those times he had eight sacks full of gold, stones, cash and silver.

'He loaded these sacks on several mules and left for the dargah of Peer Shabaz Qalandar in Sehwan district of Sindh. He reached there and prayed that he had come, with himself and his treasures. He said that he had absolutely no use of those since he was without an offspring. Instead of leaving the wealth to be wasted away in the wrong hands, he offered his treasures in the service of the peer and wanted to spend the rest of his life living there.

'The caretaker closed his eyes and by the order of divine intervention instructed him to go home. He said, "You need not give up your treasures nor your hope—return home, you will be blessed with a boy. Come back with the child, in a procession of celebration, beating drums and dancing in joy."

'Sure enough, he returned home and soon after, your great-grandfather Arjan Singh was born. As instructed, he went to seek the blessings of the peer, in a procession with dhols. The caretaker further instructed him, "Peer baba blesses your family and the pure of heart will choose this household for themselves. Your treasures that you so kindly offered also remain blessed and will always return to you, one way or another."'

Maya was fascinated. 'And then, Bhua? What happened after that?'

'After that, they lived happily and the child was raised in the protection and great love of his two mothers.

'One night there was news of dacoits raiding the area. A messenger informed them that they would attack their home that night. He urged them to flee the haveli. The men of the house however, refused to leave insisting upon dealing with their fate and dying a death of honour. The mothers, worried for their men's lives, mixed opium in their food so they would sleep through this turmoil. They spent the entire night hiding in the storage compartment of the shed used for storing grains.

'They heard the sounds of horses and held their breath. It was a hot moonless night. A few of the dacoits walked in discreetly, and lightly spun the charkas to test the waters. The others stood armed with rifles, ready to shoot. When there was no response at all, the sardar declared, "All clear, no one is home." Slowly the army marched in and raided every closet and each drawer amassing loads of jewellery and cash. With the first light of the day, they loaded their horses and set off. They arrived at a vast open space far from the village where they sat down to distribute their loot. The family looked at the ransacked house and wept for all they had lost and prayed for the peer to give them courage to deal with this.

'After dividing up the entire loot, the dacoits realized that some of the legendary things they had heard about including the 30 tola hass, champakali, bazuband and bhawatta were missing. They were enraged. "The family knew we were coming and hid some of their treasures," said one of them. "Let's go back and kill them all," said another. It is said that in that moment, reconsidering the vast wealth including assets that were immovable, the leader of the gang had a change of heart. He ordered everyone to stop. He said, "We will go back but not with our guns. Instead, we will go with band baja."

'He fell at their feet and offered his sister's hand in marriage with my father. Legends of her beauty and spiritual inclinations ran far and wide. He returned the treasure and sent his sister off with 21 horses, 200 cows, 11 caretakers and many gifts. I hear she came dressed in gold slippers and gold parandi and her brother gave up being a dacoit for life.'

'So you mean that was the story of your mother and father's marriage?'

'Yes, strange as it sounds. And once again, they lived a long happy fulfilled life. After a few years, the grapevine was ripe with the talks of a young boy in a village close by who had some mystic connections. The political and religious leaders considered him a threat since people were starting to believe that whatever he predicted came true. One day there was a murder in the village and this young boy was accused. He was sentenced to death. His parents cried helplessly. He told them, "Do not weep for me. I am going, but only to come back. I will take birth in Arjan Singh's house in Khara village." This was little consolation for his parents. They said, "But how will

we ever recognize you? Everything about you will be different."
He said, "I will be born with a crescent on my forehead. Come
with a silver coin to greet me back into this world."

'Sure enough, my brother was conceived shortly after, he
was born with a crescent on the right side of his forehead just
above his temple. The old couple heard of the birth and came
to see the child with a silver coin. They cried as they saw his
birthmark. He was indeed special and one of the lucky few to
have the love of four parents.'

'So that was my grandfather?' confirmed Maya.

'Yes, that is the story of his birth. He was a distinguished
spirit. So when your grandfather and later your father were
born, our family went to Sehwan to celebrate the birth. We
don't know the connection beyond this for certain, but later
in life your grandfather was consumed with Sufi fervour and
left the house for nearly twelve years in search of the truth.
He eventually decided to return home on the occasion of your
parents' wedding.'

'And,' said Maya, 'continuing with the tradition, did you
know dad left behind a collection of over 200 poems that he
claimed just came to him?'

'I'm not surprised, my child.'

She patted her on the head and said, 'Maya, would you
like some Kadah?'

'Of course yes, that's my favourite.'

'It was your father's as well. He was closer to me than he
was to his own mother. As a little boy, he heard his father call
me Preetan and he addressed me as Adpeetan,' she laughed
as if she could recall the sound of his words in Maya's voice.

That evening, as Raju claimed, she stepped inside the kitchen to cook with her own hands after twenty-six long years. Maya sat on the small stool next to Bhua and looked upon her in admiration, as she cooked for her.

'Bhua, mom tells me you are an epitome of patience. How did you deal with everything? It must not have been easy. I mean, I didn't have it that bad, but even then, I did not have your wisdom or strength. I led myself to a bitter end while you are still so full of love and grace. How?' questioned Maya.

'Maya, in our times, giving up was not an option, neither on a situation, nor on a relationship and certainly never on yourself. I still don't know if that was good or bad. Nowadays, I see relationships break up just because of an available choice even though they can be made to work with a little effort and some compromise. Unless, it is physically abusive or unsafe, for most parts, it can be dealt with.

'You just heard about our heritage. Royalty and class ran in our blood. We had seen money like none others and that made it significantly non-essential to us. There was a great emphasis on culture and values. We were well-read, soft-spoken and imbued with virtues of respect for every citizen of humanity. Intelligence was greatly respected and women held a place equal to men, if not above. My father consulted my mother in all matters, business and social. I was educated at par with my brothers and had an opinion on everything that was well-received and logically argued if necessary.

'However, our family suffered an irrecoverable blow when India and Pakistan parted ways; the road of devastation travelled through many broken homes and hearts. I was all of nine years when we fled on horses with nothing but our strong faith and a weak hope that we would be back someday.

'My father and brothers worked hard to start over and found their ground again. At 19, I was married into an extremely wealthy family of the time—a first generation of self-created wealth. Unfortunately, quick money managed to destroy their value system and played havoc with their inherent regard and respect for all else, but money. Women were considered inferior and their inherent role was limited to that of a powerless housemaker whose needs would be provided for as long as she kept everyone happy. For most of the women in the family, this was the only way of life they had known. But coming from where I did, I stood up for what I believed in, and voiced my opinions. However, this did not go down well with men of my family, as if in some way, it belittled them. They kept me on the edge, they kept me dependent and helpless.

'However, it took me more than a few years to realize that no one can truly take away your power, it remains with you, until you willingly choose to hand it over.

'I find a lot of aware, educated women in my situation. Since there may be little these people can do to physically abstain us from expressing our opinions, they resort to subtle techniques.

'They start to attack your intelligence. Sadly, conviction often wins over truth. As Hitler said, "If you repeat a lie often enough, it becomes the truth." They will not spare a chance to prove you wrong. By constantly attacking your mind, your opinions and your choices, they will make your intelligence weary to the point that you start doubting your own truth.

'Once your intelligence is suppressed enough, your mind starts its own vicious cycle of defeat. At this point, the person stops telling you, but you continue to tell yourself. His prophecy takes on a life of its own and each time you falter, you repeat his words to yourself, maybe he was right, perhaps I really am not capable, maybe I should not even try. So you struggle to prove your worth harder and harder to the tyrant who is already aware of it.'

'So then what did you do Bhua?'

'I stopped trying to prove him wrong. I stopped engaging, reasoning and arguing. I reclaimed my power.

'Maya, you often make a point, when more than others, you are trying to make a point to yourself. You try to convince others when you yourself are in need of conviction. When there is belief, conflict is unnecessary.

'If someone came and told you that you are a bird. Would you fight, would you try to convince him, would you get really angry or offended? Would you tell him, "Look at me, I have two legs, I walk and I talk, I cannot fly, hence I'm not a bird but a human?" It is too ridiculous to even bother to start explaining. You know so well that you are not a bird, that you do not engage in an argument. You laugh and say, "Let him believe I'm a bird if that makes him happy." You do not fight to prove yourself. Maya, knowing is your greatest strength.

'Given our culture and values, I never was offensively rude or argumentative. I understood we must treat others the way we want to be treated by others. But I also came to realize that more importantly, we must treat ourselves the way we want to be treated by others. What you experience is in some ways related to what you believe about yourself. If you are confident yourself, others will place their trust in you. If you respect yourself, others will regard you as well. If you love yourself, others will too.

'But if you don't see your own beauty, no one can show

it to you. If you cannot love yourself, no one else can. If you don't believe in yourself, no one will. If you don't enjoy your own company, others certainly will not.

'Be gentle with yourself Maya, treat yourself with kindness and that will give you the strength and the perseverance to treat others well. The rest comes easy.'

Maya gave her a mighty hug.

Bhua left her a note that night. 'My child, leave without bidding me goodbye. It will be too much for my frail heart to bear. I will wake up tomorrow morning believing you visited me in my dreams. I give you my blessings. May you continue to see your own beauty, may the great spirit show you the way home and may your treasures return to you manifold.'

Maya gently opened the door to her room and blew her a kiss. She felt she was leaving richer, greater and wiser than she had arrived.

Flight of the Falcon

'No *bird soars too high*
if he soars with his own wings.'

–William Blake

$\mathscr{P}$IA WAS OUT OF SORTS as she walked around the house holding a few black outfits.

'Which one guys? I can't seem to decide and you all seem totally disinterested in helping me figure this out.'

All the outfits were black, appeared more or less same to an untrained eye; there wasn't really much to base the decision on other than perhaps the neckline or the slits.

'Any one,' came a monotone reply.

She threw her hands up in frustration. 'No one wants to help me. So be it. I will wear whatever I will wear and then you, especially you Mom, do not come complaining to me about how your kitty party friends were discussing my unappealing appearance.'

Dadi called her over. 'Pia, first of all, I know you don't care about the kitty party friends but that was a good weapon to extract a response out of your society-fearing mom. And second, no matter what you wear, you will look beautiful, as long as you dress it up with a smile. Silks wrapped around frowning faces look humble compared to a piece of khaddar graced by a genuine smile. And all the ornate diamonds will not add a sparkle to a withered soul with lifeless eyes.'

Pia gave her a big hug, 'You always have a way with your words Dadi, it's an unfair advantage. Once again, point taken, argument sealed. Eeny Meenie Miny Moe, catch a tiger by the toe, if he hollers let him go... Eeny, meenie, miny moe, this one for tonight.'

Maya, in the meantime, stared through the window as she lay on the daybed, with her head rested on the silk bolster, reminiscing the beauty of an enchanting tale she had recently discovered. A story that had started over one hundred years ago and had somehow led to her or rather led her to itself.

'MAYA,' screamed Pia. 'Hurry up Ms Happy Dreams, Abhay will be here in an hour. By the way, you might need a stiff drink before we head out. He just informed me that Veer will be with him.'

Maya bounced off the bed and nearly hit the ceiling as if a powerful electric shock just ripped right through her. 'You've got to be kidding me. Why him? I'm not going.'

'Stop it Maya, maybe you just need to get over whatever it is about him that you're battling with,' insisted Pia.

'I'm not fighting any battles with him. These are my own battles and he keeps getting in the way. A soldier can't afford to be distracted or he will lose his life,' said Maya, sounding certain.

'What if the person appearing is a messenger of peace or perhaps the soldier's saviour?' suggested Dadi with a wink, 'The possibilities are endless!'

'A knight in shining armour, how romantic!' cooed Pia.

'Maya, never say no to life, gently allow whatever wants to come into your life and make way for that which is ready to pass. Running after things and running away from things are both signs of resistance. Open up and make space for good things to happen,' added Dadi.

Maya started to calm down, maybe her reactions were a bit extreme and maybe she was being too hard on herself. After all, she had been in control all her life and where exactly did that land her?

Once again, Pia held out the black dresses and with a smile, questioned, 'Which one?'

Abhay, for one, was known for his punctuality. He believed that being punctual was showing respect for others' time and, more importantly, to his own commitments. The signature double beep sent Pia running down, holding her sandals in her hands. 'Yes, yes... I'm here. Nope, not late again!'

'Phew!' she sighed, looking at her watch and said to Abhay as he smiled with his dimples flashing in a naughty grin, 'Abhay, I think you weren't just inspired by Cinderella, you were Cinderella in your past life.' All four of them broke into a laughter that instantly melted the distances and dissolved the apprehensions. Maya added, 'And since Abhay is Cinderella for the evening, maybe it will not be too out of place to call you Abhay,' she giggled, extending her hand out to greet Veer, diluting the awkwardness of the memory from last time.

Maya looked at him directly in the eyes. Tonight, dressed in her confidence and accessorized with her smile, she looked divine. 'Yaay,' Pia instinctively clapped her hands, almost as a celebration of Maya's emotional triumph. All eyes turned towards Pia and she blurted, 'Well yaaay...I mean, we are all set to go, in time, so my Cinderella won't have to walk without his dainty shoes and the car will not turn into a pumpkin.' She shrugged her shoulders and winked.

The town was bustling with activity as they drove past bicycles, autorickshaws and an occasional car full of young boys and pounding beats. Finally, the town grew quieter and the road became steeper as dim lights started to appear in a distance. Tonight, Mehrangarh Fort resembled a beautiful shy bride eagerly awaiting the arrival of her better half to come venerate her. The guests walked in on the red carpet to the sound of shehnais and a welcome of flower petals. Earthen lamps lit up the winding path to the fort appearing as though hundreds of setting suns had briefly halted their journey, to descend upon the earth and witness this union of souls.

'Maya, this takes me back to our apartment in the city. Remember your Zen oasis in our apartment with perpetual Henri Bendel "Vanilla Bean" candle flames and soft white lilies you would splurge your last bit of savings on?'

'Yes, crazy me! Still love that!' responded Maya.

'And remember Maya, your Soho and Chelsea weekend plans that started and ended with art galleries and art museums? I can't believe you signed me up for MoMA's annual membership. A visit to MoMA (Museum of Modern Art) was like Sunday church. Could not skip it for anything. And that crazy artist! Who was that revivalist who painted abstract illusionism? Gosh, just thinking about all the torture you inflicted upon me is terrible!' exclaimed Pia. Maya laughed dismissively.

Gradually, the evening grew deeper and the music more

intense. From instruments to folk songs, and ghazals to qawaalis, these varied forms of music seemed to be strung upon a common thread of love. Maya could feel the ecstasy of the music throbbing in her pulse. The crowd cheered and swayed to the songs, the singers appeared to have transcended into another world, obediently following wherever their music led them. Some of them appeared to be tuned into another beat, perhaps one meant just for their ears. The passion and the experience was magical. Interestingly, all there was, was a flood of music and thousands of souls drenched in it. Conversations ceased, questioning minds found their momentary rest and hearts communicated, unbarred and free.

For a moment, Maya's eyes were met by Veer's gaze, and in that brief collision, Maya caught a glimpse of eternity. It was her and him, and all else around them faded into a blur. She quickly and intentionally diverted her glance. She was so in love!

Just as she felt herself losing her pulse, on came, 'Oh Lal Meri, Pat Rakhiyo Bala Juhle Lalan.' Maya applauded and jumped in joy, 'Hey Pia, this is the song.' She was listening to it for the first time since she had discovered the story behind it. Veer smiled tenderly. To Maya, this song conveyed an aloof heritage, like she owned it in some strange way. She felt like she had a connection with it no one out there shared. She listened intently, following barely a few words here and there. But something about this music triggered an unnecessary and unstoppable flow of tears that trickled on. 'Silly girl,' said Pia as she extended her a hug.

Soon after the song ended, Maya disappeared into the crowd eventually making her way backstage. She met an old man from the song crew, who could almost be described as the universal grandfather, the kind who holds little children in his lap, allows them to play with his beard and tells them tales of faraway lands. The cheerful kindness in his eyes spilled out unbounded, like he had something to give to everyone along the way. His presence was calming, Maya started to relax. The old man in his brown sherwani, intricately carved walking cane and black Karakul hat said in a deep tender voice, *'Baitho beti. Khidmat mein kya pesh karen?'* (Come sit my child, what might I offer you in service?). The delivery of his speech was akin to an eloquently mesmerizing poem, to say the least.

'Um,' hesitated Maya. 'Could you explain the meaning of this song to me?'

'That is a strange request,' he said, 'but a very delightful one at that. It is promising to see that among our modern youth, there still remain a handful who seek an understanding of the lyrics, the meaning and the significance. I'm honoured and obliged to share.'

'Thank you,' she continued, 'by the way, I'm Maya.'

'And everyone refers to me as Chachha Jaan,' he responded graciously.

'So once upon a time, there lived a Sufi mystic, philosopher and poet named Shabaz Qalandar—the red king of falcons adorning the limitless skies. To put it in perspective, he was a contemporary of Rumi. Literally speaking, Lal stands for red, after the attire he wore, Shabaz means the king of falcons and Qalandar means free of boundaries. His name sums him up pretty descriptively.'

'Well, from what I hear, this song was originally a kalaam or a prayer written by Amir Khusrau and was given an altogether different dimension by Bulleh Shah who turned this into a devotional qawalli,' Maya interjected, 'Bulleh Shah of Kasur transformed it?'

'Yes, Bulleh Shah of Kasur,' confirmed Chachha Jaan.

'Sure I wasn't making history up in my head, facts are speaking for themselves,' whispered Maya.

'This ballad then, is an ode to the powers of this master from Sehwan, Sindh, to grant everyone their wishes. He granted sons to mothers and brother to sisters, he is the ultimate truth, the one and only. That is the heart and the gist of the song.'

'Wow,' said Maya with a long breath. This world-famous legend seemed uncannily close to home.

Chachha Jaan continued, 'Let me narrate an incident from his life you will find interesting and could perhaps utilize in your own life. One time, Lal Shabaz Qalandar arrived at a village that was full of faqirs. Upon hearing about his arrival, the faqirs sent him an overflowing bowl of milk. It was meant to symbolize the message that there is absolutely no room for more. He returned the overflowing bowl, just the same, only with a beautiful flower floating on top.'

'Beautiful!' she said.

He added, 'Yes, a reminder of the fact that each situation in life can be viewed for its limitations or for its possibilities.'

'So can reality be greater than our belief?' questioned Maya.

'It always is,' said the old man.

'You are so much more than you know,' he stated, closing his eyes. You are more than you believe, you are more than you achieve.

'Scratch the surface, just a little, right behind the appearance lies the ever peaceful, all knowing, confident, completely abundant Maya.

'It's the most powerful truth of our lives—The Real Truth—which is sometimes revealed in a flash of a moment and sometimes eludes an entire lifetime of searching. But we need not worry, your truth never leaves you. It just becomes a stranger in you.

'This truth neither changes, nor evolves...however, it sustains all change and contains all evolution. This truth is what sets you free, that transforms you into a Mast Qalandar—free to soar like a falcon and reach for the limitless skies.'

'Maya, who you know as yourself today is a familiar appearance, not the inherent reality of yourself.'

'Then who is the real me? How do I find her?' asked Maya.

'Rumi says, "That which you seek, seeks you." The journey of this Maya going to meet the real Maya is driven by an equally compelling desire on both sides.

'The path unveils itself, but only a few steps at a time. The truth starts to reveal itself but in bits and pieces, sometimes through coincidences but often through random, disconnected, scattered events. When you start looking, these will start to appear. There will be a strange pull, a silent calling, signals that only you will understand—follow it faithfully. Initially, these might not make a whole lot of sense but you must believe and remain true to this path.'

'When you arrive on the other side of the bridge and look over your shoulder, there it will be—your "Aha" moment, where every piece of the puzzle fits perfectly together and the dots connect and light up. Only from that vantage point, you will begin to see how perfectly synchronized and greatly instrumental every event, every accident and every person in your life has been in order to drive and deliver you exactly to that point.

'Let me ask you something. Do you have this intrinsic desire to find something that will always stay and never change?'

'Well, I guess I do. For that matter, I believe we all do.'

'Yes, we all do and we do because inherently there is a constant within us, the part of us which always was, is and will remain, which is lost and seeks its expression. We know we're incomplete, we know we're seeking something, we desire it so. We simply do not know where to look for that which beckons us. In fact, we don't even know exactly what it is that we're looking for so we follow the crowd.

'So we spend our days searching for that which we do not know, and in a place where we can never find it. Then disappointments should come as no surprise.

'The road that takes you home only begins on the inside. Directions may be everywhere but those are indications, mere dead ends.'

'But what is this reality, what is my truth?' insisted Maya.

The old man answered, 'The truth of what we do not know cannot be described...it can only be arrived at. You reached where you stand today by accumulation. Time, roles and experiences led you here, each casting another layer, each projecting one more shadow. Now, you must deconstruct. You must peel away one layer at a time until you reach the centre, your core.

'This process of elimination or subtraction is not something new. It has been described in various philosophies and numerous religions via negativa in some philosophies, and neti–neti in Vedanta, which literally translates as neither this nor that. So we eliminate or subtract what is not, we carefully excavate one layer at a time, peel away one mask at a time until we reach the treasure of what remains.

'The real Maya stands on the other side of the bridge, holding the keys to your authentic joy, your home. After your crossing, she hands them over and together you walk merging into the sunrise of glory.

'Maya, discover your real truth; remember:

- Who you are today only shows where you've been, not where you're going.
- You can view life for its limitations or its possibilities.
- Tune in to your heart often—it sees beyond creation, it recognizes inspiration.
- The real truth is your undiluted core, the reason for your joy and the path into the unchartered skies.'

'Chachha Jaan,' came a voice from behind, 'it's time to go.'

He smiled and said, 'The sky awaits the falcon as much as the falcon seeks the sky, just spread your wings, you will know how to fly.'

Maya counted down another bead of the Real Truth as she headed back into the evening, wondering how far she was from her reality. Something told her she was already on the path, signs were appearing and she was following her heart... 'For most parts,' she added, as she noticed Veer standing amongst the crowd.

'Everything alright?' he asked, sounding concerned.

'Yes, more so than ever,' she responded with a placid smile. The sentiment among the crowd had escalated. It was on the cusp of being wild with passion to elated with devotion. Abhay and Piya were upfront and the deluge of this energy seemed unyielding. Veer smiled, 'It only gets better from here, I suggest we wait for it to tide down.' They walked away towards the city views under the silent moonlight.

'This is breathtaking,' said Maya as she stood back and gazed upon the magnificently lit fort perched high above the city.

'"A palace that might have been built by Titans and coloured by the morning sun" is how Rudyard Kipling described this place. Some have even called it the eighth wonder,' said Veer.

'Even the name is exotic—Mehrangarh,' said Maya.

'Mehrangarh,' he continued, 'is derived from the Sanskrit words "Mihir" meaning Sun and "Garh" meaning Fort. So it actually translates as the Sun Fort that stands majestically on this indomitable cliff, saluting the sun as it greets the morning sky. Of course, it is also in some ways used to refer the mythical descent of this clan from sun god "Surya",' he stated, as they arrived at the famous Kilkila Cannon. 'And that right there,' he pointed, 'draped in white marble is Jaswant Thada, a memorial with a lesser known legend of a peacock that flew into a funeral pyre. As you can tell, I find history fascinating.'

'Quite intriguing,' said Maya.

'Well, that's not all, I saved the best for last,' he said as he led her to the left side of the fort with sweeping views of the city below. It was a spectacle to behold. The wind blew Maya's hair across her face as Veer looked upon. The silence that stood between them at 400 feet above the day-to-day grind, seemed to dance in midnight ecstasy upon the celestial notes of Madhuvanti, the timeless raga of love.

The electrifying intensity of the moment, the captivating seduction of music and unconquerable fury of emotions convinced Maya of Tansen's legend that could light lamps with Raaga Deepak and induce rain with Raaga Malhar.

The music was ushering a storm while silence was expressing that which could not be stated, yet could not be left unexpressed.

She silently reflected on the depth of these words as she looked at the glittering city below, caressed by the softness of the moonlight.

Utsava—A Celebration

'Clouds come floating into my life,
no longer to carry rain or usher storm,
but to add colour to my sunset sky.'

–Rabindranath Tagore

*B*ACK IN JAIPUR, MAYA FELT the same comfort checking in as she might have felt after coming home from a long hectic travel.

It had neither been long nor hectic and certainly this hotel was far from being home. The feelings, she pondered, might be owed to the distance she had travelled, how far she had come, how much more she had become and undeniably the amazing shower she had long missed. The experience felt as fulfilling as a return home after a worthwhile adventure.

Hard as she tried, she could not get Veer out of her thoughts or her mind. Her own words echoed in her mind, 'I follow my heart…most of the time,' as she recalled looking at Veer standing among the crowd and consciously diverting her steps. She knew well that in this case she was ruthlessly denying her heart.

'I understand we must follow our hearts,' said Maya to

herself, 'but sometimes the heart can be very treacherous,' she reasoned with her own self. 'The toughest debate to win is the one that goes on between the heart and the mind…am I holding on to what I should be letting go…or am I letting go what I should be holding on to…guess the heart already knows what mind can neither comprehend nor rationalize…'

'Maya,' she reminded herself, 'remember the lessons you have learnt. Step into a state of acceptance, surrender and grace. Yes. I can't tell life where I wish to be… I simply allow it to lead me exactly where I'm meant to be…' she mumbled as she fell into a restful slumber.

After a midday siesta, Maya decided to pay a visit to Ananda. As she rode past the familiar village, the taxi came to an abrupt stop.

'What is the matter?' Maya questioned.

'A goat herder,' came the reply.

'A goat herder?'

The driver responded, 'That's right Madam. Well, you will find plenty of them here, since Rajasthan alone accounts for more than 18 per cent of country's entire population of goats but this one is unique—he cannot see.'

'A blind man who herds goats, how does he even do that?' questioned Maya.

'I have wondered about it all my life,' said the driver. 'I hear these goats are the only family he has. He talks to them, plays flute to them and they never seem to leave his side. He even has a name for every member of his family.'

'Incredible,' said Maya.

'One day, an Englishman rode in this taxi with me. Interestingly, he was here in search of a great master, an old unassuming man believed to be over one hundred years old who could teach the ancient art of Dhanurveda, the science of archery, like none other. I'm not sure if he ever was able to find his master but he did explain to me this herder's phenomenon with a term called "Mushin".'

'Mushin?'

'Yes, that's what the gentleman said. He said it was a Zen philosophy used in martial arts which literally means "no mind". It is a state of mind attached to neither a thought nor an emotion thus fully open and available to the world around it. In this highly perceptive mental state, the person acts not based on what he thinks he ought to do but what he intuitively feels he must do. When a person enters this state of mind, he leaves his intention, plan and direction outside the door. Fighters trained in this technique stand with swords in their hands and their lives on the line, only to follow the dictates of their hearts, without a technique or carefully chalked out plan to protect themselves. Some masters believe that Mushin is the state of realization where an understanding comes about, where people finally let go of their dependencies, cut the ropes and become truly free to flow. Such people often refer to themselves as living beings moving through space.'

Maya listened intently.

'He further told me about an interesting offshoot of this. In the Japanese martial art called Kudos, Mushin refers to the act of "non-doing". The master can hit the target with a bow and arrow in complete darkness. In fact, what is even more interesting is that hitting the target accounts only for 10-20 per cent of the points. The person should have no obvious desire to hit the target, he just needs to demonstrate the experience of release directed towards the target. These masters believe that the target does not lie outside but it lies within them and is demonstrated by shooting it right on dot in total darkness. It appears to be a calm act of being rather than a planned act of achievement.

'To prove this theory, they even conducted a brain experiment on the master versus a beginner. The brain activity was scanned to track the level of activity and the blood flow. The novice's brain was fully engaged with high level of activity and a corresponding red image which indicated increased blood flow signifying that the brain activity in this case, peaked right at the time he released his bow. This was the most natural response based on the way we act and think which means action gets result.

'However, quite interestingly and on the contrary, the master's brain registered very low activity, and a blue scan indicated no heightened sense of engagement. His brain pattern was similar to someone in a meditative state, calm and restful. It was stable and in fact, the activity actually dipped at the point of release amounting to perfection through non-doing.

'When questioned, the master responded, "It is our thinking that leads us into believing that effort gets result, effortless actions are far more efficient. This practice has a less than 1 per cent success rate since everyone believes more action leads to better result." Non-action is apparently much harder to learn.

'Well. His logic did seem plausible and that's how I understand this blind goat herder now. A master in sync with his surroundings. He carries the world within him.'

'If you wouldn't mind, I would like to be dropped off right here,' requested Maya.

Maya walked behind the herder watching his every move. She doubted for a few moments if he really was blind, his sure steps neither tripped nor shook. He knew exactly what lay ahead of him.

Finally, the old man sat down on the concrete that surrounded the trunk of the large shaded tree. Some of his goats sat next to him, others by his feet. He took off his turban and pulled out a flute from his sack. The music he played echoed a story of love and kindled a flame of devotion. Maya was filled with admiration and wonder.

'He has been singing this song of love for possibly as long as you have been alive, if not longer,' prompted a voice as Maya turned around. It was Leela holding a stick of sugarcane that she chewed on and occasionally spat as she headed towards Maya.

'So you are back! Did you meet your masters?' Leela asked in a snippy tone.

'Yes, I did and I learnt enough, but I'm still two beads away from returning to you,' Maya said with the proud sense of accomplishment. 'Very well,' said Leela, 'so I will see you after you have strung the remaining two beads.'

'Leela,' called out Maya, urging her to stop. 'I need help.'

'What do you need help with?' asked Leela.

'Save me from love,' urged Maya meekly.

Leela laughed out loud. 'Say that again. How can you be saved from love when love is what saves you?'

Maya insisted, 'I'm not talking about the idea of lofty universal love, Leela. It's the love for one man—the trifling kind that comes with pain and heartbreaks.'

The flute stopped playing. There was a moment of silence and then the blind old man recited:

Mohobbat mohobbat hai...
Aur phir ye zindagi ki kahani hai

Ek hai gumnaam talaash sitaron ki
Doosri saada si haqiqat ki bas, rawaani hai

Zindagi mein mohobbat ko na khojo mere yaar
Aur mohobbat ko zindagi banane ki tamanna na karo

Ek zamin hai kuch thehri simti
Ek hai aasman—zara bikhra udta

Paas rehten hai dono magar sath nahin
Milte hain to sirf afaq—who bhi farebe nazar se

Zindagi hai woh zameen jo buniyaad de chalna sikhaye
Aur mohobbat woh aasman jo roshni de rah dikhaye

Rahon ke humsafar hain dono magar manzil nahin
Humraah na hote agar—to yeh safar bhi nahin

'Wah,' said Leela. '*Bahut khoob.*'

Maya looked a little perplexed, not quite understanding the exchange that just happened. Maya was struggling to get on the plane with them but clearly felt she had lost the plot.

'Maya, the language of love is universal. He expresses what he comprehends through his music and his words. He suggests that life is the earth that offers us a foundation and teaches us how to walk while the love is the sky that lightens our path. Let each remain where it belongs for both are your companions along this journey but not your final destination. These remain apart yet come together...merging into a horizon promised by an illusion of the eye.

'For something you might understand, let me share with you what Kahlil Gibran states about love and togetherness. It is profound. Listen:

"Let there be spaces in your togetherness, and let the winds of the heavens dance between you. Love one another but make not a bond of love: Let it rather be a moving sea between the shores of your souls. Fill each other's cup but drink not from one cup. Give one another of your bread but eat not from the same loaf. Sing and dance together and be joyous, but let each one of you be alone, even as the strings of a lute are alone though they quiver with the same music. Give your hearts, but not into each other's keeping. For only the hand of life can contain your hearts. And stand together, yet not too near together, for the pillars of the temple stand apart, And the oak tree and the cypress grow not in each other's shadow."'

'An incredibly beautiful expression,' said Maya.

Leela continued, 'Love is a strange creature. I say, you cannot dictate it, you cannot create it. When it comes knocking on your door, you must answer and follow it. You can neither convince it nor reason with it, question you may but surrender you must, for it renders you powerless. Love walks you to its kiln where it transforms your being, it forges you with pain and colours you with ecstasy, it reveals to you your finest identity.

'When you find love wandering through the streets, walk a few steps holding its hand, cling not, possess not but offer yourself to it unconditionally, selflessly and completely. Allow it to sweep you away like a feather that blows in the wind, aimless and free, neither seeking the sky above nor refusing the street below. Like the dark clouds that usher the rain, pour, unburden your heart and let the torrent of this shower wash upon the dancing trees and cascading rivers.'

The old man played his flute again and whispered, 'Love is the breath that flows through my flute and makes music. Music is because love is. Flute becomes what love makes of it and look what it creates.'

'Love is a discovery, not a conclusion...explore it,' stated Leela.

'But I tried finding myself in love and nearly lost my life,' spoke Maya in dismay.

'You were looking to find yourself and you were looking to find happiness, you were looking for outcomes, you were not looking for love.

'Love to you came as a relief from the pain and struggles of everyday life. You sought the pleasures that came with it, you were compensating. This relief slowly turned into a need, with need came the demand for fulfilment of the need and the fear of losing the relief.

'It was the need and the fears that created the pain, love misunderstood, was left with blame. The desire to own love is what drove love away. What you held onto was a dark shadow, left somewhere along the way. Love cannot be bought, it cannot be owned but it will always be there long after it's gone. Love compliments, it completes not. It enhances, it compensates not. It expects of you a song of love itself. It returns to you the joy that you give. Love seeks its expression; it demands its fulfilment. It is growth, it is healing.'

'Maya, it is awful to be empty...but it's a sin to be full yet keep your love from overflowing. One of the greatest regrets people have at the end of their days is words left unsaid and love remained unexpressed.'

'Leela, I am afraid of being vulnerable,' said Maya.

Leela responded, 'You are vulnerable without it. Love is the shield that allows you to tread through life with light steps. This is what enables you to dive into the richness of life and gather its treasures. If you protect your vulnerability, you cast a shadow on the sun, you deny life itself.

'Life and love are playmates that do not need reason, but ask for passion. Live your life at the point of exuberance, touching and forever altering all that basks in its glow. Be like an overflowing river that rushes to its sea dancing in ecstasy and pouring in joy—the day it starts to hold back its flow for the fear of losing itself will be the day it starts to stagnate and die.

'Maya, dictates of love come from a world beyond, we merely follow the command,' said Leela.

'I know exactly what you mean, Leela. Honestly, I feel like I have known him all my life or for many lives perhaps,' said Maya.

'Now you speak what I already know,' Leela laughed aloud and walked away.

Maya did not try to stop her.

Maya stared at her phone as the music from the flute floated around her and the goats started to bleat. She thought about Leela, love and Mushin—'acting out of instinct rather than a plan.'

'Siri,' she said, 'call Veer.'

'Are you sure you want me to call Veer?' came the digitized voice of apprehension speaking through Siri.

She smiled 'Yes, I'm sure.'

'Calling Veer,' said Siri.

'This is Veer,' said a deep discerning voice.

'Hi, Maya this side.'

'Hello Maya, how are you?'

'Well, I'm good, I just arrived this morning and ended up in your neighbourhood, perhaps if you do not have much else going on, I could stop by for a few minutes?' suggested Maya.

'Of course,' he said. 'Come on over. Do you know where I live?' Maya bit her tongue, not wanting to appear as if she'd been stalking him.

'Oh no. I just had a vague idea from a conversation with Pia. Why don't you give me your address; I will see you shortly.' Maya caught her breath, 'Phew!'

The clouds came in dark and heavy carrying in their bosom a promise of relief for the parched land and hope for release of their own joy.

Maya was dressed in a white kurta with cropped pants, her hair pulled towards one side, revealing the delicate pearls that hung in her ears. Her simplicity was graceful. As the taxi approached the gate, the guards rushed forward to open it. Maya got off by the main entrance and thanked the driver.

She walked softly towards the mansion surrounded by the lush manicured gardens on both sides. Maya spotted an outdoor seating next to the gazebo. An elaborate set-up of tea cozies and tiered platters containing colourful macaroons, pastries and scones was visibly inviting.

Maya proceeded towards it.

The wind picked up blowing leaves and kicking dust. It was strangely symbolic of the conversation Maya had had a little while ago with Leela—the rain pours its joy, the leaf surrenders to the wind aimlessly floating around. Maya smiled as if nature was reinforcing the message in actions that Leela had just stated in words. She looked up and whispered, 'I get it!'

Birds added to the excitement of this impending storm as they chattered louder and louder and flew back and forth. Peacocks strolled in preparation for their rain dance.

As she walked up behind Veer, she heard the words:

I seem to have loved you in numberless forms,
numberless times...
In life after life, in age after age, forever.
My spellbound heart has made and remade the
necklace of songs,
That you take as a gift, wear round your neck in
your many forms,
In life after life, in age after age, forever.

Maya's lips turned blue, her body shook, her hands trembled as a voice interrupted, 'Welcome Madam, please take a seat.' Veer turned around. Maya noticed a book in his hand and colour returned to her face again. She was both relieved and embarrassed.

Veer spoke, 'I'm so sorry. Of course I was expecting you but I just didn't realize when you arrived. I apologize, books have a way of consuming me and Rabindranath Tagore's poetry is my absolute favourite. I have read it innumerable times, yet each time it brings with it something new.'

Maya smiled, 'I can totally understand, it happens to me too often.'

'So I guess we both share a common love...of reading of course!' Veer added with a smile as he watched Maya's expressions fade in and out, yet again.

'Why don't we have tea first?' he said. He indicated to the server who stood close by. 'Madam, this is your cooked tea in the white pot and Sir, your black tea is in the silver pot.'

Maya's eyes lit up. 'How did you find out?'

'I do my research,' he laughed. 'No, I believe it is not important how many people we know but how well we know those that we claim to know. Besides, in my experience, personalization has never failed to impress,' he said with a wink.

'And your words haven't failed to impress me either...' added Maya.

'My words?'

'Yes, Ananda, he's my friend.'

'Memsahib from New York?' exclaimed Veer.

'Yes, that's me!'

They broke into laughter, 'It's a small world after all!'

As soon as they were finished with tea, Maya felt a few drops of rain on her face. 'Seems like it's going to pour,' she said as they ran to the corridor for cover.

'Come inside, Maya,' came a firm voice.

'Did I hear that right?' asked Maya.

'Yes, you did.' said Veer, 'That's my Dadisa.'

Maya stepped inside the sprawling entrance with winding staircases and shiny marble floors, accented with bold silk carpets. Decorated mostly in cream, white and gold, an understated elegance ran through the house.

Out of the kitchen walked Dadisa, wiping her wet hands with a towel before handing it to the helper. She hugged Maya and said, *'Jug jug jiyo beti'* (May you live long).

Maya softly responded with a 'thank you.'

'Veer tells me you are here on a big research project,' asked Dadisa. Veer stood smiling behind her. Maya turned around to look at him and smiled in return, 'Yes, the most critical research project of my life.'

'Good,' she said, 'and how about your family?'

'Well, my mom is the only family I have left and we live in New York.'

'I love that city,' said Dadisa. 'His grandfather loved taking me there on holidays. We would sail for weeks and then spend time with his golf buddies. The final week and my most favourite of all was all about dining and entertaining in Manhattan. He went to Harvard so we always had great company there. So nice, you brought back memories that were gathering dust. Those indeed were beautiful days.'

'You should come visit me one of these days. A lot has changed since then, but I'm sure it will be special nonetheless,' offered Maya.

Dadisa answered with moist eyes, 'I stopped travelling after he passed away. It was mostly to give him company, I am quite a homebody, you know. This community gives me so much love and their service gives me immense fulfilment. I love the simple abundance of life here. That was wonderful then and this is wonderful now. When small things in life are so good, the big things get taken care of.'

Maya responded, 'I hear you. My mom is the same way and yes, we immensely miss Dad but I guess to live in the hearts of others after one leaves is to never truly leave. My mom often says, "Unfortunate are not the cherished ones who leave or are left behind, for they will live in each other till eternity, truly unfortunate are those who may have a place in your everyday life but never find a place in your heart."'

'She is a wise lady,' said Dadisa.

'His Dada had a simple approach to life as well. "Celebrate life," he would say. "Life is a beautiful gift in your hands...create something that is larger than yourself and that continues to exist beyond you. Let your life be remembered by all the lives you touch and the difference it makes. And when comes your day to move on, leave content, knowing you loved truly, lived fully and emptied out completely." And he did.'

She laughed nodding her head, 'He was the life and soul of this house. Well, you children should head out. Veer, why don't you show Maya around? Maya, ever since Veer was a child, each time it rained, he insisted that I cooked malpuras with my own hands. It is a ritual now,' she smiled. 'And Veer, the filter coffee should be on its way as well.'

They were walking towards the corridor when Maya paused to admire the lovely collection of artwork displayed along the steps leading upstairs. 'Are these family portraits? And how about the rest of the artwork? It is a gorgeous collection.'

'Some of this are made by family, some collected by family and I personally love a good piece of art. I'm not as enamoured by the name or the reputation of the artist but if the art calls out to me, I bring it home,' said Veer.

'Of course, a lot of what you will find scattered around the house is thanks to Dadisa's effort. She was Dada's muse for art. He got her hooked on to it, as he would say, "To keep her engaged with purpose and surrounded by beauty,"' added Veer.

Maya looked on in wonderment as she stepped closer to the frames, almost as if she had been transported into another world.

And then she spoke, 'Art really can be quite captivating and communicative. It speaks volumes behind its obvious display. I love how all the elements of it come together to depict a person, his world, and the relationship between the two.

'In expressing life, the artist also expresses himself. We live in this world where things take on a meaning based on how they address our needs, desires, emotions, and joys. One without the other would be meaningless. It's the interaction of the two that delivers a purpose to both.

'Art simply captures the inspiration that life offers, an inspiration that arises like a tempestuous wave, washes over our hearts and mind and crashes onto the shores of our canvas.'

'That's fairly deep Maya. Not many people I have met uphold art to this standard,' said Veer.

Maya contributed, 'Well, art is an undeniable aspect of human existence, Veer. The greatest minds of all times are known to have leaned heavily on art despite all their worldly pursuits. Einstein played violin and piano. It is even said that if he had not been a scientist, he would have been a musician. Darwin read Shakespeare extensively. Leonardo da Vinci was an inventor, painter, sculptor, a writer and a poet. He maintained a journal which has over 13,000 pages full of drawing on scientific illustrations. Art is such a powerful catalyst to provoke thought, stimulate imagination and stir curiosity, so essential to all achievements.

'One summer while I was quite young, my mom took me to the Salvador Dali Museum in Figueres, Spain. It was the most delightful place ever, a playground for my mind. In addition to many paintings from his personal collection, it housed sculptures, three-dimensional collages, mechanical devices and other curiosities from Dali's imagination. We also visited the Museu Picasso in Barcelona, touring one of the most extensive collections of Picasso's work. I was so fascinated and captivated by what I saw that I drew hundreds of illustrations over that one summer,' smiled Maya, lost in a sweet recollection.

'Really, without art, an individual's tryst with life would remain forever unconsummated.'

'Maya, you really do belong on the other side of the canvas, I suggest you think about it,' implored Veer.

'Sorry, I tend to get carried away,' said Maya abruptly pulling herself back, moving on from art and the stairway on to the outdoor corridor.

'How about your life in London? Do you have family there?' Maya knew he didn't, but she just wanted to hear it nonetheless.

'Well no family per se but I have lived there long enough so I have a large circle of friends who are like family.'

Maya's eyes shone with delight.

Maya's greatest shortcoming, she believed was a face as transparent as glass. She knew he could see right through it.

'What do you do for a living?' she asked in an attempt to conceal her obvious elation.

'I run a real estate investment fund,' he answered. 'Other than that, for most part I like to spend my time in literary communities. I would rather relax and talk in good company than be out there among the thronging crowds late on weekend nights. Most of my friends typically are twice my age, but age is never a barrier when you are mentally aligned.'

'I quite get it,' said Maya, 'I have spent some very fond days with Ananda. We connected perfectly.'

'That's right. I'm glad he looked after you well,' said Veer.

'Besides that, this community of ours keeps me very involved. There still remains a lot to be done.'

'Achievement is a great thing Maya but enabling achievement

is a different ball game altogether. I'm sure you've heard of Maslow's hierarchy of needs theory.'

'Well, I hope you do know that you are talking to a psychiatrist,' said Maya.

Veer paused, 'Impressive! Good field to be in given the times.'

He continued, 'Well, in that case you understand how the pyramid goes. Physiological needs like food, water and shelter, followed by need for safety and security, followed by need to belong and be loved, followed by self-esteem, pride and achievement, but on the very top of the pyramid lies our most important need, the need for self-actualization. Achieving of one's potential.

'For every human being, whether he lives in London or New York, Tibet, Africa or a small village in Rajasthan, the fundamental needs do not vary, inherently we are all the same. I sincerely believe that each person should realize his or her potential. Whatever he can be, he must be.

'What I try to do here then, is to offer them a platform to find themselves. I help them get education, some might realize they are made by geniuses, others may have a love of technology, some might have soccer running in their veins and other, a painter rising to his glory. Even women with homes and children have aspirations, some may contain an artist within them, a dancer perhaps or a leader, who knows. Each life that blossoms in its full glory uplifts the entire mankind in ways untold.

'There is all this talk about wars and crime and we spend billions of dollars trying to fight it. You know what lies at the very root of it—potential that wasn't harnessed—it is the pain of unfulfilled lives that spreads in the world.

'If we are looking to create love and world peace, we need to nurture individuals who grow to love themselves and are at peace with their own lives.

'I earn to give and I learn to share. What comes to me goes back out into the world and multiplies a thousand fold. At the end of the day, what you create doesn't matter as much as what you make of yourself and others in the process.'

Maya paused. 'I'm impressed again. And thank you for all that you did for me along this journey.'

'Don't thank me Maya, thank yourself. It was your courage that made this journey possible, I just happened to meet you along the way. If it wasn't me, it would be someone else but your journey would still remain your own. You owe it to none other than yourself. You know what is the single most important quality I value in an individual?'

'What is it?' questioned Maya.

'Authenticity,' he responded. 'The courage to be genuine. The ability to stand up for one's truth. I deeply respect your journey Maya. Very few have the courage to question their choices and fewer the strength to deal with the answers and only a handful muster the fortitude to step out and seek a change. I'm proud of you.'

As they spoke, a group of women ushered in and walked hurriedly towards the back of the house. They giggled and chattered under long veils and chunnaris clinched between their teeth. 'Rain is quite the festival here,' said Veer, changing the tone of the conversation. 'Dadisa initiated this tradition at our house. They call it "Utsava". These women sing songs and welcome the arrival of rain. Did you notice the numerous swings hanging off mango trees in the courtyard behind the house? Well, that's what that courtyard was built for.'

'Could I possibly join them?' asked Maya with the innocence and impatience of a child standing in front of a huge toy store.

'Be my guest,' said Veer as he took a sip of the steaming filter coffee. Dadisa and Veer watched Maya as she happily stepped in the puddles and braided flowers in her hair. She swung back and forth reaching for the mist, as women sang songs, danced and frolicked in the rain. Peacocks spread their feathers and walked around in gaiety. It was delightfully refreshing...like the blossoming of flowers after a long harsh winter.

One String That Binds All

> 'To see a world in a grain of sand and heaven in a
> wild flower hold infinity in the palms of your hand
> and eternity in an hour.'
>
> —William Blake

*M*AYA SAT AT THE BREAKFAST table overlooking the splendid gardens. She enjoyed her glass of mimosa that complemented her continental spread. Birds chirped. Pigeons cooed. Peacocks called and the flute payer played a lilting tune.

Across from Maya was seated a peculiar family. The head of the family was a man with unruly hair, big glasses and an awkward appearance. His two daughters incessantly tapped away on their cell phones while the mother, a seemingly simple woman with a maroon bindi nearly as large as the moon appeared content relishing her Punjabi parathas in Rajasthan.

As the flute player completed his symphony, there was a loud applause, most of it from that family's table. The flute player bowed and started to pack up his instruments. This man, who stood distinctly apart in both his looks and demeanour walked down to the garden, and touched the young flute player's feet as a mark of respect. Maya intently watched this interesting development. It is rather rare to find this humility in a world that acclaims status and prestige, she observed.

The two men spoke for a while. Both seemed equally pleased as they faced each other in a similar stance, hands joined and folded in gratitude in front of their chests.

Maya lingered on.

The man sauntered back and leisurely sat down on the steps. He looked at the sky and started to hum a tune, soon the hum transitioned into a song. If she recalled it correctly, it was one of her mom's favourite songs, 'Dil Dhoondta Hai Phir Wahi Fursat Ke Raat Din.' A song reminiscing the golden days spent in the yard, lounging under the cozy winter sun and cherishing the summer breeze on the rooftop terrace on cool starlit nights. One after the other, spectators walked over and joined him on the steps. Before long, the entire breakfast community was gathered around him, tapping their feet, clapping their hands and snapping their fingers. Maya was one of them. The girls, of course, preferred clicking selfies over listening to their father sing.

After a loud applause, the crowd dispersed and Maya went up to the man and shook his hand. 'That was a very deep song and you sung it with great emotion. Are you from the music industry?'

'Thank you,' said this man adjusting his glasses. 'I'm a quantum physicist.'

'Really! I couldn't have guessed that in a million years. Very interesting!' expressed Maya.

'Not so much for my wife,' he laughed. His wife was quiet

but rather pleasant; her small eyes becoming even smaller as she smiled, neither denying the claim nor arguing it.

Maya could tell by his accent, that he was from her part of the world. 'I live in California, Los Angeles to be precise. Yes, science and music have both been my passions ever since I was a little boy. One gives me a peek into the unlimited reality and the other gives me depth to comprehend it. It is quite a fascinating intertwined perspective you get to form over time. I mean the way you view this world.'

'That's a compelling statement,' said Maya, 'I would love to take in some of this view and hear all about it.'

'Of course, with pleasure! I'm around for a few days. In fact, my wife and daughters have planned a shopping spree this afternoon. Stop by at your convenience, you should be able to find me at the coffee shop or the tavern,' said the man as he shook her hand.

Maya said, 'I look forward to that.'

Maya's phone beeped. She looked at her text notification unassumingly. It was a message from Veer. Maya fumbled to open it. It contained a picture, and as the saying goes, a picture is worth a thousand words. It indeed was worth a thousand words, a compelling interplay of intricately woven expressions and emotions. Maya, caught in the upswing, rain drops trickling down her face, leaves blowing around, her eyes shut tight, her exuberant smile and undisguised simplicity—riveting, to say the least. Below the picture were posted these words:

'When the soul lies down in that grass
the world is too full to talk about.'

—Jallaluddin Rumi

222 • *The Indigo Sun*

Maya watched upon in daze and wonder. This by far was the highest compliment she had ever received and that too without words to address her. She was as confounded with Veer's ambiguity as she was pleased with the relevance of this message.

'Maybe I'm reading too much into it,' thought Maya, shaking off her feel-good emotions that were now taking on a life of their own. She decided not to indulge these thoughts any further but her heart was leaping in joy.

Before long, Maya stood knocking at Ananda's door. Amma answered the door and Ananda came rushing over. 'Maya Memsahib, we were worried for you.'

She held him by his shoulders and spun him in delight. 'There is no reason to be worried anymore, Ananda,' said Maya in an obviously delighted tone. 'I am discovering the art of "Ananda" and projecting it onto "Maya". Today I got to see a glimpse of how splendid she appears in the hues of bliss!' Ananda and Amma looked at her, perplexed.

'A cup of tea please?' requested Maya in an upbeat pitch. Amma tapped herself on her head, 'Of course, I forgot to ask, I was just so captivated to see you like this. It will be just a few minutes.' She stroked some kohl off the edge of her eyes and placed it on the corner of Maya's forehead. 'God bless you,' she said as she walked away feeling emotional.

They gathered under the shade of the kikar tree sipping on tea from kullhars as she told them all about Pia, Abhay, Bhua and Veer. The mention of Veer caused Ananda to break into a dance instantaneously. Maya giggled and happy hours passed by in a matter of minutes it seemed.

She hugged Amma and told Ananda, 'You still owe me the

game of rocks, they have been intriguing me for many sleepless nights,' she said as she bid them goodbye for the day.

Birds flew across the motionless sky returning to their nests and the mellow sun embraced the city for one last time in its fading light. It was nearly 6 p.m., a little late in the day for coffee, presumed Maya and headed towards the tavern.

Sure enough, the man appeared comfortably spread out on the three-seater dark brown chesterfield sofa, smoking a cigar as he browsed through a newspaper—hair still ruffled, glasses hanging off the edge of his nose.

The lounge was elegantly covered with Burmese teak wood, accented with elephant tusks and a grand fireplace. Maya felt silly not having remembered to ask him his name.

'Good to see you again, by the way, I'm Maya,' she said, extending her hand. 'Good to meet you Maya. I'm Shankar. Make yourself comfortable,' he said pointing towards the seat next to the sofa. 'Something to drink?' he asked. 'Yes, I ordered myself a glass of Malbec on my way in. But thanks for asking,' responded Maya politely.

'So I've been thinking about you quite a bit, this quantum physicist from California who has a passion for singing, how do you bring the two together?'

'Easy! It's actually a complimentary package, one stimulates my intellect and pays my bills, and the other rests my heart and rejuvenates my soul. I enjoy both of these but I do not bring them together, I mean, at work, I do not sing and I do not sing about my work,' he said in a serious voice before breaking out into a roaring laughter. 'That was meant to be funny,' he said. Maya still found herself groping for a reaction.

He was an interesting creature, deep and complicated,

224 • *The Indigo Sun*

brilliant and awkward. Maya decided she would refer to him as the complicated mad scientist with two left feet, perfect vocal cords and a brilliant brain.

'Well, life comes full circle,' said Shankar. 'I grew up in a small town. My father was a civil judge and we were transferred from one station to another very often. For the lack of consistent friendships, I often relied on my own company for entertainment and discovered two passions to keep me engaged—singing and reading.

'One time, I stood first in my school for an interstate mathematics competition. As a prize, I received a book called *One two three... Infinity*, by George Gamow. It talked about the three levels of infinity in addition to other cool sounding and thought-provoking concepts including number theory, spacetime, relativity and cosmology. That book triggered such a deep interest that I was completely hooked.

'Looking back, I think so much else could have been, had it not been for that one victory and one prize. What if it was a book on music? But while it all could be, this I believe was just meant to be. One thing followed another and it became a series of happy coincidences.

'My father with his strong academic background encouraged me to pursue my interest all the way and suggested I explored further education overseas. I enrolled for a Masters programme in the US, and went on to finish my PhD and postdoctorate from Harvard. Since then, I've written several research papers and published a few books pertaining to the concepts of relativity.

'During this time, I became good friends with a professor of philosophical theology. He was like a Zen master, spoke little, mostly in terms of simple questions that would provoke my thinking and ignite a burning desire to uncover the answers. The love of music also brought me very close to a renowned Indian mathematician. He ascribed to a theory about how various elements of music could be related back to the measurement of time and frequency.'

He laughed, 'It was quite the melting pot of inquisitive minds questioning the frontiers of everything known and experienced. We were forever restless and dissatisfied.'

'So tell me, comprehensively, combining science, music and theology, how does this world appear to you?' asked Maya. 'It must indeed be quite colourful.'

'Maya, excuse me when I start to blur the lines between science and spirituality but I believe, science simply is that aspect of universal nature which we have been able to prove. It's a small subset. Gravity existed even before Newton's discovery but it became a science because he proved it. There lies a truth beyond the workings of the world, outside the limits of our comprehension. I refer to this as The Universal Truth. This world is simply a collective reality that can often be experienced but not always explained.

'There is a primal web of energy that connects our bodies and minds, the earth, the universe, the void, and the space, as one vast quantum field. Philosophically speaking then, when you take a breath, you have merged with the winds, when you touch a rain drop...you've touched the deepest ocean. Spiritually speaking, our Vedas refer to Bhraman or Akasha in various ways describing it as an energy that is timeless, formless, infinite, unified field of pure consciousness, which cannot be created or destroyed, but simply moves in and out of form.

'When you come to describe Tao, they call it the one that

defines everything but ultimately remains beyond description. The eternally nameless, that is non-conceptual yet alive.

'"As above, so below; as within, so without," states Hermeticism. Some of our greatest early scientists including Issac Newton were known to have studied in great detail these Egyptian-Greek wisdom texts and ancient scriptures in which secrets of the divine, nature, cosmos and mind have been revealed. He was better known then as a natural philosopher who had a very deep interest in alchemy which he extensively wrote about in his papers.

'Fundamentally then, all religions point towards a creator (the macrocosm), that cannot be created but lives in each creation (the microcosm). Whichever religious belief you ascribe to, it will have different names to refer to one unified force that does not change but causes all change.

'If we extend the attempt to define it scientifically, in addition to the above, perhaps we already have partial evidence to suggest that this energy is non-local.

'In physics, the principle of locality states that an object is influenced directly only by its immediate surroundings. However, in recent experiments, the principle of locality has been violated wherein photons "interacted" or "communicated" with one another instantly or "in no time". Our reality then is connected outside of spacetime which suggests that distance may be a limitation of our mind more than an actual reality.

'This reality of ours might also be non-linear, not necessarily moving step-by-step further down an "arrow of time". Think of the possibility that it might all be happening simultaneously.

'I understand this can be tough to wrap your head around

but Albert Einstein himself might have suggested that the past, present, and future all exist simultaneously. Instead of quoting his scientific works or references, let me give it a human perspective. Upon Besso's death in 1955, Einstein wrote a letter of condolence to the family that contained these words, "Now he has departed from this strange world a little ahead of me. That signifies nothing. For those of us who believe in physics, the distinction between past, present and future is only a stubbornly persistent illusion."

'Now practically speaking, if we converge what religion believes, philosophy indicates and science proves in layman's terms, this universe, may be summed up as below:

'Alive

Intelligent,

All-knowing,

All potential and possibility,

Constantly evolving/dynamic,

Ultimate provider

and a perfectionist

that moves from implicate to explicate, from unseen into the seen, from formless into form, from mind into reality, from energy into matter.

'Our passage to this intelligence lies in our thoughts. Our conscious thoughts or mind, impacts the subconscious mind which in turn is connected to the vast super conscious awareness. Now what does all this mean to you as a person? A few different things.

'Best options are the best kept secrets. This universal mind keeps from us the best options right up until the point where we're ready to plunge. A blind deal of sorts where big chances often lead to best consequences. It is a test of your faith in universe and its ability.

'The human mind will evaluate its options based upon human thinking, it can't go beyond what it already knows. It is a very limited pool of possibilities. We often force our own limits on the solutions, when we try to come up with a solution rather than allowing a solution to emerge.

'The truly great options, options that can transform our lives, the innovative solutions, the breakthrough realizations are not the ones we can think our way to, but rather the ones that are created in the universal intellect, perfectly synchronized, amazingly orchestrated and revealed to us when the moment is right. Someone out there already knows it.

'These might appear as an omen, an insight, a thought, a coincidence, a struggle, an accident. Who knows how they may come about, we just need to be prepared and receptive.

'We don't arrive at answers Maya; answers arrive in our life when we're ready to receive them. And only that which you could not have thought about, can take you to a place you could not have dreamt of being.'

'That is actually right!' Maya responded.

'So assuming life comes our way and we remain open, are we merely passive passengers in this journey?' asked Maya,

'Good question,' said Shankar. 'No, we are not.'

'We participate in this world through the power of our thoughts. Thoughts are the seeds of creation. The universal language, timeless as the soul itself. Language is often taught to a child, but he is not taught how to think...he's born with it.

'When you adopt a thought, you create a bundle of energy that is on a certain wavelength of frequency, your mind holds the power to squander it or to release it into this world with intention, a deep belief that then nurtures it to maturity and one fine day your paths cross again. It meets you in all its glory somewhere along the journey of your life and you hold it and say, "Look, we did it." When we move in alignment with nature's goals, and surrender to its flow, the current of life delivers you to your ocean.

'Well, Maya, try asking any person if they reached where they are in their life by exactly planning it such. You will be surprised. Life has a plan for those that have a plan. It also has a plan for those that have none. Einstein said, "God does not play dice with the universe." I guess, he knew what he was talking about.'

There was a riot of chatter that grew increasingly louder and a palpable excitement seemed to draw closer. 'There they come,' said Shankar. Soon after, the door of the tavern flung open and three happy women walked in with colourful shopping bags appearing visibly delighted.

'I can see it was a day well-spent,' said Shankar.

'Bapu Bazaar delivers nothing less,' said Maya sounding wise to the ways as she counted the bead of Universal truth.

Maya lay on her bed basking in her positive emotions. She picked up her phone and glanced at her picture again. Still as precious. She read the quote a few times over and said to herself, 'Maya now that you've taken your time and won't appear as desperate as you are, how about observing the basic courtesy and responding with a simple "Thank you" before the day is over?'

'Thank you,' typed Maya.

The reply was instantaneous, 'Anytime!'

It was followed by, 'Seems like you accidentally dropped your watch by the swing.'

Veer added, 'Any plans for this evening? Join us for dinner if you're available, I owe you the watch anyway.'

Maya thought about it for a moment and responded, 'No worries, I'm sure it's safe with you... Been quite a day, now I just want to hang out and take it easy.'

Veer responded, 'Totally understandable, I will come and drop it off at the reception and have it delivered it to your room.'

'Really!' Maya insisted, 'This is so unnecessary, please don't inconvenience yourself. It's not like I need it now.'

'Not an inconvenience at all. Have a good night,' texted Veer back.

Maya was waiting on the couch in the lobby, flipping through a magazine when Veer walked in. 'Hey Veer,' she called out, appearing relaxed in her lounge pants and flowing soft cotton tee, with no trace of make-up.

'Oh hi! Why are you waiting here? You didn't have to,' said Veer, looking surprised.

'You didn't have to either,' said Maya softly. 'But thank you. And now that you are here, how about a coffee or a drink? I could use some company.'

That was hard to argue.

'Absolutely. Whatever you prefer,' responded Veer.

Maya and Veer sat on the patio beneath the huge tree, as they sipped on coffee and music played on.

The dark blue sky was now pitch dark, and everything looked prettier in a soft romantic glow of string lights and lanterns hanging off the tree branches.

Maya was delightfully tickled by the thought of how seamlessly this man had slipped out of her dreams onto this chair in front of her.

'So Maya,' questioned Veer, 'have you lived in New York all your life?'

'You will find it interesting Veer,' she answered, 'but my recollection begins in Jaipur, this is where it all started.'

Slowly, Maya kept retreating deeper back in time and further along the journey from Jaipur, back to Jaipur. The starting, the summit, the vertical drop and the return, she held nothing back. She felt a sense of ease and connection that was hard to explain. She was speaking without filters, she was speaking her thoughts just as they streamed—raw and real, reassured that it was falling into trusted hands that would sift the chaff from the grain, blow away the dust and retain what really was worth keeping.

The typically tongue-tied Maya was eloquently flowing in her narration—she was honest, articulate, expressive, poignant and vivid.

Strangely, Veer or his mere presence, seemed to evoke in Maya what she herself hadn't quite realized. She was explaining it better to him than she had ever been able to explain to herself, reflecting upon her conclusions as she was arriving at them.

Veer exuded the same sense of comfort and non-judgement that could only come from family or a trusted friend.

She beamed at her thoughts which contained another question and a conclusion, 'Why do I feel like I'm sitting across from my girlfriend, and not the man of my dreams?'

She was further amused at her own inference. Projection of a dissociative identity disorder. She muttered softly, 'Hey Veer-2, you are such a great friend but soon I might ask you to leave and have the other Veer return instead. I am missing my silly Maya and the butterflies in her stomach. This is all too comfortable and one more thing, you can't share with him all that I just shared with you. It strictly stays between us.' She laughed. She was incurable.

Veer said, 'You look rather amused Maya, some secret joke?'

Of course, she thought to herself, *he's also blessed with mind reading skills or I'm cursed with emotion revealing ones.*

'No, nothing really,' she replied hoping her expressions would somewhat stand behind her words.

Before long, they were the only ones left on the patio as the last orders were taken. Veer stood up, 'I guess we should call it a night.'

She looked at him again, nothing had changed, but Maya felt a strange sense of liberation. He hadn't said much yet he had heard everything so patiently, and it is true that the way you listen determines what you will be told and there are those who hear you, those who listen and those who understand but Veer seemed to have understood the silence between her words.

As they walked along, Veer said, 'Maya never question yourself, many people would forever be stuck in the vain glory of a glittering life, if you were shallow enough, you would have complacently fit right in. It wasn't your glory that gave you pain but your depth that had to break through the shell. It had to breathe, it had to roam free, it had to sing in the rain—and look how it did!'

They exchanged a long silent look; it spoke volumes.

🍁

Upahaar—A Thought That Counts

'It is when you give of yourself that you truly give.'

—Kahlil Gibran

*M*AYA WAS AT THE SPA getting her hair blown out when her phone beeped.

Message read: 'Coming down for a few days. Polo match fundraiser this weekend. Will be fun to watch. See you then. Oh yes, btw staying with Veer, and Dadi insists on coming too, she's a huge fan of polo. Not surprising eh?'

Maya responded, 'Yaay! You just made my day. Correction, you just made my year. Get over here soon. I've been having withdrawal symptoms. Cannot wait.'

Pia texted, 'I figured as much, hence the plan;-)'

Maya was ecstatic. She wanted someone to share this news with. 'Ananda! I should go see him', decided Maya as she requested a car.

Maya found Ananda feeding the sheep. 'Hey Ananda! Maya screamed as she waved through the taxi window.'

'Maya Memsahib! How are you?'

'I'm well,' she said as she quickly stepped out of the taxi and paid the fare. She turned around with stars glittering in her eyes, 'Guess what? My friend Pia that I told you about will be here day after. Abhay and Dadi are coming as well. It will be fabulous. Ananda, I can't wait!!' said Maya, completely exhilarated.

Amma walked in with a glass of sweet lassi, 'What is all this excitement about?' she asked, handing the glass over. 'Pia my friend, and her family, they are coming to Jaipur,' explained Maya. 'That is wonderful!' smiled Amma.

'So then there is a chance we might not see much of you for a few days,' said Amma as she softly nudged Ananda.

'Well, since last time you left without notice, we have a few gifts for you that we might as well deliver today. We never let a guest leave empty-handed.'

'What gifts?' asked Maya. 'But I did not buy anything for you,' she said with an air of candidness.

'Maya, gifting is not a social act or a transaction. It need not be returned, just received gracefully. It need not be expensive, just thoughtful. A heartfelt compliment, a sincere wish, a flower, and a hug are all perfectly beautiful gifts.'

Ananda skipped with joy. 'Follow me this way for the first one.'

'First one?' questioned Maya. 'Yes, from Baba, come this way,' indicated Ananda.

They walked together into the shed. In the middle of the vast room, where Maya had first learnt her lesson through the art of carving, stood a table. On top of it rested what seemed to be a sculpture of some sort covered under a sheer pink fabric. 'Ta-Da!' chimed Ananda as he pointed his hands towards the sculpture.

'What is this?' asked Maya in wonder.

'Father carved this—especially for you. He also spent many hours explaining to me the significance of this sculpture.' He said, "This one gift will sum up everything Memsahib has learnt and everything she ever needs to know." It was the most comprehensive symbol he could share with you that will guide you throughout the journey of your life. Go ahead, this is for you.'

Maya slowly unveiled the sculpture to reveal a stunning image of Nataraja. It was large and intricately carved. The sheer serenity of it left Maya speechless. It spoke volumes in its very still depiction. She gazed at it in admiration, and uttered 'This is out of this world Ananda, simply magnificent.'

'Well,' said Ananda, 'this is not an ordinary sculpture. You will not truly comprehend it until you understand its significance. So listen.

'This is called Nataraja, which, literally translated, stands for "King of Dance". As Nataraja, Shiva embodies both the apocalypse and creation as he performs the two dances of life— "Lasya", the gentle dance of bliss and creation and "Tandava", the violent dance of destruction.

'This image is a symbolic depiction of Shiva. He stands within a circle which symbolizes cosmic cycles of creation and annihilation—rhythmic pattern of birth, life and death that goes on indefinitely.

'Surrounding the circle is a ring of flames—the universe, encapsulated cosmos of matter, time and space that produces pain and suffering.

'Shiva is depicted with four arms indicating the four cardinal directions.

'In one hand, he holds a damaru which depicts the eternal sound of creation and the consistent passage of time. In the right hand, he holds fire or agni, depicting the flames of destruction that annihilate all that the sound of damaru brings into existence.

'This lower right hand depicts the Abhay Mudra (fearlessness) directing us to remain fearless in staying true to our course. And, the lower left hand points towards the left foot which is raised in upliftment and grace, indicating the way through the forest of ignorance.

'Shiva's matted locks like that of an ascetic or a yogi, whirl around spreading into space, indicating contemplation as the path.

'And then the crux of this symbol, Shiva's right foot is firmly planted on the back of the demon called Apasmara, the embodiment of sloth, illusion, and forgetfulness. His right leg is raised, representing victory over the demon and freedom from the enthralls of Maya, attained by breaking the ego or the self, represented by the demon. This upliftment is comparable to the releasing of the mature soul from this bondage.

'The most interesting aspect Memsahib, is that through all this chaos of creation and destruction, suffering and release, illusion and enlightenment, Shiva depicts a sense of tranquility within. His calm stoic expression balances the vigorous activity around him.

'Baba says that Nataraja's dance is not just a symbol. The dance is taking place within each one of us, this very moment. The centre of movement is depicted to be the heart where the dance and the dancer merge into one another, Shiva becomes one with his creation.

'Baba has studied this in great detail. One time, a hotel

guest told Baba that the Nataraja is well-known and respected as a symbol, not just in India, but the world over. He told him that a famous French sculptor Auguste Rodin, I believe was his name, wrote that the Shiva Nataraja has "what many people cannot see—the unknown depths, the core of life. There is grace in elegance, but beyond grace there is perfection."

'Such,' stated Ananda, 'is the Nataraja, an image worth a thousand words.'

Maya walked up to it softly, as dust particles scattered through the sunlit room. Maya extended her hand and touched it, trying to decipher all the meaning and lessons it held.

'This truly is the most beautiful and most thoughtful gift I have received in my life Ananda,' said Maya. 'I will cherish it deeply and it will never let me forget the lessons I have learnt here in this amazing land.'

Ananda stepped forward, 'I will wrap this up for you,' he said as he stepped on a stool to gather newspapers collected on top of the shelf.

'I don't know how I can ever thank Baba for all his hard work, effort and love,' said Maya.

Ananada expressed, 'One, you can either thank him or you can call him Baba, you can't do both. Two, if you still feel a compelling need to thank him, make a promise to remain fearless and happy as you dance with life. Nataraja is the witness here, he will remind you of this pact,' he laughed.

Amma stood by the door silently watching over them. She walked in with a box in her hand, 'This, Maya, is my humble gift for you,' she said, handing it over to her.

'And now what is this?' asked Maya.

'A treasure box,' answered Amma.

It depicted a beautiful image of a woman holding a sitar walking away into the woods with a doe following. On the inside of the lid was a mirror carved around the edges with ornate details.

'This is quite a famous artifact from Jaipur. These artists use gemstones like pearl, onyx, emerald and agate to create this art called gemstone painting,' elaborated Amma.

'It is beautiful,' she said as Maya stepped forward to give Amma an affectionate hug. 'I really will treasure this treasure box.'

Amma said, 'It is warm in here, why don't you sit outside while I bring you some sharbat?' They sat in the open courtyard as Amma prepared lemonade, and poured it from one glass into another like a perfectly contained waterfall.

As they sipped on the chilled lemonade, Amma reached out to the box once again.

'Maya, this box also holds a message for you. I thought you will remember it each time you use it.'

'What message Amma?'

'Go ahead, open the box, you will find it in there.'

Maya excitedly flipped the box open. 'I see delicate carving and a beautiful mirror, other than that it is empty, I don't see any message.'

'And what do you see in the mirror, Maya?'

'I see myself.'

'Correct. This empty treasure box contains your reflection. Always remember, you are your greatest treasure. And what is empty is also full of potential. This empty treasure box contains the potential and the possibility of your greatest self.'

'Amma wait!' paused Maya as she dug in her bag for that last bead. She carefully placed it inside the treasure box and said, 'And there goes the last bead of Potential Truth. Now tell me what this treasured bead of potential truth holds for me?'

'It holds the truth of your best possibility. You do not see it today but it is there, you are holding it in your hands right now. This empty treasure box contains your life, that is waiting to be lived.

'It contains the power of dreams. You must be thinking what Amma could possibly know about the power of dreams.'

'No, It's not that at all Amma,' clarified Maya.

'Maya, many years ago, UNICEF organized a roadshow across sixty-four rural villages in Rajasthan screening a documentary titled "Girl Stars". It was the story of three women who held an unconventional dream and despite all odds managed to realize it. I watched it in admiration alongside nearly 300 villagers who could relate to these constraints and the struggles, which we all faced but these girls were different. They weren't looking at what stood in front of them, they were looking at what stood on the other side of their challenges.

'Maya, that day I learnt something—dreams remain dreams until someone starts believing in them, and turns them into a reality.

'Anuradha, one of the three, was a girl to begin with, disadvantaged in means, and impacted by polio, yet it could not debilitate her spirit. She somehow managed to put herself through education with a goal to become a doctor. She could have been held back by her limitations, by her challenges, by the orthodox mindset but she tapped into this limitless potential and manifested it.'

'Amma, this is both commendable and inspiring.'

'Maya, it may not sound like much, we hear about greater

achievements, but those, we believe belong in another world. We tell ourselves only if we had the means and the circumstances… but these girls…they were one of us, they left us with no excuse.

'That documentary inspired me and I concluded that the reality we start believing in becomes unlimited, potentiality, caged and confined.

'I cannot read fluently yet, although I have recently enrolled in the adult learning classes, but Ananda's Baba reads newspapers and often narrates to me stories of people who achieve astonishing feats all the time. Recently, he told me about a mother who lifted a car off her trapped child. And there was a dancer who defied gravity as she leaped in a movement of grace. A runner who broke what they believed was the human barrier of speed. What are these I wondered? Only a tiny glimpse of the vast potential within us. Why should we define the possible when life remains an unimaginable possibility?'

Maya looked up towards the bird resting on the tree branch. Soon it spread its wings and soared into the sunset. Her eyes followed its flight as her heart whispered, 'Maya, set yourself free, hear the song of your soul, it invites you to the swaying winds of change.

'Dare to dream once more…and this time offer it wings. Let it soar as far as it may reach, and then freeze it, right there, at the pinnacle, at the helm of its brilliance. Look at it often. Look at it enough. Extend yourself and take a step forward. Touch it, hold it, lend it a hand and pull it into the world of your reality.'

Maya felt reassured as she said, 'Thank you Amma. I will take care of both this box and my treasure.'

Ananda stepped forward and handed her a blue velvet pouch.

'And now what is this Ananda?' asked Maya, overwhelmed with gratitude.

'My promise, our introduction—the pebbles,' he laughed.

'Of course,' said Maya. 'How can I forget that?'

'These pebbles will help you in arriving at answers when the noise around you is too loud to decode the subtle messages.'

'How does that work Ananda?'

'It is simple Memsahib. I have formed a relationship with water, it talks to me. When I need a clear answer to a question or I'm in a dilemma, I simply go to a still body of water, ask my question out loud and urge the water to reveal the answer to me.

'I throw a pebble, sometimes even three, and observe the ripples as they form. An odd number of ripples indicates a yes and an even number means no. Also, the speed and the distance between the ripples holds meaning, indicating delays and obstructions or quick and fast results but you start to comprehend those gradually over time.'

'Hold on to these pebbles,' said Ananda, 'and when you really need to hear the answers, toss these in the water and count.'

Maya was deeply touched and greatly moved. She thought about the art of gifting, and what an inadequate introduction she'd had to it all along. In a time of click and share, gifts were synonymous with brand, monetary value, convenience and entertainment appeal. However, these gifts were neither lavish, nor instantaneous. These were personal, thoughtful expressions that contained a part of both the giver and the receiver.

Amma was right when she said that a gift need not be something expensive but it must be something that enriches your life.

Maya collected her gifts, and bid them goodbye.

As she drove back to the hotel, Maya opened the treasure box and stared at the emptiness within. *What possibilities did it hold for her?* she wondered.

The Grand Reunion

'Each friend represents a world in us, a world not born until they arrive, and it is only by this meeting that a new world is born.'

–Anaïs Nin

Maya's phone rang. It was a little past noon, on a clear sunny day. 'Almost there,' came an excited voice from the other end of the phone. 'We will pick you up in 15 minutes, will have lunch together at Veer's. See you in a bit.' Maya was ready and waiting by the front lobby when the gleaming Mercedes-Benz S-Class pulled up. Dadi's window was rolled down and she waved her hands vigorously. Maya was sure she would open the door and jump off the car if it did not come to a halt soon enough. Maya ran towards them and hugged Dadi. Pia was next, and then came Abhay's turn.

'All set?' came the crisp question from Abhay.

'As always,' was the swift reply.

As they approached Veer's mansion, both Dadi and Pia looked on in wonderment.

'How incredibly exquisite,' cried Pia.

'So majestic and regal. It seems to be a historical landmark,' added Dadi.

'Well, it was built in 1924 by Veer's great-grandfather,' said Abhay in introduction to this majestic mansion.

'He wanted to leave a legacy for the generations to come. Veer's grandfather too was quite the man with his fleet of vintage cars and private jets. You will enjoy touring his collection. Let me warn you though, Veer is a very private and humble person, you will really need to dig and implore him before he will share any of this with you guys. He would much rather talk about his great library and his lofty social goals,' joked Abhay.

'I have heard all about it,' said Maya.

Both Pia and Dadi's heads turned instantaneously in her direction with big question marks on their faces.

'When? Where? How?'

'Well, I was here the day before,' admitted Maya.

And the two heads swung briefly towards each other before returning right back to Maya.

Before they could get to the bottom of this subject, they were dropped off by the front door. One of the drivers ran up to take the keys from Abhay to park the car. Pia stepped closer to Maya and whispered in her ear. 'I need to hear all about it. No details spared.'

Maya assured, 'Of course I would have, anyway.'

By the main door stood Dadisa and Veer. Dadi's eyes narrowed as she pushed Pia aside and walked up the steps, constantly staring at Dadisa. Everyone seemed a little taken aback at her reaction.

Eventually, she stood face-to-face with her in an unusually

close stance, as she leaned in even closer. 'SAADI?' she questioned.

'MEERU?' came the reply.

They hugged each other tight and mumbled words that were hard to understand. It seemed like a blend of love and blabber, laughter and tears all the same. Everyone stood awfully quiet, both surprised and pleased at the fortunate turn of events. What are the odds of events leading to something like this?

After their BFF and 'forever together' hugs, the two women turned around, Dadi's hand extending behind Dadisa's shoulder as she announced, 'Santiniketan. Both of us. Best friends.'

Everyone broke out into a cheer and applause.

'We didn't have Twitter and Facebook to keep us connected,' she continued, 'we exchanged letters for a while, which turned around in thirty days if we were lucky. And then I left for Switzerland abruptly,' explained Dadi.

Dadisa added, 'I wrote quite a few letters after that but there was no reply. I assumed you moved, were married or dead,' she laughed.

'I remember,' said Dadisa, 'my sacrosanct trips to the stationery store, the shopping spree that consisted of rare and pretty writing pads with matching envelopes. Each day between 11 a.m. and 1 p.m., I would visit the mailbox approximately five times. And then our old postman in his khakhi uniform and matching cap would appear on the horizon waving his hand indicating no mail,' she recollected fondly.

'And we meet here today, after what, well over sixty years?'

'Those were the days!' said Dadi.

'Come inside first,' insisted Dadisa. 'We have so much to talk about.'

Everyone appeared pleased to witness this aspect of their grandmothers. It was a joy to watch them let go and be essentially themselves, in light of a history they shared, made richer perhaps by many secrets that lay buried within their hearts.

Dadisa seemed obviously fired up, running in and out of the kitchen with last-minute instructions and menu changes. Soon it was time for lunch. The lunch was served in the formal twenty-seater dining room which hosted a grand teak wood table, perfectly laid with silver platters and elegant cutlery, that shone brighter under the crystal chandelier. The glasses were engraved with some kind of a personalized seal. Maya couldn't make sense of it but it was a treat to the eyes nonetheless.

Small talks and loud laughter surrounded the strange setting of friends across ages, genders and connections. There was Dadisa and Daadi, Maya and Pia and Abhay and Veer and then there was Abhay and Pia and, oh well, it was complicatedly perfect.

That evening, the tea was served in a vintage musical tea set that Maya was absolutely fascinated by. 'This is my outright favourite,' she said. 'It is mine as well,' said Dadisa as she continued to pour tea while the soft music lasted to the unwinding of the key.

'Santiniketan was another world,' recalled Dadi fondly, putting her tea cup down. 'Initially I was hesitant to go there, but my father who was an avid believer in Bhramo Samaj and had great respect for the Tagore values, insisted it would be more than an academic experience. And it was!'

'Brahmo Samaj?' asked Pia.

'Brahmo Samaj was a renaissance of Hindu religion that

believed in Brahman or one eternal, ultimate reality of this universe. It came together as a community of like-minded people who did not discriminate on the basis of caste, creed or religion. You must read about it when you have some time to spare,' suggested Dadi as she continued on.

'Well, Santiniketan, defined literally as an abode of peace, indeed was every bit so. With groves of shaded trees, colourful red sand and tiny sparkling streams, it was paradise on earth. We climbed trees, fought with boys, rode bikes, swam and even did physical work around the ashram. It made us stronger, more confident individuals, ones who related to themselves as human beings before defining themselves as women.

'There were a lot of conflicting opinions and controversial assumptions. Some were dismissive of this concept as a place for dreamers with low intellectual goals. However, what we actually found was that this place developed all our faculties including our intellect, in a manner that far exceeded any academic standards. We were bright and ambitious yet we celebrated life as if it were a festival.'

Dadisa added, 'You know Maya, that day when I saw you swinging in the rain. It took me right back to Santiniketan where each time it rained, it was celebrated by taking a walk outdoors, barefooted and without umbrellas. We often studied in natural light under the shade of dancing trees, free to follow the wanderings of our heart. As a result, self-discipline rather than enforced rules got woven into the fabric of our very being.'

Dadi continued, 'We were like one large family. Gurudev's legacy of emphasis on each one being true to their own self and in tune with nature was deeply ingrained. Unlike many other platforms, he valued the creative spirit within each one of us. He believed, "The main object of teaching is not to explain meanings, but to knock at the door of the mind, for what happens within is much bigger than what we can express in words."

'It wasn't just a place where people dreamed on the sly, it was a place where dreams were encouraged and pursued. It was not a cage designed to replicate success, it was a stage created to display your wonder.

'One of our teachers there would often say that excessive dependence on knowledge can be a dangerous thing, it is reflective of what was, and is already known. If we focus too much on it, it will displace our natural intelligence and curiosity which contains the future, the possibilities, the creating, the experimenting and the inventing. If the cup is too full, there is no room for more.

'He was so right. As children, we believe in this intelligence and question the norm—"but I'm not sleepy, but I'm not hungry, but I want to play." Unfortunately, as well-meaning parents, we sweep their intelligence under the garb of discipline. We trade intelligence for obedience and teach them that the answer to all their questions is "because we say so" or "because that's how it's done."

'Somewhere we remain fearful of where their intelligence might lead them, what if they grow up to be different? What if they go wrong?

'We prefer order and safety of the tried and tested, we want them be like everyone else, to not talk about big dreams and unknown possibilities. As parents, we hand them a future and deny them a life. We provide them answers to the point where questions become irrelevant.

'Slowly the child stops questioning and starts accepting.

Instead of looking for answers within he starts seeking them outside.

'This situation offers safety and conformity on the surface but underneath the repression continues to manifest itself in forms like pain, anger, frustration, hatred, jealousy and emotional troubles. So we are led to counsellors, therapists, medicine and conflicts.

'Sadly, once again, we are containing the symptoms and not the problem.

'Gurudev recognized this way ahead of its time and created Santiniken on the premise of this powerful thought—let nature be the guide.'

Dadisa added, 'As much as it connected us with the vastness of nature, it also brought us in close touch with our roots. It made us value our inheritance, it gave us a foundation in our tradition that we bring to our families in principles we lived by.

'Meeru or Meera as you may know her,' said Dadisa pointing towards Pia's grandmother, 'loved to play instruments, write her songs and perform on them.'

'Oh, so that's where the love for music goes back to!' Pia observed.

'Certainly!' affirmed Dadisa, 'And she was brilliant at it.'

'And, Sadhana as you may know her,' revealed Dadi as she chuckled, 'detested her name, and so we came to call her Saadi, which means simple, or joyful, and it also happened to be the name of a famous Persian poet, and that fact, she took great pride in stating.'

'My father,' clarified Dadisa 'was very involved with Tagore's works, and his favourite book besides *Geetanjali* was *Sadhana—The Realization of Life*. So when I was born, I was named Sadhana.

I always saw the book in that name and never myself. Until of course much later, when I did get to read the book and came to deeply admire the name I had been given.'

'Saadi was fascinated with art. Being at Santiniketan, we bore a personal association with Bengal school of art. Abanindranath Tagore, Gurudev's nephew, or Aban Thakur as we knew of him was a believer of Swadeshi movement in Indian art forms. He stood up for modernization of Rajput and Mughal art as opposed to the Western influence that seemed to be engulfing the traditional art scene like a wild fire in the woods. She was especially enamoured by his depiction of his famous patriotic artwork "Bharat Mata" on canvas. We were certain she would either take to art or a patriotic mission if it wasn't for her love of theatre that saved her,' said Dadi breaking into a boisterous laughter.

'We jokingly referred to her as the drama queen. Santiniketan had a rich heritage in theatrics given that most of Gurudev's plays were written there. The students during our times wrote, directed an acted in these plays. Saadi, of course, was always in lead.'

'It is interesting to see that back in the day there was such a huge emphasis on performing arts. It is rare even in this day and age,' said Abhay.

'Yes, he was a true visionary. He believed education was more than knowledge. Satyajit Ray, Indira Gandhi, Gayatri Devi, Amartya Sen—look at the brilliance that was created. Not to mention the two amazing women who sit in front of you,' Dadi laughed.

'I can see clearly where Veer's love for Tagore's poetry comes from,' said Maya.

'Yes, his words are a staple in this household,' added Dadisa.

'Remember the "Basant Utsava!" It was the highlight of the year,' exclaimed Dadisa.

'Utsava,' repeated Maya, 'I heard this word the other day—Veer mentioned that you celebrate Utsava here when it rains.'

'Beta, Utsava simply stands for the convergence of two words "Ut"—removal and "Sava"—negativity or grief. So Utsava is any celebration that drives negativity away and welcomes joy. In fact, Gurudev started the tradition of Basant Utsava celebration at Santiniketan to welcome spring with songs, dances and abeer or colours that people smeared on each other, restoring this forgotten Aryan festival to its former glory.'

'Essentially, life itself was a celebration there. The very mention of it takes me down the road of nostalgia,' said Dadisa.

Chit-chat continued, and the evening came upon. Tea transitioned into wine, musical tea set was replaced with shiny flutes, tea cozies with ice buckets and the party moved from front porch to the poolside in the backyard.

'This calls for a real celebration,' declared Dadi. 'Pia, arrange for a bottle of champagne and I know this is not my house but I can treat it my own by virtue of my friend and all the intertwined relationships going on in here. I can't even factor who's related to who and what came first—chicken or the egg,' she stated speaking as fast as ever with visible signs of extreme euphoria.

The pool with its cascading waterfall was beautifully lit up and so was the palatial house.

Dadi ordered Pia to run upstairs and fetch her portable Bose bluetooth wireless speaker.

'I travel with my technology and my music,' she said

sounding fascinated with her own self. Music came on.

'This was your song, Saadi,' Dadi chuckled.

Dadi's retro playlist started to permeate the air.

Pia, Abhay, Maya and Veer converged by the other end of the pool. Suddenly the quiet of the night was broken by a blaring song. All four of them turned around instantly.

It was Dadi and Dadisa, with sarees pulled up just above the ankles and tucked around the waist. Soon, they were swaying and swirling to the timeless Bollywood classic, 'Aaj Phir Jeene Ki Tammana Hai'. Household help peeked from the kitchen windows and rooftop terrace. They had never remotely heard of something like this, let alone witness it.

These two women were graceful, elegant and on fire, but most of all, they were happy. Everyone clapped and cheered as they finished their performance breathlessly and bowed down to touch the ground and then their ears. Thunderous applause followed.

Veer was deeply indebted to this moment for allowing him to witness this unfiltered look of joy on his grandmother's face. In his eyes, Dadisa had been the lady who had consistently replaced her dreams with his, every step of the way. And it didn't end at him, everything in her life was about others. Yet, she was always grateful and always smiling. Today was the first day in all the years that Veer could recall, he saw a reflection, an identity of a woman in her own right expressing her personal joy and he appreciated it very much.

Following a delicious finger-licking good meal, Veer invited Maya, Abhay and Pia for coffee in his study.

'I should be heading out now,' said Maya.

Pia resisted, 'Stay a little longer. It's not every day that we get together like this. Besides, it is not like you have starving kids waiting for you to get back home.'

'Come on Maya,' said Abhay.

Veer just smiled with his eyes, and it was enough to melt Maya into a puddle.

'Alright,' said Maya playing along as they made their way up to the magnificent library. It was every book lover's dream. Covered in books from floor to ceiling, the commanding bookcase with a tall ladder leaning against it stood majestically in the warm glow of the wooden fireplace. 'Too bad we live in the middle of a desert, but a study would be incomplete without it,' said Veer, pointing towards the fireplace.

Maya was mesmerized. She walked up to the books and brushed her fingers lightly over them. 'How did you even create this colossal wonder?' she questioned.

'One book at a time,' came the reply.

'It's the labour of love,' he smiled as he leaned against the bookshelf with a slightly tilted head, signature smile and deep hypnotic eyes that seemed to drown Maya in their bottomless depths.

Maya instinctively broke away from the unbearable gaze to stare at her manicured feet while trying to keep her palpable heartbeat in check.

The silent awkward moment was broken by the loud laughter of Dadi and Dadisa.

'Here you guys are. We did not even realize when you left.'

Maya quickly pulled out a book and joined Pia on the cherry-coloured chesterfield couch trying to appear distracted.

On the other side of the wall behind the desk was a glass window overlooking the hills that now glittered under the moonlight. Maya and Veer exchanged a few accidental glances through the huge mirror that hung on the mantel above the fireplace.

It was a silent conversation that was certainly progressing.

Abhay said, 'Pia, I hope you get some of your Dadi's traits. At least the art of happiness. It would be a great asset to pass along to our next generation.'

Pia tapped him. 'Do you doubt that?'

'I can vouch for that,' supported Maya.

'You tell us Dadi and Dadisa—what do you think of the art of happiness having lived such fulfilled and selfless lives?' asked Abhay

'Abhay let me tell you,' said Dadi, 'happiness is both an art and a craft.'

'Silly as it may sound, what really is the difference?' wondered Pia.

'Art is an open-ended, unstructured expression driven by emotions. Craft, in addition to being an art, requires a skill, a technique that is learnt, practised and improved. It can be quantified and duplicated.

'Having said that, happiness is not so much a state of affairs but a state of mind. It is not the result of fulfilment, but a precondition to it. You will find it scattered along the journey, not gathered at some final destination. It is not an outcome, simply a decision, it is not a chance but a choice, it is not a creation but a recognition.

'And laughter is a good aid to acquire this skill. Lighten up, laugh often, sometimes at your own self and sometimes at life. It isn't meant to be taken so seriously, it takes care of itself.

'We all deserve happiness, Dadi, but sometimes you just

end up with wrong people and in bad situations,' sighed Maya. 'It can be quite challenging.'

'Correction Maya,' prompted Dadi.

'We don't deserve happiness, we choose happiness.'

'Happiness is not an entitlement; it is a responsibility. It is there within you and you are responsible for allowing it or denying it. Don't expect other to create happiness, because they can't. Your happiness is not in their hands. They can create experiences but not happiness.

'Happiness is not the absence of problems either. It's a decision to be...regardless of what is or is not. Happiness can be found among people who are hungry, naked and homeless, sitting tired after a long day's work in the chill of winter, surrounding a little fire to keep them warm, and on the contrary, you'll find people driving the most expensive cars to a therapist's office. Don't look for reasons to be happy or situations to justify it. Joy is the best reason and delivery is strictly your business.

'Besides, happiness without condition is a very precious thing. What comes out of nothing will remain because nothing cannot be taken away. However, when happiness stems from the outer dimensions in our life, it's always strained with the fear of losing the condition that we base it upon. Our happiness is always in the grip of fear and insecurity, what if the person is no longer there in our lives, what if we lose our riches tomorrow.

'However intrinsic and unconditional happiness is at peace with itself, it's not fearful, it's not agitated, it's not on the guard against losing its source, it becomes its own perennial source and flows endlessly.' To distract her own mind that was still hovering around Veer and to sound engaged in the conversation, Maya added, 'So what you're suggesting is that if happiness does not lie in people, possessions or situations, maybe it does not lie outside at all?'

'Exactly. If people get this one idea, they can spare themselves from so much unnecessary suffering,' confirmed Dadi.

'And this one idea being?' enquired Maya.

'Happiness lies within us but is often projected outwards by our mind.'

'We transfer it from within us and direct it onto a situation or possession that appeals to us. We create an idea of happiness outside us by our thoughts, judgements and feelings. When we say this person makes me happy...in essence we allow this person to make us happy by directing our thoughts and projections positively towards him.'

'I love chocolates,' said Dadi 'I project the happiness I will derive from eating it on to a bar of chocolate, so it brings me happiness. I might repeat it for the second one, however I might be struggling already for the third one, and what do you think happens by the time I'm on to my tenth bar of chocolate? I am disgusted. Now, what changed about the chocolate? Nothing. My projection of happiness? It was wiped out.

'We transmit from within this idea of happiness on to objects that simply reflect it back to us. Not realizing this to be the case, we grab the objects in a quest to capture happiness but happiness eludes us because it never was in the objects...the object was simply reflecting it.

'Similarly, relationships bring us so much pain, people claim that people change. What if instead of observing the reality of another person, you were building on top of it, making him appear larger than life. You lost your sense of objectivity, you denied the shortcomings and when that awe faded away, the coloured glasses became clear! The projection was gone and the reality was now visible, but instead of blaming yourself you started blaming your partner, you kept feeling that they changed! Now that may be entirely possible, but it also might be that simply your perspective changed, and the inflated projections readjusted closer to reality.

'And remember, the amount of happiness we receive from something is directly proportional to how much value we attribute to it. Value again is never intrinsic, we attach it to things. A master once noted that humans will chase after diamonds but a dog treasures a bone above all else.

'And my two cents on relationships, since you all are just starting out and could possibly use our experience,' said Dadisa, 'Relationships need space to grow. Togetherness is two people coming together to create something better than what was, it's a synergy. However, most of the time togetherness is misinterpreted to mean giving oneself up. Two wholes can compound quickly but two halves will struggle all their lives to barely make a whole.'

'To let others be, is the greatest gift of love. When you can allow someone to shine in their natural light, to be what they are rather than what you want them to be, you enable a relationship to flourish. A relationship which destroys your freedom becomes a prison.'

'Wow, that is quite an insight. I never thought of it in those terms,' said Pia.

'Abhay, I hope you heard it loud and clear,' she giggled.

'Point taken Ma'am,' confirmed Abhay.

Dadi concluded, 'So all my children who are gathered here today listening to us old women blabber away, may you always find your happiness within you and carry it wherever you go.'

Pia gave her a big hug. 'I'm so proud of you Dadi.'

'Stop stealing my lines Pia,' she lovingly grumbled.

'Dadisa, now is there a lesson you would like to share?' asked Abhay.

She spoke in her usual soft and graceful stance.

'Lessons will come as they have for all of us, in time...we certainly learn and eventually grow but what is required of us, the parents, is simply the unconditional love and immense belief in our children which will seep through every fibre of their being both as a cement and the cushion that will enable them to withstand and absorb every pain and each lesson when it arrives.'

'But you did sacrifice so much to make Veer successful,' suggested Pia.

'Pia, there is a difference between sacrificing and giving. You choose to give when you feel abundant and overflowing. When you sacrifice, you believe that you must give up something to enable someone else to have it. The underlying belief is that of scarcity and limitation, and you sacrifice because it seems noble or right but within, you feel empty, it builds up resentment. While giving fills up your life with immeasurable joy.'

'What I gave to him came back to enrich my own life.'

'Pretty much true!' added Maya.

The conversations continued, moving on lighter notes.

The large mirror that hung silently on the wall seemed to capture more than just the conversations and more than just their reflections, it was both the audible messenger and the silent witness.

Maya fumbled as their eyes collided yet again. Veer looked

on intently. He put down his cup and picked up a book off the coffee table while everyone was in the thick of animated talks about life and happiness. He sifted through the pages, and moved the bookmark around.

Casually, he stood up and walked over to the dimmer to soften the bright lights. On his way back, he placed the book that he held in his hand on the end table next to Maya and softly tapped on it before returning to the conversation.

Maya pretended not to notice. But in a few moments, her hands made their way to the table as she picked up the book, her eyes on Dadi all this while. It was a book of Ghalib's poetry. Slowly, she opened the bookmarked page which read:

'Hum to fanaa ho gaye unki aankhen dekh kar ghalib, na jaane who aaina kaise dekhte honge.'

Maya was hesitant to acknowledge and wasn't sure if she had turned to the right page or if this really was meant for her. His ambiguity and mystery were as appealing as frustrating, once again.

There was something brewing, Maya was certain, but what and to which extent, she couldn't tell. She wanted to shake him by his shoulders and get him to just say it outright, clear and loud, if there was anything at all that he wanted to say. Perhaps he was just flirting and she was starting to read too far into it. She took a deep breath.

Veer lit up the lantern containing a white candle that rested on the coffee table and looking at Maya through the flame, Veer hummed softly before speaking aloud:

'Phir kuch ik dil ko bekaraari hai, seena zoya-e-zkham-e-kaari hai.'

(Once again my heart seems restless. This bruised heart of mine is yet longing, for another wound.)

There was a stunned silence followed by quick glances that travelled all over the room in every direction, each possible combination and permutation.

Abhay clapped and added:

'Fir kiya pyaar e jigar ne sawaal. Ek fariyaad-o-aah-ozaaree hai.'

(Again, my heart in love cries out a question, the pleading for an answer and the sigh is released once more.)

Maya responded as she bowed her head:

'Phir usi bewaffa pe marte hain, phir wahi zindagi hamaari hai.'

(Once again I've fallen for the same indifferent lover, and the story of my life repeats, yet again.)

Dadi added:

'Bekhudi besabab nahin ghalib, kuch to hai jiske parda daari hai.'

(This ecstasy isn't without a reason, Ghalib! Surely there is something that is being concealed behind the veil.)

'Wow, I love Ghalib.' Dadi exclaimed, 'Perfect ending to a great evening...'

Maya blushed, 'But it seems like we are all forgetting about the big polo match tomorrow. I must get back so I can return again,' she said with her beautiful smile.

Veer stood up, 'Let me drive you back.'

Abhay engaged in a conversation with him as they proceeded.

Pia cleared her throat and nudged Maya, whispering, 'Good luck with that. I hope you will return tomorrow,' she said with a wink.

Maya whispered back, 'Let your overactive imagination rest, it's pointless, Pia. He is so in control all the time, the wise old soul that he is. I can never see what is going on in his mind. Not even a peek. And I stand before him like an open book that he flips through and reads to his heart's content. I don't think there is much if anything at all going on in his mind. It was just his love of poetry oozing out of him.'

Veer opened the door and Maya waved goodbye to the gang.

The moonlight was splendid as it scattered across the sleeping desert. The soft blue ambient lighting inside the car was just enough to create comfort. The radio played an old song that seemed to enhance the setting, if that was even possible. It was perfect, ethereal and out of this world. Maya wished and hoped that they would somehow miraculously get lost along these winding roads and never arrive at that wretched place where he must return her.

'You are awfully quiet,' said Veer.

'I let Pia do my share of talking,' she laughed as she blushed and felt her face flush just a little. 'Oh no, not again. Heaven help me!'

'Did you say something?' asked Veer in his deep, ever so sultry voice.

'Nope, just thinking out loud,' said Maya with a soft smile as she went back to fiddling with her hands and staring at her feet.

Maya's heart whispered as she caught a secret glimpse of Veer sitting beside her. *What an incredible feeling when life grants you something you'd hoped for but never believed in an unreasonable wish, an unrealistic dream...where logic knows you're asking for too much, where practicality knows it's too good to be true. Perhaps life understands the intensity of true desire much more than reason, possibility, practicality and logic...exactly why miracles exist!* She thought.

She looked up at the stars and smiled.

Veer rolled down the window as he spoke, 'I find this fascinating Maya, when the world falls asleep, silence comes awake, speaking volumes in its stillness.

'I have been a seeker all my life but as Hermann Hesse says,"I have ceased to question stars and books"...and a lot more. Sometimes I just seem to know the answers before the questions arrive...and then I don't second guess my choices.'

Maya looked at him with questioning eyes, 'Is it that easy?'

'Yes, it's that easy. After all, it need not be perfect, it just needs to be right.

'Perfection is an overrated ideal created by our imperfect minds. Look at nature—neither deliberated nor improvised, simply experienced...in all its glory. Everything being just where it belongs...just right.'

'Yes, that's true,' said Maya impatiently.

She fell silent again. She was waiting for him to say something more—perhaps something about her.

Before long, however, they were back at the hotel.

He opened the door for Maya and she stepped out. He

looked straight into her eyes, as if he somehow enjoyed the effect he had on her. He looked on, until her eyes fell to her feet and her hands trembled.

'It was a pleasure to have you over Maya. Thanks for joining us,' he said with a smile.

Maya simply nodded her head, as she tucked her hair behind her ear without lifting her eyes. 'Good night,' he said after a pause.

'Good night,' whispered Maya.

The car drove off and she stood still, waiting for her reactions and senses to return. Slowly, but surely, they did.

Maya called Pia right away.

'So?' questioned Pia.

'So what?' said Maya sounding frustrated.

'He talked about the beauty of silence, said it was nice to have me over and drove away.'

'Really? That's it?' asked Pia sounding disappointed.

'Yes, that's it. And I'm reconsidering my plans to attend the polo match tomorrow,' Maya giggled.

'Okay, speak to you in the morning,' she said and hung up.

As she stepped into the lobby, the manager walked over to Maya.

'Madam, there was a delivery for you. It has been sent to your room.'

'Delivery for me? I'm not expecting anything. Well thank you anyway,' she said.

Maya walked into her room and turned on the light, on a black stand stood a life-sized oil painted portrait of Maya in the rain. Head titled back, eyes shut, rain drops trickling down her face, as she wore an ecstatic smile on the upswing. On the table in front of it, was her favourite Henri Bendel "Vanilla Bean" candle, an exotic arrangement of white lilies and a bookmarked copy of Rumi's poetry book. Next to it was a pot of tea, and a pouch containing tea leaves. There was a note attached to the pouch: 'Hand-picked and shipped by your Siliguri tea estate manager.' Maya was speechless.

This was an expression every bit Maya, when she was convinced he didn't know her enough...

A handwritten note next to the portrait read:

'Beauty isn't created. It is. "If a piece of art calls out to me I bring it home," I had said. Why do I feel like this one belongs there? It seems just right. Not certain if the question has arrived yet, but I seem to know my answer. I look forward to seeing you tomorrow.'

Maya turned to the bookmarked page, it read:

'The minute I heard my first love story, I started looking for you, not knowing how blind that was. Lovers don't finally meet somewhere. They're in each other all along.'

A Return to the Beginning

'All that we see or seem is but
a dream within a dream.'

–Edgar Allan Poe

MAYA TOSSED AND TURNED IN bed. Her life was in high gear. Wisdom was flowing to her from all directions and the finest people were appearing into her life out of nowhere. The pace of this change was way too fast and most of everything taking place seemed too good to be true.

Did she have a reason to back up and slow down, perhaps to make sense of where she was heading?

A tiny voice whispered to her, 'When you let go of control, life takes over, remember you are riding on the current of life, don't disrupt it, don't try to alter the pace, you will meet your waterfalls, you will find your rapids and your plateaus, go along, allow it to deliver you to your ocean.'

Maya's thoughts then turned to Leela. Maybe she did not have much of a reason to worry about her situation but she owed Leela the six beads of truths she had discovered. Leela had asked her to return for the seventh one, one that would bring the remaining six together.

Where was she to find her? Maya drifted off to sleep.

It was a beautiful morning. Maya checked her phone, it had a message waiting.

'Be ready sharp at 9. Abhay is in the driver's seat, and you know what that means! Dadi, Dadisa and Veer will meet us there.'

'You bet,' Maya responded back.

Maya walked down the steps, caught up in adjusting her delicate white chiffon saree.

Pia ran out to meet her, 'OH MY GOD! Someone is dressed to kill today.'

She looked spellbinding in her large crescent shaped jhumkas and hair tied in a messy bun.

Abhay stepped out to greet her as well.

'My oh my, I can't help but be cheesy today. Watch as the moon descends to earth in broad daylight. Sun, you look pale in comparison, *Duniya main ghazab hai to yahin hai yahin hai yahin hai.*'

'What a drama!' laughed Pia as she continued, 'Abhay, at least be original in your appreciation. You stole the idea from Amir Khusrao who said, *"Gar Firdaus bar rue Zameen asto, Hameen asto, Hameen asto, hameen asto"*, meaning if there is paradise here on earth, it is here, it is here, it is here. And well, he was referring to Kashmir, not some woman.'

'Close enough, both are equally enchanting!'

'Well you get my point!' said Abhay, 'Madam, you look splendid.'

Pia announced, 'This calls for a selfie right here,' and they flashed happy grins to the sound of cheese.

They arrived at the polo grounds, Veer was already there waiting anxiously to see her after last night's surprise. They had neither spoken nor texted.

Interestingly, Veer was dressed in his white Sherwaani with hair pulled back into a sleek gelled look. His dark sunglasses looked handsome on his tall frame and prominently sharp nose. He reminded Maya of a blue-blooded prince, charming as always. Her heart skipped a beat...or two.

Abhay walked towards the entrance with Pia and Maya. Maya smiled, unsure of what to say yet her eyes expressed acceptance and appreciation for his thoughtful expression as she made a bold eye contact and bowed her head slightly. Veer could not take his eyes off her.

Just short of the entrance, Veer extended his hand to Maya and asked Abhay, 'May I?'

Abhay smiled, 'Of course!'

Maya blushed.

Pia nudged Abhay, 'Does he like her?'

'Shush,' dismissed Abhay, 'Let them figure it out, stop being the curious cat.'

They stood by the red carpet as bagpipers began to play their pipes. Rose petals showered on the guests as they walked across. Dadi and Dadisa were on the other end eager to receive them. As they approached closer, Dadisa instinctively reached out and kissed Maya on the forehead, took out a two-thousand-rupee note and spun it around their heads in delight. Maya couldn't quite make sense of what was going on.

'You look beautiful Maya and you both look lovely, I am just warding off the evil eye and blessing you with prosperity.'

Pia screamed in the back, 'It's almost official.'

Maya gave her the dirty look. 'Zip it!' she expressed. And so Pia did, although her excitement continued to spill out through her animated gestures!

Dadisa repeated the act with Abhay and Pia and so did Dadi.

Maya was still baffled. She did not know where the line blurred between custom, tradition, welcome and seal of approval. Veer after all still hadn't said anything.

They took their seats upfront on the white sofas next to the centre table that housed an enormous and beautiful fresh flower arrangement.

Announcements were made. The teams arrived. The players looked sharp in white Jodhpuris, pink and white polo shirts, brown leather boots and equestrian helmets.

The game progressed as did the social conversations. Players swung their mallets riding on black beauties and the crowd cheered. Veer seemed to know everyone around and graduated from one social conversation to another.

Maya hung out with Pia.

'And what is this supposed to mean?' questioned Maya.

'Not sure,' said Pia. 'I don't quite know what's going on either! But again, what do you have to worry about?'

'I don't have anything to worry about, but I just need to know,' said Maya.

Pia retorted, 'What happened to all the Zen lectures—let go of the need itself; find contentment. For god's sake, in your search for contentment, you have found a man who you could not have found even if you went searching through the world with a diya in your hand. I never knew contentment can come with bonuses and fat ones at that!'

'Pia, stop being mean,' said Maya as she laughed.

'Relax, enjoy what is happening; there is no urgency to predict. Be graceful in whatever happens,' said Pia.

'I guess you are right,' answered Maya.

'Coming back to polo, not sure if I ever mentioned to you, but my dad had a great love for horses, he was a very gifted polo player,' expressed Maya.

'Really?'

'Yes. He even named his niece Filly, of course people assumed, he would name the next in line Silly, so that was the end of his naming career!' she chuckled.

'From what I hear Maya, your dad appears to be quite a colourful personality,' said Pia.

'Yes, he painted, played polo, collected art and wrote poetry. He even wrote a couple for me.'

'That is so special Maya.'

'Yes Pia, I'm spoiled for his love or...the lack of it.'

'Come on, not anymore,' said Pia. 'We all love you and well, you might soon come to know yourself as Hukum Sahiba Maya Veer Pratap Singh. How's that for an introduction?' laughed Pia.

'Shut up!' dismissed Maya.

Maya knew she was in love, had always been with this man who had just shown up in her life. Veer turned around to acknowledge her with a smile ever so often during his social conversations.

The game grew more and more interesting as the end drew closer. The two teams were neck to neck and the audience was completely engaged. The game concluded with the Jaipur Polo Club in lead, taking the winner's cup home. The local crowd broke out in cheer and Dadi was in an ecstatic jubilation.

Veer was invited to speak. He was impressive, eloquent, charming, funny and genuinely human—all in all, a lethal combination. He spoke of service, community, giving back and its social impact with such fervour that he received a standing ovation from the crowd.

Maya was completely swept away, yet again.

Lunch was followed by a vintage car rally to Rambagh Palace.

Dadisa mentioned, 'This Rolls Royce is the same car that we have been bringing to this event for the last forty-nine years. It was quite the story that used to go around in these circles when we first bought it. It is said that Maharaja Jai Singh of Alwar was on a vacation in England. He was walking along Bond Street in his casual attire when he came across the Rolls Royce showroom and went in to enquire about the price. The discerning salesperson did not think much of him and passed him off for perhaps another ordinary Indian man. He was shown the way out.

'Upon reaching the hotel, Maharaja instructed his crew to inform the store that Maharaja of Alwar is there and would like to visit the showroom. He walked in once again, down the red carpet this time with all sales people waiting hand and foot upon him. The store had six cars in stock and he purchased all six, paid in cash, and arranged for them to be delivered to India. Upon arrival, he instructed the local municipality to use these cars for garbage collection.

'The word spread like wildfire, greatly hurting Rolls Royce's reputation as the world's leading luxury car meant for the discerning elite. Revenues started to plummet. When the management found out about the incident, they sent a telegram of apology to the Maharaja and offered him an additional six cars for free. Maharaja accepted the gesture of regret and recalled the luxury cars from their job of trash collection.'

She chuckled, 'Our Maharajas truly knew how to respond without reacting. They were brilliant at strategy.'

Veer held the door and Dadi and Dadisa sat down in the car as they drove off waving to the crowd.

Later that evening back at Veer's home, it was decided on demand by Dadi and Dadisa that the evening would be a tribute to their old times. They were to arrange for a vintage-style open-air movie night.

Torches were lit in the garden, crisp white sheets covered comfortable mattresses decorated with bolsters and cushions. A huge projector screen was displayed in front. The ambience was stunning with lanterns and trays of jasmine to lend an element of charm.

Ananda was included as an honorary guest of the evening. Soon after sunset, everyone arrived and took their seats in the garden. *Pakeezah* started to play as rounds of appetizers and drinks started flowing. Half an hour into the movie, there was a brief static followed by a sign, '*Rukavat ke liye khed hai*' (sorry for the interruption). A commotion followed, muddled with questions and complaints—'What happened, it was just starting to get interesting, call the electrician, this is not fun.'

And then it reverted to complete silence.

The lounge version of 'Aao Huzoor Tumko Sitaron Mein Le Chalein' (Come my dear, let me take you to the enchanted land of stars), started to play in the background.

A slideshow of pictures appeared on the giant projector, in the following order:

Maya, the baby
A birthday
A puppet show
A photo of SD-52 Ambabari
Her mom and dad
The family together
The first day of school
The prom
The graduation
College and doctorate
Friends and travels
Paris and Rome
Her first job
Her city apartment
A picture at the airport on the way to India
It was then followed by the questions:
What next?
Will you marry me?
Maya was startled as everyone broke into a cheer.

And then her mom appeared on the screen saying, 'Please say yes.'

Dadi appeared next with her message, 'Maya, say yes to love!'

Dadisa simply said, 'Jug jug jiyo, beti.'

And Ananda exclaimed, 'I told you your life was going to change!'

Pia said 'Yes' with a thumping of her fist.

Abhay's message said, 'Are you still thinking?'

Finally, Veer said, 'Will You?'

The messages were followed by her picture on the swing. Below it, the words appeared, 'And I promise to preserve this

Maya and her "Happily Ever Laughter".'

Maya could not stop the torrent of her tears, 'So it was a conspiracy, you all knew and mom...really, of all the people, she was involved! And Ananda you too. Pia, Abhay, Dadi, Dadisa?'

They all clapped looking at her in anticipation of a 'yes'.

Veer walked closer and looked her in the eyes, 'In case you have forgotten, I'm still waiting for my answer, so what do you say?'

'You have asked me this before, and I have answered you many a nights... Oh wait, but that was a passing dream...forever is a delight!' she cried uncontrollably.

She continued, 'By the way, you had me at hello. *Jerry Maguire*, of course! It was a yes, has always been a yes, and yes it is today. Yes again it will be tomorrow and for eternity, it will be that way. You know it too! I would like to finish the poem you had started,' said Maya as everyone cheered. She began the poem by Rabindranath Tagore:

'I seem to have loved you in numberless forms,
numberless times...
In life after life, in age after age, forever.
My spellbound heart has made and remade the necklace
of songs,
That you take as a gift, wear round your neck in your
many forms,
In life after life, in age after age, forever.

'Whenever I hear old chronicles of love, its age-old pain,
Its ancient tale of being apart or together.
As I stare on and on into the past, in the end you
emerge,

Clad in the light of a pole-star piercing the darkness of
time:
You become an image of what is remembered forever.

'You and I have floated here on the stream that brings
from the fount.
At the heart of time, love of one for another.
We have played along side millions of lovers, shared in
the same
Shy sweetness of meeting, the same distressful tears of
farewell-
Old love but in shapes that renew and renew forever.

'Today it is heaped at your feet, it has found its end in
you
The love of all man's days both past and forever:
Universal joy, universal sorrow, universal life.
The memories of all loves merging with this one love of
ours-
And the songs of every poet past and forever.

'And I mean it.'
Fireworks lit the sky and Abhay popped open a bottle of
champagne in celebration. Ananda was the ring bearer as he
walked in with the ring placed on a silver platter covered with
a red fabric.

'I have another surprise for you,' said Veer, 'look behind you.'
In walked Maya's mom with Bhua from Bikaner, Amma
and Baba.

Maya flung into her mom's arms, sobbing uncontrollably.
'I thought you nearly missed the best moment of my life. Not

sure what I have done to deserve this. I don't even know who to thank anymore.'

She hugged her Mom and Bhua and cried some more.

Dadi exclaimed, 'Crying is therapeutic too, it will help her get this shock out of her system.' Everyone laughed and the party continued...now as a family.

Maya stared at her ring into the wee hours of the morning. And interestingly, it reminded her of her promise to Leela. 'I must find her. Is she angry with me? Have I lost sight of my goals? Why wouldn't she call me? Could she be calling me and I've been too busy to hear her?'

Maya struggled with a vague sense of unease on what clearly had been the most momentous night of her entire life.

It was still only 4 a.m., and Mom was fast asleep. Maya sneaked out to take a walk and absorb everything that had just unfolded. The sky was still, the breeze was cool, birds were starting to arise and chirping, and the moon was high and clear.

'Was it really happening and was this really what she wanted?' she questioned.

She reasoned with herself. 'Getting cold feet and wedding jitters are emotions everyone deals with. I'm not the first one here. I'm sure it is all perfectly fine,' she asserted, staring at her ring again.

She walked out into the gardens and sat on the steps gazing at the diffused twilight sky. She whispered in desperation, 'May the wind be my messenger to you, Leela. Call me. We must meet soon.'

'Congratulations,' came a voice from behind her.

'Leela? Here? Now?'

'I told you, I will come find you,' said Leela in a loud voice.

Maya swiftly looked left and right to see if any guest or hotel staff was present. It was quiet and they were alone.

'Thank you,' said Maya, stumbling a little as she thought, *No she didn't just make herself appear on demand, maybe she planned it and she was here first, and then plotted a plan to call for me, and made me think of her and send her a message, as if I was the one directing it. Oh well, whatever it is, she's here and I need her. Desperately.*

'You're welcome,' said Leela. 'So you did find them, the beads of truth!'

Maya was surprised to learn that the congratulations had been in response to her meeting the teachers as opposed to finding her soulmate.

'And now that you have your six beads of truth that stand for:
The Whole Truth
The Material Truth
The Created Truth
The Real Truth
The Universal Truth
The Potential Truth,
I will give you the seventh one. The one that brings all of these together and is the bead of your truth.'

Leela reached into her bag and took out a bead. 'Here, string this one in the bracelet. This bead will set you free.'

Maya tried to talk, 'Leela, last night...'

'I know, Maya,' she interjected abruptly as she started to walk away. 'Congratulations, this bead will set you free.'

Maya stared at her long after she was gone, trying to make sense of what she was saying. She went back to her room, strung the bead in her bracelet and fiddled with it before passing into sleep again.

Maya had the dream once again. A little girl ran through the cobbled street alley under the bright sun and shimmering sand as she arrived at a blue door. She laughed, a laughter that reverberated in every direction. And then she paused and said, 'Thank you for coming home. I've been waiting for a long time.'

She unlocked the latch and invited her through, 'Maya, come inside.' As the little girl stepped over the threshold of the blue door, she transformed into little Maya as she was years ago, Maya of SD-52 Ambabari—innocent and happy. That little Maya of the past held grown-up Maya's hand after twenty-five years, and said, 'I'm happy I found you, I'm delighted you came. Did you see the flowers on the table? I bought these just for you. Sorry my hands are messy from the paint but the messier they are, the prettier they seem. Isn't it? Come see my creations. I painted a house on the golden sand under the brilliant blue sky. Look I even painted myself and the birds returning home.

'When I paint, it makes me so happy that I want to dance. You know how I dance? My paintbrush, my steps and my heart rise together. Look, let me show you how.'

The little girl spun around in delight and drew a circle on the canvas, filled it with colours and laughed blissfully, 'My heart is still dizzy from the dancing,' she laughed.

'What are you painting?' Maya questioned the little girl.

'I am painting a sun and I will colour it blue—it will be my indigo sun.'

'Do you remember what inspired you at Picasso's museum?' she asked Maya.

'Yes, I do, it was his quote that read, "There are painters who transform the sun to a yellow spot, but there are others who with the help of their art and their intelligence, transform a yellow spot into sun,"' Maya responded.

'Right,' said the little girl, 'and you promised yourself and said, "I will use not only my art, and my intelligence but also my imagination, and one day I will paint an indigo sun."'

Maya nodded as her eyes welled up at the recollection.

'Maya,' said the little Maya to the grown-up Maya, 'why are you crying? Don't you like my art?'

'I love it,' said Maya, 'I just didn't recognize it soon enough.'

'Don't cry,' said the little girl, 'I will show you everything. You will remember it all. Here, hold the brush and colour my sun.' And together, they painted.

The little girl held Maya's hand and they ran across the room that contained every image she had ever painted, and the ones she had wished to paint. And blissfully they laughed as the sun shone upon the blue door.

Maya was jolted awake. She looked at her beads. She then stared at her hands and her ring. She sat in a daze for a few moments and then she kissed her hands and the ring on it. 'Sorry,' she whispered, 'I kept you waiting too long.'

Maya opened her computer, and put in her resignation request. She sent an email to her supervisor that read, 'I am very thankful for all your guidance and support. However, I have come to realize that there is someone who is meant just for this work, who will do this better than I ever will. I need to make room for them so they can come and take this place, and I must fill in a space that awaits me.'

She then logged in and processed a rush order to print custom invitations. That afternoon, amidst the family gathering and the wedding planning, Maya excused herself to take care of some unfinished business.

She bought herself a bicycle, the one thing she missed about her city life. She purchased some fresh white lilies and went in to pick up her order. The sealed package said, 'Maya Memsahib.'

Inside, the black, white and red invitations read:

You are cordially invited to the launch of
Maya's first painting exhibition
"Return to the beginning"
on
Sunday April 8th, 2018
at 3:00 p.m.
Galleria de Art
East 67th street, New York, NY

She smiled. She kissed her invitations, felt the sun on her face and smelled the flowers. She was finally home.

Home—neither a place you live in, nor a place you arrive at… It's where you belong, and ultimately return—a return to the beginning, a return within.

Maya's phone beeped. 'Where are you?' read the text from Veer.

'Um…home!' she chuckled,

'But I don't see you here,' responded Veer.

'Never mind,' she wrote, 'you won't get it, I'll be over soon.'

He nodded his head and smiled, 'That's so Maya!'

Maya stormed in, 'Hey guys, check out my new ride,' she giggled as she introduced her purple and silver Trek.

'That's cool Maya,' said Dadi, 'get me one of those as well. I read about that app, which one was it, Pia?'

'Strava, Dadi.'

'Yes, Strava! We can track our performance and be virtual riding buddies,' she said, 'I will beat you at it!'

Maya laughed, 'With pleasure, Dadi.'

The house was buzzing with festivities. Strings of marigold adorned the house that was flooded with vendors and visitors as Dadisa, Mom and Dadi finalized the orders for sweets, clothes and jewellery.

Soon, the evening came upon and the full moon hung low in the sky. Maya sat next to Veer with her feet dipped in the pool. 'Veer,' she said, 'I want to share something with you. Remember the dream I told you about, that was leading me somewhere but the door remained closed?'

'I saw that same dream again last night and finally the door opened,' she continued.

'And what was on the other side of the door?' asked Veer.

'Me and myself, leading me back to the beginning, leading me back home. Here,' she said, handing him the invitation, 'and I'm on my way. Strangely Veer, you saw this long before I recognized it. You even suggested it, I just didn't realize. And Veer, when I finally step into the reality of my dreams, I want you there through the end of this journey, standing beside me looking on with pride, standing behind me to catch my fall and leading the way when I lose my path.'

'Congratulations, Maya. Of course, we will walk into it together, after all, your dreams are not different from my dreams, when you extend them far enough, they merge into the same horizon, colouring it with brilliant hues.'

'Veer, I no longer want to question life, I simply wish to live it. I want to flow with the streams and bask in the sunlight.

I want to dance with the trees and pour with the rain. I want to sing with the birds and I want to blow with the wind. I no longer wish to find myself, I want to lose myself over again.

'I finally understand what that Sufi mystic meant when he said, "When you find her, you will lose her, when you lose her, you will find her." I died to my past the very instant I discovered my truth or perhaps I discovered my truth because I let go of my past.

'And for us, I don't want to complete you, I want to complement everything that you do. If you sow a seed, I want to water it. If you tell a joke, I want to laugh at it, if you sight a sunset, I want to capture it, if you make the money, I want to spend it,' she laughed, 'just kidding. Veer, I don't want to change your life, I only want to make it better.'

'You already do Maya, why do you think I knew it could only be you. It could never be someone else. I didn't need a woman who cooked for me, I didn't need a woman who cleaned my house and folded my laundry, I didn't need a woman who was a trophy on my arm either. I didn't want someone who needed me to tell her how desirable she was, or how much I loved her. I wanted someone who just knew that I did. I didn't want someone I could talk to, I wanted someone who could understand my silence.

'Marriage isn't a need fulfilled, it is an abundance shared. Love doesn't ask to be followed in its footsteps, it leads to a path jointly charted. Maya, I liked you from the moment I first read your prose. I liked your depth, your innocence, and the burning desire for the simple abundance. I liked you a little more for your fierce independence and immense pride which refused my help, and yet some more when you gave away your feelings at the get go. A piece of advice, don't try your luck at poker,' he laughed.

'Honestly, what wasn't there to like about you—your search, your motivation, your intelligence, your brilliance, your beauty, your love of books and family. You seemed like an answer to every question, I could see you in every poet's composition, you were my every dream's realization.

'Speaking of it, that night when I drove you back to the hotel, I had a compelling realization. I realized how tremendously I had enjoyed your company...despite the fact that you had barely spoken.' He laughed and continued. 'Your presence was enough... and if this short ride could be so pleasurable, I wondered what the journey would be like. Interestingly, you were everything I was looking for but you weren't looking for me, you already had me! I just showed up a little late.' And they both laughed.

'By the way, as you wanted Maya, I have updated the paperwork to add you as the chair of our education fund and women's charity, Jaipur chapter, called, "Dreams in Pink."

'Follow your dreams Maya and flame some others. Dreams exist to be realized and enabling is the greatest achieving.'

The peaceful mirror reflection of the moon danced upon the pool, there was neither a ripple nor a current. Maya reached for the blue velvet pouch and skipped the rocks on the water...

She smiled and thought, *It tells me I have found my happiness and my home...*

Acknowledgements

To Mr Kapish Mehra of Rupa Publications—if it wasn't for you, these words wouldn't have come to be. I am grateful to you for this fabulous opportunity, your guidance, support and power-packed wisdom, and above all, for placing your belief in me.

To my brilliant editor, Ms Elina Majumdar, for adopting and nurturing this story, and for the consistent reminders that prompted me to look deeper into it. In the light of her keen vision, this book grew tremendously. I couldn't have done this alone.

To every team member at Rupa Publications whose contribution helped further this book along, from concept to execution, thank you.

To the team at Moes Art, for your unstinted support, thank you.

I would also like to express my sincere gratitude to His Highness Maharaja Gaj Singh Ji of Jodhpur for graciously accepting to review the first copy of this book.

Papa, if I know how to live, and I know how to love, it's because you showed me how. It's your kindness that makes me believe in the goodness of this world and it is only your love that makes everything possible!

Mama, for your unconditional love, unquestioning heart, selfless smile and unwavering hands which are ever-ready to contain my slightest stumbles and my greatest falls. For being the epitome of beauty, love, grace, simplicity and celebration. For being our mom.

To my husband Armeet—for showing me that there is no substitute for hard work and that the only thing that matters is how you deliver along that extra mile. I have a lot of respect and love for you.

To my sisters Filly and Maina—for the long hours and patient listening, for the silent brooding and the incessant questioning. For being my sounding board, my critics, and my champions. For celebrating tiny victories and shouldering the storms. For nudging me on, for keeping me going, for the craziness and laughter, the tears and the songs. I love you both.

Finally, but earnestly, to my amazing friends for seeing the light when I saw the tunnel, for believing that this book would be a reality much before it came to be. For the abundant love, tremendous support and relentless reminders.

Thank you!